Harlem Moon / Broadway Books
A Division of Random House, Inc.

Dear Reader:

It is with great pleasure that I introduce to you a fresh new voice in women's commercial fiction.

Her name is Cris Burks and she has written one of the most charming characters to come along in African American fiction in a while. In *SilkyDreamGirl*, we follow Katie Coomers, a thirty-something star-crossed everywoman who finds hope and a new sense of self in a chat room. You'll find yourself sympathizing with Katie during her trials, and cheering her on through her triumphs.

I know she'll win your heart, just as she won mine. Please join us in celebrating Katie, and Cris Burks', debut on the launch of the Harlem Moon list.

Best,

Toisan Craigg
Assistant Editor

HARLEM MOON ✳ BROADWAY

SILKYDREAMGIRL

CRIS BURKS

HARLEM MOON
BROADWAY BOOKS · NEW YORK

SILKYDREAMGIRL. Copyright © 2002 by Cris Burks. All rights reserved. No part of this book may be reproduced or transmitted in any form or by any means, electronic or mechanical, including photocopying, recording, or by any information storage and retrieval system, without written permission from the publisher. For information, address Broadway Books, a division of Random House, Inc., 1540 Broadway, New York, NY 10036.

Broadway Books titles may be purchased for business or promotional use or for special sales. For information, please write to: Special Markets Department, Random House, Inc., 1540 Broadway, New York, NY 10036.

The figure in the Harlem Moon logo is inspired by a graphic design by Aaron Douglas (1899–1979). HARLEM MOON and its logo, depicting a moon and woman, are trademarks of Broadway Books, a division of Random House, Inc.

PRINTED IN THE UNITED STATES OF AMERICA

Visit our website at www.broadwaybooks.com

Library of Congress Cataloging-in-Publication Data [tk]

FIRST EDITION

ISBN 0-7679-1295-0

10 9 8 7 6 5 4 3 2 1

ONE WORD

Mitch

ONE THOUGHT

for you

CHAPTER 1

Hubby announced he was leaving me at the Labor Day barbecue. Right before my brother LaDell took the last rib off
the grill. Right before my sister-in-law Georgie poured another round of her weak-butt, non-alcoholic margarita.
Right before Mama stumbled out of the house with the ice
cream maker. Right before my son-brother Alex dragged his
friend Tameka into the backyard. Right before my friend
Donna and her husband, Mike, arrived. The children (my
niece Shanna, my nephew Terrence, and my stepsons, CJ
and Darius) ran around LaDell's perfectly landscaped backyard. Hubby and LaDell stood at the grill like buddies, pals.
They both wore light khaki shorts and T-shirts that accentuated their muscles. Both were short and dusky brown as
Idaho potatoes. LaDell's eyes, nose, and lips gushed gener-
ously across his face. On the other hand, Clarence, my
hubby, had a tight, stingy face. His dot of a nose sat between

his small mole eyes and thin lips. Only his bushy eyebrows added depth to his face.

Up and down the block, smoke drifted from backyards up to a perfect blue sky where downy clouds sailed under a blazing sun. The mouth-watering aroma of barbecue permeated the air. Laughter and music from the backyards meshed into a continuous holiday medley. It was a storybook perfect day, and for once, I didn't envy Georgie's new things. Even Rover, their ferocious rottweiler, lay passively in his house.

"I'm going to California Saturday," Clarence said above the crackling explosion of distant fireworks. He slapped barbecue sauce on the chicken and spareribs.

"Yeah," said LaDell who was never interested in anything outside carpentry or home improvements.

"Yeah," Clarence said.

I knew he was not going to California on business. The man had no business and no job. He didn't even have a damn hustle. But if he said he was going to California, he was going to California. We didn't have enough pocket cash to buy sandals for the boys, yet there he was, planning a trip.

"My sister is sending me a ticket."

I rolled my eyes to the sky. Bertie or Roberta as she preferred, was Clarence's sister. I placed the potato salad on the picnic table and busied myself by arranging the food. A feast of fruit salad, tabbouleh, roast vegetables, and barbecue chicken sat on the table.

It should have been a good day. For once, Mama and I were not at each other's throats. For once, I had managed to pay our bills on time. For once, the extra fifty pounds on my tiny frame was not causing me grief. Clarence destroyed my smidgen of joy with his announcement.

"For how long?" Georgie asked.

Georgie poured a drink and passed it to LaDell. She

towered over me by a good six inches and over LaDell by
two. Flat-chested and the color of peanut butter, she had a
mop of chestnut brown hair that she wore in some sort of
Afro centric style. A flight of freckles soared from one side
of Georgie's face to the other. Georgie liked stars: Movie
stars, stars in the heaven, and stars on her clothes. She wore
sparkly crap like rhinestones, sequins, or anything else with
flash. Her clothes came from catalogs specifically designed
for women who wanted to look unique: Bold colors, animal
prints, and designs that resembled Juan Miro's artwork. A
jingle, jangle something—bracelets, earrings, necklaces, and
rings-covered every part of Georgie's body from her head to
her toes. She was a walking bell. Clarence said California
and Georgie saw stars.

"I'm going to stay," Clarence announced.

Unlike the shoebox backyards of the city, LaDell and
Georgie's suburban backyard wallowed in spaciousness. Any
backyard that was big enough to hold a patio set, a picnic
bench, a kid's play set, a custom-made brick grill, and a veg-
etable garden was capacious. In Chicago, developers would
have built an apartment building in that space. When
Clarence made his foul announcement, the space between
the patio furniture by the sliding glass doors and the picnic
table near the barbecue grill shrunk from eighteen feet to
six inches, shrunk until I saw the sweat seeping out of
Mama's nose. Mama crossed that space in two steps. She
dropped the ice cream maker on the corner of the bench
and glared at me.

"Katie," Mama accused, "you didn't tell me you were
moving to California."

"Kay-Jay isn't going," Clarence continued.

His stingy, tight lips spread into a wide slit of a smile. In
my head, I heard my daddy telling a fable about a woman
and a snake. The woman found a half-frozen snake in the

forest. She took it home, nourished it, and loved it, until the snake was well. In gratitude the snake bit her. *Why? Why?* The foolish woman asked. The snake grinned, like Clarence did that day, and hissed, *you knew I was a snake.*

Everyone paused, turned, and looked at me as if I had committed a sin. I wanted to say *this is all new to me.* I wanted to shrug it off, but I was too busy burning. My ears, face, neck, and body burned like the embers in the grill. Perspiration oozed from every pore in my body. My sack of a dress shrunk like wool in hot water, until it kissed the thick folds of my porcine body. My heart raced. A hole spread in my guts. I poured a glass of honey lemonade, took a sip, and ignored Mama who stared at me across the table. I ignored Georgie's intake of breath behind me. That glass of lemonade was an oasis. I closed my eyes and sipped. I imagined myself, in the middle of the Sahara, waited on by half-naked and succulent men. One massaged my foot, and one gave me a delectable belly rub.

"Katie?" Mama asked.

I opened my eyes and smiled at Mama. She was a good-looking woman with a flawless cinnamon complexion. She had small features, dark hair, and fudge brown eyes. Mama's only gifts to me were my dark eyes. I loved my daddy but I have often looked in the mirror and wondered what genie decided I should get his bulbous nose. I was as fat and shapely as a walrus with crooked teeth. Mama's teeth were so white and straight that most people swore they were fake. They were real. The only thing fake in Mama's life was her only daughter.

"It's okay, Mama," I said. I stretched my lips into the biggest, brightest smile of my life. When you don't know what else to do, smile.

"Me and Kay-Jay always gonna be close," my jerk-faced hubby said. "I'll miss all of you."

"Have mercy!" Mama exclaimed and flopped on the bench next to the ice cream maker. "I'm gonna miss those boys."

She looked over at the new swing set where the children played. Everything about LaDell and Georgie was new. Their cars, their house, and even their marriage of fifteen years sparkled with newness. Clarence and I were old married folks in a rickety canoe, paddling against the strongest current a marriage could face, financial devastation. Obviously, Clarence had decided to jump overboard and swim for a brighter shore.

"The boys will stay here and finish the next school year. I don't want to uproot them," Clarence informed us.

"Katie," Mama said, taking a non-alcoholic margarita from Georgie, "you ain't said a word about any of this."

"Mama, some things I can't discuss intelligently," I said. *Especially*, I thought, *if I don't know what is going on. Besides, Mama, why would I give you another reason to condemn me to hell?*

"Well," LaDell said, looking at me with one raised eyebrow. "I'm glad y'all friendly about this. Many couples breaking up would be at each other's throats."

Why did I take that mess? Why didn't I cuss him out and rip him to Kingdom Come? I floated around that backyard playing catch with the children, playing tag with the children, playing *Captain May I* with the children, and avoiding inquisitions from Mama and Georgie. I didn't look at Clarence who had hurt me again.

My seventeen-year-old son Alex arrived with his skinny friend Tameka. One look at Tameka and two ancient words popped into my head, chaste and modest. The girl was a throw back to another era. I've never seen her belly button. I've never seen her thighs. If a skirt didn't drag the ground, it didn't grace Tameka's lithe frame. She was a *yes ma'am, no ma'am* kind of girl. Mama, who was ever disappointed in me, grabbed the bony thing and embraced her in a bear hug. Tameka's droopy eyes popped as she looked over Mama's shoulder at me. I smirked and shook my head.

"You're a sweetheart. A real sweetheart," Mama said. She held Tameka at arms' length. "I know your grandmother is proud of you."

"Are you and Mama at it again?" Alex asked me. Beads of perspiration glistened on his chocolate skin. Immediately after his birth, my best friend Regina took one look at him and nicknamed him Cocoa Bug. Only she called him that.

I shrugged. He draped his arm across my shoulder and pulled me against him. He smelled of mountain fresh deodorant, mint mouthwash, Gray Flannel aftershave, and yes, tobacco. The top of my head barely made it to his armpit. Alex was six feet five inches and lanky. When he was fourteen and six feet, I dreamed of him playing professional basketball. Oh, yeah. I wanted to be a courtside mom, to sit behind the players' bench, and shout *that's my baby!* But Alex played basketball like Strawberry Smurf. He was terrible. The boy dribbled the ball as if his hands were coated with Elmer's glue. He couldn't make a lay-up, couldn't block a pass, and most definitely couldn't make a basket from the free throw line. On the other hand, the boy was a walking brain. He had scholarship offers from every big-ten school east of the Mississippi.

"What?" He laughed. "Did she find out that you're a bigamist or something?"

And the sense of humor of a jerk.

"Something like that," I said.

Alex didn't stay around to find out what disgusting thing had pickled Mama's nerves. He and Tameka gobbled down two huge plates of food, then said their goodbyes. Tameka had a humongous family with thirty or forty uncles and aunts and a gazillion cousins. I think she had ten thousand cousins between the ages of sixteen and nineteen. Alex had no cousins in his own age group, so he spent more time with her family than with ours.

Donna and Mike arrived with two large watermelons. I latched onto Donna like a clasp. While the other adults played spades at the patio table, Donna and I sliced the watermelons at the picnic table. The children snatched the melon as quickly as we sliced it. I stood under the shadow of Donna's arm like a lost child. Donna was as tall as Georgie but, unlike Georgie, she had a provocative roundness that, at times, she desperately attempted to hide beneath flowing outfits. At other times, she buttoned or laced up her voluptuousness beneath blocky jackets and coats. On Labor Day, she wore a cream haute-couture pants set that was more appropriate for a cocktail party than a backyard barbecue. The top flowed down to wide-leg pants, which ended in gold sandals.

"Georgie told me that Clarence is leaving," she whispered.

I shrugged. She looked at me from the canyon of her eyes. Her long sloping nose lay between deep-set and almond-shaped eyes.

"You can talk to me about anything," she said.

"Donna, you know we don't agree about love and marriage and stuff," I said.

"Well, I'm not a dreamer like . . ."

She broke off the sentence before the name slipped out. Regina was a sore subject between us. Donna, Regina, and I had been inseparable since birth. Donna was born in the spring, I was born in the summer, and finally Regina was born in December of that same year. We crawled across each other's floors, walked around each other's backyards, and ran with the same crowd of people. We thought we would grow old together, but Regina opted out.

***

On the ride home, my stepsons, CJ and Darius, chatted nonstop about the day. I drove. Bitterness crawled up my swollen ankles, my legs, and my thighs. Finally, it curled and nestled in the bowl of my belly. Clarence should have sensed that a dangerous, stab-you-in-your-sleep rage was growing in me.

"You okay, Kay-Jay?" he asked.

I bit my tongue. I focused on the bumper-to-bumper traffic of the Dan Ryan Expressway. I didn't glance his way lest I ram us all into an eighteen-wheeler. In the backseat, CJ and Darius's laughter tugged at my heart. Tomorrow was soon enough for them to discover the destruction of their family.

"Katie?" Clarence called again.

"Don't say a word," I hissed, hoping the boys were too enthralled with their conversation to feel the rage pulsating in the front seat.

When we arrived home, CJ and Darius rushed up the steps. Clarence followed. I trailed behind. Seven years before, when I weighed a hundred and thirty pounds, I had run up and down the three flights of stairs with ease. Back then the weight of a bad marriage didn't drag me down. On the second floor I was out of breath. I leaned against the banister and rested.

"You okay, Kay-Jay," Clarence called down from the third floor.

I didn't answer. I knew once I was inside the apartment, he would try to reason with me, to placate my ruffled feelings. By the time I reached the third floor, the boys were in their rooms, and Clarence was waiting for me by the door.

"I don't want to discuss this," I said. I got right in his face and stood toe-to-toe with him. Although he was two inches taller than I was, my large frame smothered his smaller body.

"I don't want to discuss this tonight, tomorrow night, or ever," I said. "I want you gone, Clarence, and when you leave this time, don't even think about coming back. This door will be closed to you." I closed the door and locked it.

That week, Clarence was as nice as ice cream on apple pie. I ignored him and went about my life as if nothing was wrong. The boys took his leaving as they had in the past, nonchalantly. In seven years, Clarence had left me twice. That Saturday, we escorted Clarence to Midway Airport. The boys hugged him good-bye. I looked at him with contempt. When your husband leaves you, you can crumple into tears or get on with living. It took a year for me to crumple into tears.

***

Everybody wanted to talk about his leaving. Georgie called and asked if I were okay. Sunday, Mama just happened by after church, although she lived way out south, on 86th Street and I lived up north, near Touhy and Sheridan. An hour drive separated our homes.

"Are you all right?" she asked when she came through my door.

Mama wore a hat as big as a sixteen-inch pizza pan and just as flat. A mess of flowers and stuffed birds filled the crown of her hat. She was a chest-heavy woman who loved clothes that puckered around her big bosom.

"Where are the boys?" she asked.

"Outside," I said and walked into the kitchen.

She followed the four steps behind me. See, that was the thing about being plain. I didn't expect much out of life and as a result I didn't get much. Take that apartment for instance. It was a tiny two-bedroom box. I could stand in the hallway and see into every room. The two bedrooms faced each other. There was a spit of a bathroom between the bedrooms. From the hall, I could step into the living room and immediately make a right into the kitchen. My foyer (yeah right) was two feet by three feet. Clarence, the boys, and I constantly tripped over each other in that apartment.

Anyway, Mama stood in the doorway of the kitchen. My kitchen was not a cook's dream. The sink, stove, refrigerator, and an old-fashioned cupboard circled the oak table like horses around a carousel. Two windows and a window in the backdoor overlooked a staircase of tenement buildings. Mama noticed the sink full of dishes, the freshly made chocolate cake with two slabs missing, and the half-full coffee maker.

"You can't eat your misery away," she said.

"You want a slice?" I asked and flopped into a chair.

I cut another wedge, my third. She shook her head and stared at me. Her flying saucer hat touched each side of the doorway. She stepped back and removed her hatpin. Her hair laid immaculately smooth. Mama had that type of control over everything. She walked to the cocktail table and set the hat on top of my photo albums. By the time she returned to the kitchen, I was pressing the fork into the crumbs on my plate. She pulled a chair out and flopped down.

"Maybe, if you didn't eat so much . . ." she began.

"I could keep a man," I finished her statement.

See, Mama thought that my weight and my husband's leaving were interdependent. Clarence was husband number four. Mama never uttered the words, but I knew she thought of me as a cauterized sore. I've heard the story of my birth often. *Felt like the child was tearing my insides out*, Mama said often enough. Indeed, I scratched all the pain, the horror, and the ugliness of childbirth from Mama's womb. My birth made it possible for LaDell to emerge from a glorious and loving womb two years later. Mama biggest complaint in life was my appearance. I cannot tell you the number of times I've heard the expression, *girl, you need to fix yourself up*. Remember that showy hat on my cocktail table? That was Mama's idea of fixing up, showy.

"I guess if I made cakes this good, I would be wide, too," she said and pulled the cake plate to her.

"You want coffee?" I asked and rose from the table.

"Milk," she said and sliced a big hunk of the cake. "So, did you and Clarence talk?"

"Of course we talked," I said, being deliberately vague. "Why wouldn't we?"

"Girl, don't give me any lip!" Mama barked. "Why did you agree to keep the boys? He could have taken them with him, and who's gonna take care of them while you work? I'm not babysitting. I don't understand how you let him go like that. Every time I look up, you got a new husband."

I shook my head, opened the refrigerator, and removed the milk. I didn't dare open my mouth. When Mama was on a roll, I listened. That was another thing. Mama and LaDell never argued. From the second of his birth, he was Mama's angel boy, the perfect child. I felt no resentment as Mama cooed over his perfect beauty, his quick intelligence, and his loving spirit. I had my daddy, who plucked stars from the heavens and placed them in my hands. Even later, when Daddy died, LaDell and I allowed no resentment to spring up between us. Our family had dwindled from four to three. Even Mama, bellying aching about the imperfections of my life could not drive a wedge between LaDell and Me. I loved my brother in spite of his "perfection."

Everything about LaDell and Georgie was perfect. He owned a little construction business. She was a nurse. They had two point five children. I swear they treated that dog like a child. They lived in Country Club Hills, a suburb, in a beautiful four-bedroom house with a sunken family room. I lived in a cramped two-bedroom apartment in East Rogers Park, a neighborhood on the North Side of Chicago. Mama always lectured me on the state of my life, and I always felt obligated to listen.

"What is with Bertie?" Mama asked, waving the cake server. "This is the second time she has sent for him. Seems mighty strange that she sent for him and not the whole family. What's she got against you?"

"I don't know," I lied and poured her a glass of milk. Unlike Clarence I can lie like a lobbyist, especially under pressure. I knew that I had offended Bertie from the very day of my wedding. Bertie took one look at my wedding dress and went off.

"Why are you wearing white?" Bertie had asked.

I had worn white twice before, and nobody had said a damn thing. Mama, who criticized everything about me from my shoe size to my college degree, didn't raise an eyebrow when I chose the white tulle gown for my first wedding. Nor did she object to my appointing five-year-old Alex as my ring boy. Mama skipped my second marriage. However, when I married for the third time in a lovely white calf-length dress with a short veil, she fussed more about the man than the dress.

"Joe Robinson got his name carved in the walls of St. Charles reformatory. The county jail is his second home. I hear he got his own special cell down on Twenty-sixth Street. So somebody please, tell me why that girl is marrying that hoodlum?"

Still, Mama sat in her appointed place and tucked her disappointment in her bosom while I exchanged vows with Joe Robinson. So, I thought why not wear white again. After all, the third time had to be a charm.

Bertie, I concluded, was simply jealous. Although, I was not the prettiest girl in the world, I had been married three times before. Bertie had never been married. The cow. She was beautiful with a damn good business. Money gushed from Bertie's hand like an oil gusher, overflowing. But, she couldn't buy a husband.

Our animosity really began over my stepsons. After their mother's death, Bertie latched onto the boys. She pampered them with expensive gifts and allowed them to do whatever they wanted. They had been unruly, cry babies. I laid down strict rules. However, I had a natural affinity with children. The boys took to me like the dwarves to Snow White. They loved me. I was *mom* before Clarence and I said our vows.

After Clarence and I married, Bertie tried to maintain her position in their lives, but there can be only one Queen Bee. The boys loved me, deferred to me, and Bertie had to concede defeat. Within a year, she moved to California and opened a frozen yogurt shop.

"You're not gonna take this lying down, are you?" Mama asked. "You gonna fight for your marriage?"

I looked at Mama and smiled. She blanched. She hated when I smiled like that, right in the middle of an argument or discussion. What else could I do?

"Yes, ma'am," I lied. "You are right. I'm gonna fight for my marriage."

"You need to make a commitment to at least one marriage!" She snapped. "Jumping around like Zsa Zsa Gabor or Liz Taylor, like you don't come from decent stock."

Yeah, that's what the woman said. *Stock.* Last time I checked the records my daddy had been ten years younger than Mama. Ten years younger! Regina told me that my daddy dated her Aunt Phyllis. I believed that because Aunt Phyllis, at fifty, was a fox and as sweet and gentle as lemon pudding. Regina said that my daddy went south one summer with some friends and came back with Helen Hill as his wife. People's tongues flapped for days. Aunt Phyllis, who never married, cried for years. So, when Mama said *decent stock*, I wasn't sure whether she were referring to herself or to daddy.

"You know, Katie, I did the best I could for you," Mama said. "I tried to bring you up in church. I tried to keep you from acting like the other girls, but some things are in the blood line, and you can't get it out."

"What things, Mama?" I asked.

"You're hopeless, Katie," she said. "Just hopeless."

I set the glass of milk on the table. We sat in silence. I watched the fork rise to her mouth. Her fudge brown eyes softened with pleasure as she closed her cupid-bow mouth around the cake. After she had swallowed, the hard glint returned to her eyes.

"You can't sit by and watch another marriage end, Katie," she said, pointing the fork at me like it was a dart. "You can't."

CHAPTER 2

"Katie!"

One of the other call center supervisors waved at me as I stepped from my car. I pulled my briefcase and shoulder bag from the backseat. I bumped the door closed with my butt, pressed the automatic lock, and made my way through the maze of cars. We met at the end of the row. The woman was one of those beautiful redheads with creamy skin, an Irish lass. I knew the tall, skinny thing had a crush on Clarence. I knew she wondered why a man as fine as Clarence stayed with a big-bellied woman like me. At company functions she cooed around him like a lovesick bird.

"You've driven yourself to work every day for the past month," she said. "Is Clarence well?"

"Clarence is perfect," I said and led the way to the glass structure of Luft's Catalog Company.

"You hate driving out here," she reminded me.

Out here was forty minutes from Chicago. We worked

down the road from the Discover Card Corporation and close to Baxter Laboratories. Deerfield was the hottest growing business district in northern Illinois. We each managed a squad of eighteen people who handled calls from disgruntled customers around the world.

"So, why are you driving?" she asked.

She would not let the subject die, and I would never tell her the truth. I smiled, turned, and gestured toward my Mercury Mystique.

"You see that beauty? It's a dream car!"

"You are a nut," she laughed.

That's the way it went after Clarence left. Everybody who knew him-the neighbors, the people at the supermarket, and the gas station attendants-asked about Clarence. I gave them all my quirky smile and told them nothing. What ticked me off the most? If I had left or died, those same people would have shaken their sorry heads and mourned with Clarence. They would have said, *Poor man. What a rough spot she left him in.* Everybody loved the man. Clarence was, is, will always be, a charmer. He could charm the funk out of a skunk, make the poor creature give up its only defense mechanism. Didn't he charm all sense and logic from my feeble brain? Didn't I surrender all, every nickel and every minute to Clarence Coomers? The first moment I set my eyes on the man I was doomed.

Donna and I had agreed to attend Wednesday night Bible study with Mama. Rather, Mama had insisted that we attend a series of lectures on *The Virtuous Woman*. So, there we sat in a front, side pew, watching the congregation flock in, when Roberta Coomers strolled victoriously through the doors. She wore an unnatural smile on her face and had a strange glint in her eyes. On each side of her was a small wide-eyed toddler. A yummy, palatable man in navy whites followed her. Honey, the ripples and bulges of his muscles strained the threads of that uniform. His muscles liquified every bone in my body.

"Here," Donna whispered and waved a fragrant handkerchief under my nose, "saliva is dripping from your mouth."

I brushed the handkerchief aside and closed my mouth. I followed that man's every move as he walked up the aisle and took a seat next to Roberta and the toddlers.

"Girl, do you see him?" I whispered. "That man is fine."

"Yes, but he's short," Donna replied.

"Yeah, but so am I."

"There must be a Mrs. Fine somewhere," she warned, "because those are not Roberta's children."

Everyone knew Roberta Coomers had no children, no husband, no suitor, and no prospects of obtaining any of those things. The taste buds on Roberta's tongue contained poisonous gasses and bubbly acids. Every time she opened her mouth, negative words shot out. She seasoned her good mornings with *this snow is murderous or this heat is gonna kill me.* Her conversations revolved around calamities and sorrows. She was a regular bearer of foul words. That fine man, we learned during visitors' recognition, was her widowed younger brother, Clarence.

Clarence Coomers married me four months later. Trust me. Fine does not feed you. My first three husbands had agendas for our marriages, and so did Clarence. His agenda cost me more than the others, combined. Maybe if I had known the truth about Valerie, Clarence's first wife, this story would not exist. Before I married Clarence, I learned that Valerie had died in a car accident. The rest of her story I learned one-hundred-thousand-dollars in debt later.

I could have told all that and more to the Irish lass. I could have told her of Clarence's latest desertion. Yes, I could have shown her the depths of my ruin. Like everyone else in my life, she too would have pointed the finger at me.

So, I let her laugh at my silliness as we entered the catalog center.

The functionary departments of the company slogged along the basement corridors. Those employed in the mail/supply room, the records department, the cafeteria, security, and the call center had no view of the pond, and little hope of moving up to the golden offices on levels one and two. The Irish lass opted for morning coffee, so I continued down the corridor without her. Clamorous noises besieged me when I entered the call center. Seven days a week, twenty-four hours a day, relentlessly, the murmur of sixty-odd voices, the hum of sixty-odd computers, the clickety-clack of keyboards, the ringing of phones, the whish-whirr of copiers, the metallic creaks of desk drawers and file cabinets, and the continuous drone of the HVAC undulated around that center. I endured the noise with selective listening and a raised voice. Yet, I could not endure the foul odors that rose, one-by-one, from the work stations' occupants: The feral funk of unwashed bodies, the swinish stench of a day-old drunk, foul feet, beastly breath, and yes, once, an odor akin to a fiendish fish. Daily, I armed myself with a can of disinfectant spray and charged through the center.

As usual, the noises and odors saturated the center with discomfort. However, that day a charged undercurrent added to the discomfort. Something was wrong. Marjorie, the call center manager, stood in the center of the room, waiting. Marjorie was a hefty silver blond with jowls that wobbled as she talked. Her neck was so short that her head appeared to rotate in its socket. She was taller than I by a foot.

"Katie," she greeted me. "Let's go into my office."

The woman didn't allow me to store away my purse and briefcase but, with a beefy hand that had diamonds around red knuckles, propelled me toward her office. A

huge steel gray desk with a large comfy leather chair commanded the center of the office. A second chair (a gift from
the Marquis de Sade, perhaps?) sat in front of the desk.
That chair had an unnaturally high back and a hard seat
that pressed against the flesh like stone. Knobby studs
strolled along the arms of the chair. Along one wall ran a
bank of steel gray file cabinets that dated from the 1950s.
A delicate rose-print, old-fashioned settee with chintz pillows graced the opposite wall.

When we entered the office, the director of human resources sat on the settee. He was a thin boy of twenty-four.
His red, mousy face twitched continuously. Flakes of dry
skin covered his dark suit as if he had walked through a
shower of uncooked oats. A career change might have
helped his psoriasis. Luft's was not an easy place to work.
The three-hundred-page employees' handbook covered
everything from benefits to where to place the date on a
business letter.

Marjorie closed the door behind me. She walked passed
the HR Jerk and around the huge steel desk. She plopped
into the big comfy chair. Pointing to the chair in front of her
desk, she ordered me to sit. The structure of the chair forced
me to drop my briefcase on the floor, place my purse on my
lap, and to sit straight and demurely like a school girl before
the principal.

Marjorie peered at me with milky blue eyes. I noticed a
wart on the side of her nose. She leaned forward and
steepled her fingers. I knew the matter was serious. Something mean was about to happen on the floor. I glanced at
the HR Jerk. He squirmed and ran his fingers between his
tight shirt collar and his neck. I looked at Marjorie again.

"Those are the production numbers," she said.

Marjorie had strategically placed the production report
before the Marquis de Sade's chair. She was not a people

person. Why the company put her in charge of the call center was beyond me. I scooted up in the chair until I could reach the report. I flipped the pages until I found my squad's number. I ran down the list of eighteen employees. The squad's production rate was low. I turned the page. Large, bold, red circles corralled exceptionally high error rates. I'm no fool. I understood the implications. The report said my squad did little work and what little they did was wrong, wrong, wrong.

"Bottom line, the company must cut staff," Marjorie said and tapped her fingers.

Oh, my goodness, I thought. *I have to fire somebody.*

"And, Katie," she continued, "we're going to start with you."

I waited for her to say something more. Nothing more came out of her mouth. She looked at me, expecting me to say something, but nothing came out of my mouth either. I looked from her to the HR Jerk. He began his spiel on what I could and could not expect from the company as far as severance pay, references, and COBRA. The one-sided conversation was over in fifteen minutes. The HR jerk escorted me to my cubicle, where I removed all the things that made life at work bearable: Extra pantyhose, toothbrush and paste, a package of Oreo cookies, dental floss, deodorant for those stressful days, comb, mirror, a bag of Hershey's kisses, my can of disinfectant spray, lipstick, a box of tissue, my Rolodex, a bag of Snickers, pictures of my three sons, an old birthday card from my squad, and, of course, tucked away in the back of a drawer, my outdated resume. I drove home with my small box of possessions in the next seat. When I entered my quiet apartment, the first wave of panic hit me. I was jobless and broke.

I dropped my briefcase, the box, and my purse by the

front door then headed for the kitchen. The remains of a sock-it-to-me cake sat on the table. I got milk from the refrigerator, a fork from a drawer, a glass from a cabinet, and sat down to feast. There was nothing else to do.

***

I kept my firing to myself until Clarence called that Saturday. I was in the kitchen with the backdoor open, the rustling autumn leaves filled the air with a soft whisper. The smell of barbecue drifted up from the second floor. My downstairs neighbor barbecued all year round. In the winter, she shrugged into her down-filled jacket, pulled her grill out her tiny apartment, and created a roaring fire. The aroma of barbecue and the sight of all that glorious autumn orange, red, and gold made me long for a thick book like Tolstoy's *War and Peace* or Morrison's *Song of Solomon* and a glass of Pinot Grigio. I could laze on the sofa and not worry about losing my job.

"How are you and the boys getting along?" Clarence asked.

"I lost my job," I said. I clenched the phone with my chin as I mixed the shredded cheeses, green onions, and chicken together for my famous enchiladas.

"You what?" Clarence asked.

I didn't respond. The man heard me. Clarence said nothing. The silence between us was the silence of two people battling for power, for control. He who spoke first was the weakest, the loser. Clarence could out wait a snail's pace. I always lost that battle. Always. I felt the words boiling in my throat. I quickly stuffed some enchilada mixture into my mouth. You can't fuss with a mouth full of food. Clarence remained silent.

"You wanna talk to the boys?" I asked, chewing and smacking in his ears.

"Yeah, put my boys on."

"Your boys?" I challenged him. I felt the fight rising in my blood. "Your boys?"

I had fought for four years to adopt the boys. Each year, Clarence had argued that we had no available funds for legal fees. On our fifth wedding anniversary, the funds dropped like manna into our laps. Mama, bubbling with emotions and generosity because I had crossed the five-year mark in a marriage, gave me a healthy check as a present. I used that money to pay court cost and lawyer's fees, and the boys became my sons, legally.

I slammed the phone on the table and yelled, "CJ! Darius! Pick up the phone!"

"Is it dad?" CJ called.

I didn't answer him. He was so much like his father. The boys talked to Clarence, and I wrapped my enchiladas. The sun was bright, and I would be happy if it made me cry. Movies waited by the VCR: *Godzilla*, *Lost in Space*, and *The Empire Strikes Back*. I would bake my enchiladas. I would drink my margarita. I would gorge on my homemade hemorrhoid-hot-salsa. I would top it all off with my sensational key lime pie. Yes! Yes! Yes! I would enjoy the day with *my* sons. It was a good life even if my money disappeared. I had unemployment compensation coming. I had my cakes. Maybe, I would finally get a chance to finish my novel.

I placed the enchiladas on a bed of sauce. I poured more sauce over them. Cheese, sprinkled heavily over the top, completed the creation. I slammed the works into the oven and took a swig from the tequila bottle. I always kept a fifth of tequila for medicinal purposes, in other words to doctor up my pathetic store-bought margarita.

"Mom, Dad says pick up the phone," Darius called.

"Yeah," I barked into the phone. I swirled the golden liquor around the bottle.

"Maybe, I should come back and help you out," Clarence suggested.

"What?" I asked.

"You got a lot on your plate with no job. I know the boys can be hard to handle."

Oh, no. I knew that spiel. The first time Clarence deserted me, he managed to weasel back into my life when I was in a vulnerable state. I knew at the Labor Day barbecue that this day would come. Hell, everybody knew it.

"You think?" I asked coyly.

"I only left because I couldn't make it there," he said.

"And you think you can make it now?" I asked.

"We are a family. We need to try to make this thing work," he said.

I looked out my back door. No matter what season, even in the bitter cold when my toes were achy (because I never wore heavy, ugly boots), I loved Chicago. When I drove along Lake Shore Drive and looked at the superficial beauty of the city, I pretended that I was an independent woman with the world on a string. Nothing could stop me. Everything was okey dokey.

Clarence broke into my thoughts, "Kay-Jay, are you listening, or are you dreaming?" He knew me so well.

"What do you want me to say?" I asked.

"Do you need me to come back?"

In days of yore, I would have said *We need to save our marriage. The boys need both of us. Why are you breaking up our marriage? Etcetera, etcetera.* It had been seven years, and I was growing older. I wanted to be loved simply because I was Katie Jeffries of the South Side Jeffries, educated at Billings Elementary School, Parker High School, and Chicago State University, a Chicago girl from birth to death. I wanted a man to reach for me because my touch evoked spiraling, dizzying desire in his loins. I wanted a man who would dissolve in my kisses and the pleasures found only in my thighs. I wanted a man that would work.

"Clarence, what's the problem?" I asked. I took another swig from the tequila bottle.

"What?" he asked.

"You've only been out there two months. You need to give it time, at least six months," I said. I read somewhere that after a six-month separation there was a good chance a couple would not get back together.

"We got the boys to think about," he said.

"I am thinking about the boys," I said. I swirled the Tequila bottle. I didn't take another swig. I loved tequila but I didn't love drunkenness.

"You're not working, and the apartment is probably in shambles," he said.

I looked in the living room. Papers and clothes were scattered everywhere. I knew my bedroom and the boys' bedroom were equally messy. However, I sat in a clean kitchen, cooking a great meal, and looking at a glorious autumn day.

"No," I said, "You would be surprised how clean this kitchen is. I'm actually keeping it tip top." I turned my back on the living room. If I didn't see it, I wasn't lying.

"I'll come back and get a job, and we'll buy a house," he said.

Oh, my goodness! The man was using the same tired lines. Next he would dangle his GI bill before me. On cue, he began:

"We'll use my GI bill to get a house in Bolingbrook, in that development you like. I'll talk to Thomas at the VA about that position."

Clarence always spoke about strangers as if they were on a first-name basis with him. He met Thomas once, a year before.

"That position is gone, Clarence," I said. "That guy offered you that job a year ago."

"So, what are you saying?" he asked. "Do you want to make this marriage work or not?"

"I can't do this anymore."

"I know this has been hard on you," he said.

"I don't want to do it anymore," I said.

"You're upset because you lost your job."

"No."

"When I get there I'll give you a back rub and . . ."

"No!" I snapped before he could plunge into his sex talk. "I don't want this anymore. You find a job out there and send for *your boys* at the end of the school year."

"Oh, they are my boys now," he said.

"Well, that's what you said to me."

"You knew what I meant."

"Clarence, I don't want to fight," I said. "I'm tired."

"Well, what are you gonna do?" he asked.

"It doesn't matter what I'm going to do!" I said. "You are going to call either the VA or the Department of Defense and have one of those checks sent to me."

"That's all you're about, money!" he snapped.

"You got two sons here, and Christmas is a few weeks away," I snapped back.

"You don't celebrate Christmas," he said.

"No, but you and the boys do. They expect presents. You send the damn money," I hissed. "If I don't have one of those checks by the fifth of December, I'm going down to DCFS and filing a complaint of abandonment, then I'm suing you for custody of your boys. Then I'm coming after you for seven years of child support."

"Why are you bitter?" he asked.

"Send the money, Clarence."

"That's all you got to say to me."

"Yup," I said and hung up the phone.

***

I never considered myself a rich woman. True, Mr. Pete, my second husband, had left a small inheritance at my disposal. The house he left me brought in an extra seven hundred dollars a month, and I received about two hundred a month from his retirement fund, but I had debts crawling around me like maggots. When Clarence fled to California, he took his retirement income with him, but he left two growing boys, a new car with a new car note, credit card bills, my student loan, and debts from his failed business ventures. He left a heart that was fast becoming as black as the Sears Tower.

I have avoided discussing Clarence's business ventures. I have never shared this with another soul—not Donna, Mama, LaDell, Georgie, or Alex. Whenever I looked back down the path that led to my financial ruin, shame chomped at my guts. The continuous rumble in my stomach was shame chomping, chomping, chomping. Debt overwhelmed me so much that I had difficulty holding my head up. Yes, it's true. Do I have to say it? The further in debt we got, the more shame weighed me down until depression joined the club. The more depressed I became, the more I baked. The more I baked, the more I ate. I went from a curvaceous one hundred and thirty pounds to a big blob of shame and depression. Here's the truth of the matter:

Clarence retired from the Navy with a small wad of money, a retirement income, and a dream to leverage time into money, so he could buy back time or something like that. I couldn't explain his theory with Cliff Notes. I half listened to him when he explained it to me. I was too busy nibbling his ears and fingers or rubbing my toes up his pants legs. His explanation was a jumble of hot words and hot air on my ears. When he shoved a pen and application under my nose for my signature, I signed and became a partner in a buy-from-yourself business. Yes, we bought everything from socks to a new bedroom suite.

We zoomed up and down and across I-94, I-80, I-65, and I-70 at breakneck speed. We attended conferences that were supposed to teach us to be successful. Like thousands of others, we paid hundreds and hundreds of dollars to attend those professional pep rallies. Yes, Clarence and I rah-rah-rahed as men in tuxedos and women in sparkling gowns paraded their successes across stage after stage. At every conference some washed-out musicians played a loud mixture of classic rock music and folk songs. At every conference, some almost famous motivational speaker confirmed that we too could have the American dream.

Mama, Georgie, or Donna kept the boys while we went on these junkets. Six months and five thousand dollars later, I stayed home with the boys while Clarence continued to chase that dream. A year and fifteen thousand dollars later, he came home fired up with a different dream, government auctions. Clarence had attended a seminar on how to get rich buying and selling government surplus items. His initial investment consisted of the cost of the seminar, the cost of a sleek black Dodge Ram, and the monthly rental for a storage unit. The first big auction that Clarence attended offered little reward. He purchased seventy-five IBM Selectric typewriters. When I examined them, I found missing balls or bad motors. Some were repairable and others were total losses. I didn't have the heart to tell him that typewriters, especially old Selectrics were becoming obsolete. Next, he purchased a slew of office furniture. He broke even on that purchase, but gave up on wealth through government auctions. Next came a string of multi-level marketing schemes. Clarence sold products that promised to revolutionize auto care, health care, the aging process, and weight loss. One business venture gave way to the next business venture. Every time Clarence turned around, I slapped him with another "I told you so." I was the drum of damnation, beating his stupidity into his head. One day I looked up and Clarence was gone. No ta-ta, goodbye, see you later, just gone. Three days later, he calls me from California. That was the first time he left. He was gone for three months and only returned home after Darius was hospitalized appendicitis.

While Clarence pursued his dreams, I continued to work, take care of home, mother his sons, and flounce around like June Cleaver. My family and I bonded with CJ and Darius. The boys clung hungrily to us. Soon, we could not imagine life without them.

We were approaching our third anniversary when Clarence ran into an old Navy buddy and his wife. Clarence thought the couple had a great business idea, a typing center in downtown Waukegan. That time I did speak up. I waited until the man was sated and drowsy.

"Clarence," I whispered in the darkened bedroom. The street light seeped through closed mini blinds and fell across his face. His eyelashes fluttered. He was not asleep.

"Clarence," I called again.

"Huh," he answered.

"I've been thinking," I said and snuggled deep into his side. "Most companies are moving toward in-house word processing centers. They are finding it cheaper than hiring temps or sourcing out work. You know, as more people become familiar with personal computers, the need for dedicated typists will vanish."

"Kay-Jay," he said. "You really don't understand business. Everyone can't type. I can't type. In the Navy, we had large typing pools. Trust me. There will always be a need for typing centers. We are getting state-of-the-art computers and word processing software. I wish I hadn't sold all those type-writers. We could use a couple to type the forms and documents that can't be done on a computer."

"Clarence, I think eventually computers will generate forms."

"Go to sleep, Kay-Jay," he said and pulled me into his arms. "You're thinking too much."

I shut my mouth on the venture but signed my name to a sixty-five-thousand-dollar loan. Clarence sank that wad of dough into an antiquated idea. In the summer of '94, A.C.E. Support Services opened shop in Waukegan, fully equipped with state-of-the-art hardware and software, fully furnished in beautiful teak and royal blue, fully staffed with two typists and a secretary, and fully run by three simpletons with myopic vision. Each morning they donned expensive business suits (they had to look successful for success to follow), opened their offices, brewed expensive coffee, chatted on the phone to relatives and friends about A.C.E., held strategy meetings, created flyers and ads, assigned the few assignments those ads generated to a typist, and spent much time yakking with the staff. Not one of the three thought to visit local businesses. Not one of the three thought to make cold calls. They waited for their ship to crash through the doors of A.C.E. and spill gold upon the floors. Unfortunately, their ship never arrived.

Even in the winter of '94, there were firms that required the work of a typing center. Those firms bustled in adrenergic downtown Chicago while A.C.E. nestled in the coziness of downtown Waukegan. On a good day, with clear skies and light traffic, it was an hour drive between Waukegan and the Loop. In the winter, with sinister snow blanketing the roadways, that drive could expand to three hours. By spring of '95, A.C.E. closed its doors.

Clarence's next brilliant business venture burst my last

hope of having a sane family life. He rolled out of the typing center into a concept called flipping properties. Trust me, even with Einstein coaching me, I couldn't explain the concept. When I first heard it, I imagined us living a farmer's life. I imagined Clarence in overalls sitting on a backhoe. I imagined myself sowing seeds. Flipping properties had nothing to do with tilling soil.

"We'll make a killing," Clarence said to me across the kitchen table.

Clarence's bare chest showed his age more than his face. Sprigs of gray peppered his thick chest hairs. I drew my eyes from his chest to the decadent fudge cake. Thick chocolate sauce drenched the cake. Utility bills, Visa and MasterCard statements, payment coupons, and mounds of letters from debtors surrounded the cake plate. An adding machine, a legal pad, and pencils sat by my dessert plate. Except for Clarence's babbling, the distant rumble of an El, and the hissing of steam from the radiator, the apartment was quiet. I licked my finger. I was determined not to let Clarence sway me with dreams of riches. It was time for him to emerge from his fantasy world into the reality of the nine-to-five, Monday through Friday drudgery of this world. I looked past him, out the tiny window of the back door. A starless sky stretched above the neighboring buildings.

"Kay-Jay, just think, real estate is the way to go."

"Clarence, we are in debt. Serious, crippling debt."

I circled the bottom line on the legal pad, $81,294.75, and then drew an arrow from that to $7,617. I pushed the pad across the table to him.

"Clarence, we owe eighty thousand plus dollars," I said. "To breathe each month, we need more than seven thousand dollars for living expenses and debts. Now how much of that will flipping properties give us next week, next month? Guaranteed?"

"Kay-Jay, nothing is guaranteed."

"If you march yourself to the federal building or city hall or the state building and apply for a job, I can guarantee that you will receive veterans' preference," I said.

"Kay-Jay, anybody can work a job. I'm trying to do something big for you."

"I think an eighty-thousand-dollars debt is as big as I want to get," I said.

"I thought you believed in me, believed in us."

He looked at me with watery brown eyes. I saw CJ and Darius in those eyes. I saw years of living in a misty, imaginary land where wealth was always on the horizon. I looked at my hands that were as plump and puffy as Fat Albert's from the Cosby Kids. I could not go on with dreams.

"I believe two little boys have a right to food, clothing, and a nice backyard," I said. "I believe I have a right to expect my husband to provide those things. I believe I have a right to answer the phone and not hear a creditor's voice. I believe I have a right to peaceful sleep."

"What would you have me do, Katie?" he asked and shoved the pad back to me. "Get one of those dollar-an-hour jobs."

"Minimum wage is more than five dollars," I corrected him.

"How can that chump change help?"

"Let's see," I said and pushed buttons on the adding machine. "We'll use your retirement check to pay your truck note and that A.C.E. loan. Now, five twenty-five times forty equals two hundred and ten dollars a week, minus about twenty-two percent for taxes, FICA and whatever, and that will give us approximately sixty hundred fifty-five dollars and twenty cents a month."

I tore the tape off the adding machine and studied it. When I looked up, controlled anger pulsated in Clarence's face. His tight, ashy lips twitched like a fish gulping water. A syncopated beat worked in his jaws. His fingers drummed up and down on the table. *Get over it*, I thought and pushed the tape across the table.

"That is more than enough, Clarence, to pay Com-Ed, Peoples Gas, Illinois Bell, and car insurance. You can use whatever is left over for your harebrained schemes. Or," I said and stood, "you can go straight to hell!"

I walked out the kitchen and into the bedroom. I slammed the door shut. Clarence slept on the couch that night but woke me at four-thirty in the morning by flipping on the bedroom light. I burrowed under the covers. To sleep, I needed darkness and silence, or as much silence as possible in a neighborhood where sirens constantly wailed and gun-shots exploded with the regularity of a traffic light.

"Turn off that light," I mumbled.

"We need to talk," he said.

"Couldn't you wait?" I asked.

"I'm leaving," he said.

"Uh-huh," I said from beneath the covers.

"I'm going to California."

"What?" I sat up in bed. The light blinded me. I rubbed my eyes.

"This is too much for me," he said.

He leaned against the door post. He humbly bowed his head. He stroked the stubbles on his cheek.

"What is too much for you?" I asked. I adjusted the scarf around my head. I wore my hair in a wrap back then, and the scarf was necessary to keep the hairstyle in place.

"I can't make you happy. I can't be what you want me to be," he said. He stood straight up and slipped his hands into his pockets. He nervously played with the coins in his pocket.

"So, you'd rather leave than find a damn job," I said.

"I can't see myself working for pennies."

"You can't see yourself working, Clarence."

"That's not it, Katie."

"If you want to leave, leave," I said. "Don't give me that crap about you can't make me happy. You haven't tried."

"Will you keep the boys until I get settled?"

"Just go," I said and burrowed under the covers.

He flicked off the lights, and I was again in darkness.

CHAPTER 3

Right there! From the small of my back, frustration crept up my spine, balled in my throat, and shot out tentacles of panic. Many, many times I had sat at the kitchen table with my adding machine, legal pad, pencils, and bills galore. Three days after my phone conversation with Clarence, I again faced the ritual of manipulating debts. My financial life screeched with the irritation of ragged steel on porcelain.

A car horn blared on the street. In the bathroom, CJ and Darius argued over toothpaste. My next door neighbor's radio blasted through the thin apartment walls. I grabbed my head and shook it back and forth. I breathed in the robust aroma of French roasted coffee. Still, panic stretched its parasitic limbs and sucked logic and sensibility from my bloated body. Oh, woe is me. What am I to do? My chest tightened as panic made its awful descent down my esophagus and into my stomach. Alas, I knew poor Katie well. For whom the debt rattle clinks? It clinks for me. Mercy! All such phrases ran through my head.

"Think, Katie," I said to myself. "Think of something lovely."

I closed my eyes and saw a mound of fluffy pancakes drenched with maple syrup. A rich buttery pecan coffee cake rose in that daydream followed by hot buttery grits, buttermilk biscuits, doughnuts, cheese omelet, egg benedicts, and mimosa. I sighed and the panic reclined.

After a cup of coffee, after the boys left for school, and after the neighbor departed for work, I threw sausages into a skillet and turned the gas on low. I prepared my over-worked griddle and then measured flour, salt, and baking powder into a sifter. The shrill of the phone broke through my hard-earned peace. I snatched it off the hook.

"Hello!" I barked.

"Kay-Jay?" Clarence asked.

"Who else would be answering my phone at eight o'clock in the morning?" I snapped.

"You're in a foul mood."

"I've been in a foul mood since nineteen-ninety-five, Clarence," I said.

"That bad, huh?"

No reply necessary, I thought. I cupped the receiver between my head and shoulder and furiously sifted the dry ingredients into a bowl.

"Kay-Jay, what are you doing?" he asked.

"Making pancakes," I said.

"I sure miss your pancakes," he said. "I miss your cooking."

"Clarence, I know you didn't call to talk about my cooking."

"You don't want to talk to me?" he asked.

"Not really."

"I have some news," he said.

"You found a job?" I asked.

"I'm going into the movie business."

I cracked an egg into a smaller bowl and poured butter-milk over it. Ignoring Clarence was the best thing to do. I beat the mixture into a yellow froth. Anger swirled around in my guts.

"Kay-Jay, are you listening."

"To another one of your pipe dreams?"

He was quiet. I set the bowl and whisk down and leaned against the counter and took a great drink of air. I held it for a moment then slowly exhaled the ragged anger. I examined my nails as I waited for Clarence's next brilliant remark. My right thumb was ugly. A split kissed the tip of the nail. A gray line ran from that split to the ragged cuticle. Twelve to fifteen bucks for a manicure was not a line item in my budget.

"Why you gotta be like that, Katie?" He asked.

"Don't even try to shift the blame on me, Clarence."

"I only called to tell you about this terrific opportu-nity . . ."

Clarence went on to tell me about Roberta's boyfriend. That was amazing. Roberta has a *Boyfriend!?!* Hmm, let's see. Sushi with Raisenets was a more believable combina-tion. I rolled my eyes and poured the egg mixture into the flour mixture as Clarence talked. The boyfriend, an up-and-coming movie producer, had a proposal before an HBO honcho. Once the honcho approved the proposal, the boyfriend would need investors. Roberta promised to lend Clarence fifty thousand dollars to invest in the company. The whole thing smelled like ten kettles of chitt'lings on a summer day.

"Why not get the fifty thousand dollars from Roberta and pay off half your debts?" I asked as I poured three per-fect circle onto the sizzling griddle.

"You think small, Katie," he said. "This investment will make me a multimillionaire."

"Shit!" I screamed into the phone.

"Katie!"

"Shit! Shit! Shit!"

"Katie, why you have to cuss. I only wanted to share my news with you."

"Clarence, let me share some news with you. Shit is an old English word. It means foolishness, nonsense. You're talking SHIT! Instead of getting your act together and finding a damn job, you're dreaming again. Now here's a newsflash, Clarence: I don't want you calling me with delusions of grandeur. I don't want to hear anything out of your mouth except, *Kay-Jay, I've found a job.* Is that clear?"

Click.

Yes, it was clear. The man hung up on me. I slammed the phone in the hook and returned to my meal preparation. Spores of bitterness fluttered behind my eyes and in the back of my throat. I stood in the middle of my kitchen floor and screamed. Oh, the man had nerve, and yes, it was all my fault. Didn't I readily take him back the first time he left me?

Yes, he left me over that flipping property business. The morning he flipped the lights on and informed me he was leaving, I didn't really believe him. That evening, when I came home from work, his black Dodge was not parked in front of the building. Clarence was gone. I didn't tell the boys. They were used to his trips. Nevertheless, if I had known a Vinnie or Louie or Joey I would have gladly paid to have Clarence rubbed out. Instead, I crawled around in devastation. CJ and Darius eyed me with fear as I squeezed them each morning and again at night. I wept on their young shoulders. CJ tentatively patted me with *it's okay mom*. Then as suddenly as he had left, Clarence returned.

The boys and I entered the apartment one evening to find Clarence sprawled on the couch like it was a normal day.

"Dad!" The boys shouted and ran to him. He laughed and lifted them onto his lap.

I stormed through the apartment and threw my purse, briefcase, and coat on the bed. I didn't want to face him. I was ashamed as if I had done something wrong.

"I'm sorry," he whispered behind me.

The weak-butt woman that I was, I turned and jumped readily into his arms. Through my connections at Luft's Catalog Company, Clarence got a job in the warehouse. For two years, he worked, and I worked. We hammered and banged each cent into a useful tool. I squeezed and manipulated money like a Wall Street broker. Finally, a sliver of hope broke through the red. We breathed.

A dreamer dreams. Dreams puckered under Clarence's skin. The warehouse promised years of drudgery, of time clocks, and of four-percent increases. The warehouse led him down a road to old age and a small social security check. At least, that's what Clarence tried to convey to me. In early 1997, he approached me with yet another idea. For a mere thirty-five thousand dollars, Clarence could invest in a company that manufactured novelties, those small plastic items that were cute but had no real purpose in life other than to pollute the environment.

"No, Clarence," I told him when he approached me with the idea. "We are not getting involved with any more business ideas. We are going to pay off these debts and buy a house."

Thus, Clarence's period of discontentment began. Nothing I did pleased him. We argued about everything—newspaper articles, food, the weather, colors, shoes, and the real name of the kid who had played Diahann Carroll's son on television. Soon, he joined rank with those famous nags of old: Delilah and the Woodsman wife.

Imagine Delilah nagging Samson as he kissed her: *A little thing like your strength, you won't share with me. You don't trust me. How can you say you love me, when you don't trust me?* Imagine Hansel and Gretel's stepmom nagging her husband in his sleep: *How can you say you love me, when you don't listen to me? Why should I starve for you? Why are you so stubborn? Don't you see? Getting rid of the kids is the only out?* Imagine Clarence nagging me from the moment he rose in the morning, to the moment he closed his eyes at night: *I need a woman to support me. I need a woman to believe in me. How can you say you love me, and not believe in me, not see what I'm trying to do?* I had no peace. All I had left in the world was that piece of property in Englewood, a neighbor on the South Side of Chicago, so I mortgaged it. Ever see a stack of money burn? First it smokes as a warning. Next, a few sparks fly, to allow time for salvaging. Finally, there's total combustion. Long before Clarence carried that thirty-five thousand dollars away, I saw the smoke. A few flecks of sparks seared my face. How did it feel to be over a hundred thousand dollars in debt? I wanted to drown in my bathtub. I wanted to leap in front of an El. I wanted to curl in my daddy's arms and cry. I wanted solutions and absolution. Foolishness. Nonsense. Shit! Shit! Shit! What did I care about the man hanging up on me? I've had enough dreams to last me a lifetime. Dreams carried debts and ruin.

I finished cooking my breakfast. I settled before the computer with a stack of buttermilk pancakes drenched with maple syrup and a mound of smoked beef sausages. I topped it off with whipped butter and a glass of whole milk. I'm not a two-percent girl. Puleeze. If I want water, I'll drink water. By the time the pancakes were gone, I had sent out six resumes, checked out a website on Black Hebrews, and printed the articles for Mama. Mama was convinced that we (African-Americans) were one of the lost tribes of Israel. I found a new game site for the boys and book marked that. I found a site for cooks. I've been looking for a particular cheesecake recipe for years. I scanned the online recipe files but didn't find it. I was bored, and it was two hours before *The Young and the Restless*. I had nothing to do. Like a neon light out of the heavens, one of those flashing windows popped up and said:

FIND A CHAT NOW. CLICK HERE.

I clicked. Immediately, I was swished into a room called *Friends on the Porch*. The conversation went like this:

WillingGurl69:	For me?
WhiskyLips:	yes ma'am
TwoTonHarry2:	looks like gurl has been hit by cupids arrow lol
ODnthurtme:	hello Katie
SimpleMagic:	(»`' ., „ñÿ» _ñ)ª((S b&dunn~My Maria))ª(ñ_ » `ñ, „ ' »)
WhiskyLips:	hi Katie how are you?
SimpleMagic:	Hi Katie, you're in Chicago. What part?

Mercy! I thought. *They know me. They know where I live.* Without thinking, I turned the computer off. I didn't shut down. I clicked that thing off. My heart was thumping in my chest. I looked out of the bedroom window at the guy across the way. He sat at his computer all day. Was he the one who asked, *What part?* At that moment, the man looked up. I grabbed the dishes and left the room.

After I put the dishes away, I went into the living room and sat on the couch. For the first time I saw one of those sleazy talk shows. There was a man with raggedly teeth saying his big fat wife was leaving her big fat hairy lover and returning to him and their five love-starved children. The show made me forget the chat room. During the commercial break, I scanned the channels. On one channel, in big bold letters, were the words: **Are you Safe on the Internet?** A deep voice boomed from the television set. *A special report tonight on* . . . I clicked off the television. Everybody knew my shame. I had been in a chat room.

***

"Katie, put on your best dress," Donna said over the phone, a week or two later. "You're going to the opera with Mike tonight while I baby-sit."

"Kinda last minute isn't it?" I asked. Donna always called me at the last minute, like I didn't have a life. How many cakes had I baked for her at a minute notice?

"You have plans?" she asked.

"Okay, what time?" I asked.

I loved the opera. Going to the Civic Opera House was like going to another world. The production companies always found such exquisite backdrops for the huge stage. The backdrops appeared real, like the company had moved the great outdoors inside the opera house. Always, I expected the painted sky to churn. Donna hated the opera, and Mike had season tickets. Usually he took his aunt, but the old girl was ill. Mike and Donna arrived before I had finished dressing. The boys entertained Mike with stud poker, while Donna and I wrestled with the zipper of my best black dress.

"I don't understand it," I moaned. "I wore it to the company's anniversary party four weeks ago."

"Girl, you've gained ten pounds in the last three weeks," Donna said. "Weigh yourself and see."

Clarence's forgotten scale squatted in the bathroom between the sink and toilet. After I gained the first thirty pounds, I never used the scale again. Watching my weight was not part of my daily routine. Clarence was the health nut, always pumping iron and working out. The man had muscles that made me salivate. He was a good-looking man. I had to give him that.

"Go on. Weigh yourself," Donna urged.

"I know I've gained a bit," I said.

"Get your fat ass on the scale," she said and pushed me through the bedroom door.

She stood in the bathroom doorway while I weighed myself. The scale screamed. Yes it did! *Get off, fatty, get off!* I swear it screamed. I could not see the numbers because my stomach was in the way. I sucked in my gut. That did no good. I pressed in my stomach and saw that the numbers were verging on one hundred and ninety-three pounds. I fell against the sink. I wrapped my arms around myself. My head was spinning.

"Donna, why didn't you tell me?" I said. Our eyes met in the mirror. A scowl puckered across Donna's brow.

"I did. Every time I told you not to taste-test a whole cake," Donna snapped.

We squeezed me into that dress, but I tell you, it hurt. The waist cut into my stomach like a rubber band. The sleeves strapped my meaty forearms like they were rump roasts. Mike, who was always such a gentleman, said nothing when I joined him although his eyebrows rose slightly. He was a large burly man with deep-set eyes. He had a Neanderthal appearance but a sharp wit and an infectious laugh.

Mike draped my cape around my shoulders, pecked Donna on the check, and whisked a fat Cinderella to the opera. On the way, we talked about the Chicago Bulls and how sad that Michael Jordan had become a legend of the past, how sad that Chicago was once again the bottom of the NBA barrel. We had a heated debate about the mayor and the rejuvenation of the city. Mike and I differed on the politics of Chicago. I was a staunch supporter of the whatever-works-now program, while Mike always looked to the future.

"Mike, Chicago hasn't been this clean in years."

"Well, when all your homies are in the suburbs because they can't afford city housing, you'll see my point," Mike assured me.

"Ya da ya da ya da, Mike," I said.

"You're a case," he said and turned off Lake Shore Drive onto Randolph Street.

Wacker Drive had the best night view of Chicago's architecture. The ghostly Tribune Tower, the white iridescent Wrigley Building, the old-man gray of Sun-Times Building and many other stately structures sparkled at night along the Chicago River. On a clear night the lights in their windows sparkled on the river like gems. But Mike never took that scenic route to the Civic Opera House. Instead, he cut across Randolph where the only thing worth seeing was Marshall Field's stately structure, the old combination city hall/county building, and the Midland Hotel.

"How's the chatting going?" Mike cut into my thoughts.

"What?" I asked. Suddenly, my palms were sweaty. A curl of a smile played on Mike's lips when he glanced at me. I turned my head toward the hot dog stand on the corner of Franklin and Randolph. Did my Internet provider publish a list of chatters?

"You were in my favorite chat room," he said. "I'm WhiskyLips."

"No!" I looked at him and exclaimed. His smiled was wide, verging on a full-blown laugh.

"Yup," he said.

"Donna knows you chat?" I asked.

"Katie, it's not against the law to chat," he said and turned onto Wacker Drive. We were a block away from the Civic Opera House.

"Does Donna chat?"

"Naw," he said. "She thinks it will hurt her professional image to chat."

"You don't think it will hurt your image?"

"I'm at work. I'm bored. It's lunchtime. I chat," he said laughingly. "Next time, Katie, change your name and create a fictitious profile that's not so revealing."

"To what?" I asked.

"You'll think of something and when you do, create a fictitious profile."

"Fictitious?" I asked.

"Yeah," he said. "Be creative. Don't put in personal information. Remember, that a bunch of strangers will read it. You would not walk into a crowded restaurant and pass out personal information, so why do it online?"

I peered at his face trying to remember what his lips looked like and why he called himself WhiskyLips. All I could see was his nose jutting from his face like the curve of an expansion bridge.

"How did you come up with WhiskyLips?" I asked.

He turned briefly and laughed. "What's my favorite drink?"

"Black Jack, neat," I said. Then I laughed, "Oh, WhiskyLips."

"See. You'll think of something."

Later that night, I signed online and created a new screen name, *Stepmom8945*. Next I created a simple profile. Finally, I entered a room called The Corner Bookstore.

SassySteam555:	Is slide
OnlineHost:	YaMamalzhere has entered the room.

DanCanDoIt:	Ride me . . . Muahhhhhhhhhhhh back at you baby
ShoUCan2:	hi Stepmom
ShoUCan2:	wb YaMama
RideMeWild:	Crack da whip, babyDanCanDoIt: I give upppppp.

I thought the conversation would be about books, but obviously it wasn't. I left the room, confused.

CHAPTER 4

Tameka whipped the pale pink icing in her bowl until it was glossy and stiff. She scooped a finger full of frosting from the bowl and popped it into her mouth.

"This is great!" she exclaimed.

"It's my standard butter cream frosting," I said. "It's really the cake that counts."

The aroma of a luscious sour cream chocolate cake surrounded us. A twelve-inch layer cooled on the counter behind Tameka. An eight-inch top layer was in the oven, also behind Tameka. An unbearable heat filled the kitchen. I reached behind me and cracked open the back door. A cool breeze rushed. Icy rain fell from the gray sky. The angry voices of an arguing couple came from the next building. The cries of a frightened child rose from the street. A dog barked. An el rumbled a block away, and my brain ticked, ticked, ticked. I was in my third week of unemployment.

Panic rubbed against my temples. I had no idea how I was going to manage all the bills.

Last summer Mama and Donna had talked me into baking cakes as a sideline. People were constantly begging me to bake a little something for them. Some weeks I churned out four to six cakes. Members of Tameka's family called me almost weekly for cakes. Honey, when there's a trillion-zillion people in a family, there's always a birthday, a wedding, an anniversary, or some other special occasion that requires a cake. Whenever I baked a cake for her family, Tameka hitched a ride with Alex. While Alex spent the day with CJ and Darius, she spent the day helping me. That day we were making a wedding cake for one of her cousins.

Tameka and I worked around my oak table without the hindrance of kitchen chairs. The chairs sat before the living room windows. On the kitchen table was an array of spatulas, decorating bags, decorating tips, rose nails, and tiny squares of wax paper. An eighteen-inch bowl of buttercream frosting stood in the center of the table. Tameka had two smaller bowls before her. One contained the pale pink icing and the other contained a deeper pink shade. She chatted on and on about school and some dumb boy who was giving her the bum-rush. A spotless white apron was wrapped around her skinny body like a Band-Aid around a finger. I had on a purple-mad-cow muumuu. Flour, icing, stains, and a streak of chocolate covered it. My bowl of green icing lacked intensity. I dipped a toothpick into a small vial of green paste. I swirled the toothpick in the icing until the paste dissolved.

"The brother is buff, so he thinks he can pull any girl he wants," she said.

"Doesn't he know about you and Alex?" I asked.

"Everybody knows about Alex and me," she said. "Everybody but you and Mama Jeffries."

She leaned across the table and stared into my eyes. She held that stare for a full minute. Her droopy eyes were the color of molasses. The bridge of her nose was flat. A tiny bump of a nose poked from her face. I saw Regina in her face.

"Alex and I are just friends," she enunciated slowly. "Don't plan on baking a wedding cake for us. It's not happening. Ever."

"But you get along so well," I said. "You care for each other and . . ."

"Yeah, I care about you too. Do you wanna marry me?"

I laughed. We were similar peas in the same crazy pod.

"I got dreams," she continued. "There are places I wanna go. Things I want to see."

"I understand that," I said. "Most kids have high hopes. I even had dreams when I was your age."

"What were your dreams?" she asked.

I thought back to my last year of high school and laughed.

"What?" she asked.

"My biggest dream was to find Miss Prissy a date for the prom."

"Huh?"

"Mama said I couldn't go to my senior prom if Donna didn't go. Donna couldn't find a date."

"Miss Donna?"

"Oh, yeah. The girl was a dog," I laughed.

"Naw!" Tameka shouted. "She's one of the most glamorous women I know."

"Trust me. She was a bow-wow. The girl had enough pimples to start a pus bank. I wasn't a beauty queen but I had a couple of boyfriends. Regina was our star. In high school, the boys hung around your aunt Regina like she was Playboy's pinup of the century. All you Jordan women got it going on. You're intelligent, beautiful, and sensuous. A dangerous combination. That's probably why there's a quadzillion of you Jordans walking around."

"Miss Katie!"

I threw my hand up and blocked the stunned look on her face. I walked to the cupboard and pulled out two cake rounds: One plain and one ruffle. I placed the ruffle round on the cake stand and carried the other to the counter. I positioned it over the cake pan and flipped the cool cake over. It slid easily out the pan. Using a pastry brush, I dusted all the loose crumbs from the cake.

"So, you had to find Miss Donna a date?" Tameka asked.

"Girl, yeah, and it wasn't easy. I tried to pay LaDell to take her, but he said he wasn't that desperate for twenty dollars. Regina asked half the guys in your family. Their laughter rose from the South Side like a victory cry from Comiskey Park. Finally, I found a duffus guy with no hope of a prom date. I still had to beg him to take her. It cost me thirty dollars. Regina didn't want any part of my plan. She said I was wrong. Hmph! I was not going to miss my senior prom cause of Donna Anderson."

I returned to the table with the cake. Using the two cake rounds, I flipped the cake over and set it onto the cake stand. Tameka opened a plastic bag and dropped the base of a coupler into the bag. A coupler is a two-part gizmo. The base, actually a sprout, was shoved through the plastic decorating bag. Next she guided a decorating tip over the sprout, and finally, she screwed the ring of the coupler over the decorating tip. Tameka worked quickly. She scooped stiff icing out of the bowl with a large spoon-spatula combination and packed it into the bag. If the icing were not the right consistency, the rose petals would not form properly. I positioned the cake before the large bowl of buttercream icing.

"So, what happened?" Tameka asked.

Tameka held a tiny rose nail in her right hand. The head of the rose nail was about the size of a quarter. Tameka dabbed a dot of icing on the head and placed a tiny square of wax paper on that dot. The icing held the paper in place. Tameka gripped the bag of pale pink icing in her right hand. She squeezed hard from the base, relaxed, and lifted. A perfect cone sat in the center of the nail. She positioned the bag at 7:30 and turned the nail clockwise, since she was left-handed. Like a machine she moved the tip up and down. She abruptly stopped and lifted the tip away. Once she formed the center petals, Tameka used the same gesture to form three more rows of petals. Tameka wiped the tip of the coupler as she worked. A clean tip allowed the icing to flow freely and kept the petals from blurring together. I finished the prom date story as we worked.

"She accepted his invitation," I said. "Then the most amazing thing happened."

"What?" Tameka asked. She rubbed the back of her hand across the bridge of her nose and left a streak of pink icing on it.

"Your grandmama transformed Miss Prissy into a hot babe!"

"Naw!"

"Yeah!"

"When Donna stepped into the hotel ballroom, you would have thought Appollonia had walked through that door."

"Apple who . . ."

"Never mind. She was one of Prince's old girlfriends . . ."

"You mean the Artist formerly known as . . ."

"Listen, the man will always be Prince to me. Okay?"

"Chill."

"Anyway, the girl floated into the room. My date left me on the dance floor. Oh, talking about despising Miss Prissy."

"Why do you call her Miss Prissy?" Tameka asked.

"That's a long story," I said.

"We got the time," she said. "Tell it."

So I told her . . .

In some countries, parents arrange marriages with no participation from the bride or the groom. My relationship with Donna was such an arrangement. Mrs. Anderson, Mrs. Jordan, and Mama assumed that their daughters would be best friends since they were. From the moment of our births, those three biddies threw us together in cribs, playpens, Headstart programs, Sunday school, and summer camp. Mild and easy-going Regina blended well with both Donna and me. Donna and I scratched and clawed each other every chance we got. Our first real fight happened when we were mere babes-in-arms.

Mrs. Anderson, Mrs. Jordan, and Mama stood outside of church in their Sunday fineries. They held their beautiful bundles of joy. As Mrs. Anderson complimented the Reverend on his great sermon, I reached out of my blankets and grabbed Donna's fat cheek. She wailed and grabbed my hair. I wailed and dug my tiny hand deeper into her pudgy cheek. Regina wailed. Mama pried my fingers out of Donna's flesh. Mrs. Anderson snatched Donna's hand out of my hair. Mrs. Jordan pat Regina on the back and asked, "What got into these babies. What got into them?"

Mrs. Anderson used jars of cocoa butter on Donna's face. Yet, to this day, tiny brown scars marred Donna's left cheek. Did the mothers learn? No. They continued to force us together. Regina is the only reason Donna survived our childhood. I locked Donna in a closet, and Regina let her out. I slammed Donna's finger in a door. Regina ran for help. I

tripped Donna. Regina lifted her up. I ripped apart every
View Master Donna ever owned. Why? Because she was a
suck face teller-tale, that's why. I knew it from the moment
I set eyes on her. Babies know these things. I christened
Donna *Miss Prissy* in the Summer of 1971.

Whenever my daddy drove down Interstate 57 to the
bridge connecting Illinois to Missouri, a low fog always
drifted across the highway. The fog, the dense canopy of
trees, and an eerie full moon spooked me. Why was there a
full moon, each time we took that trip? Why did Mama
Verna, Mr. Pete's first wife, plunge into spooky tales of haints
and love gone wrong? Why did Mr. Pete talk about slavery
and the wickedness of the white man? Why did mama grow
solemn and heavy and hummed hymns from her youth,
blues from her youth, songs that weighed us down? LaDell
and I lay in the back of that 1965 station wagon scared and
excited. We made bets about who could hold their pee until
the next necessary stop. We munched on the fried chicken
and played Old Maid cause Mama Verna said regular cards
were the devil's tools.

We drove from our middle-class life in Englewood to the
deprived (Mama's word, not mine) life of the Mississippi
Delta. Once we arrived in the Delta, Mama and Mama
Verna swapped stories of the promise land. For seven days,
they sat around with old girlfriends and laughed at the heft
and girth they each wore. Their conversations became a continuous *wonder whatever happened to no count Rowland or
Deeves who left to fight in the war and never came back, but
didn't you see his picture in a magazine being giving the con-
gressional medal of honor and whatever happened to that piece
of trash Cleora who left home on the coat tail of some blues
playing man who had women up and down the cotton rows.*

LaDell enjoyed those trips because the Hills sprouted
boys like they sprouted soybeans, in abundance. The cousins

taught LaDell how to dig for crawdads and to down butter-milk in three gulps. My closest girl cousin was five years older than I. By the time I was nine, she most certainly didn't want me tagging behind her. So, I ripped and ran with the boys but I missed girls. The summer of my tenth birth-day, I begged my daddy to let Regina come with me. He told Mama it was a good idea. Mama came up with the big brain-buster to invite Donna too.

"Inviting only Regina wouldn't be fair," she said.

So the Summer of '71 found Donna, Regina, and me in the back of the station wagon. LaDell fretted and frowned between Mama Verna and Mama in the back seat of the sta-tion wagon. When we arrived in the Delta, my Aunt Mame grabbed me and planted one of those wet, sloppy auntie-kisses on my face. She pressed a package in my hand.

"Happy birthday, baby girl!" she exclaimed. "Happy birthday. You kneed to know Jesus for yourself."

I unwrapped the present and found a child's Bible. The vivid blue cover had a picture of the Good Shepherd and a flock of lambs. While Regina and Donna slept the first night away, I dove into that book. The tenth year of my life Regina and Donna found freedom on the Delta soil and I found Jesus.

Those Bible people spoke to my heart: Adam and Eve with their fig leafs and shame, Cain, who knew how it felt to be second in his parents' eyes, Noah and his menagerie of animals, Abraham, Lot, Isaac, Joseph, Moses, Moses, and more Moses. By the time I got to Jesus and his birth I was ready for church. I was ready to join all creation in shouting hallelujah.

Church, I knew, was the place where children sat still while adults shouted amen, lifted their voices in mournful songs, and got down on their knees. Church was the place where a tall lanky deacon led us in the benediction. That

Sunday, when the preacher preached and the choir sang, I wanted to sing too. I wanted to shout with the old sisters in the front pew. I knew the Moses in the preacher's sermon. I knew about the parting of the Red Sea. I knew how to go on when all looked lost. Wasn't Donna sitting between me and my mama? Wasn't Donna my greatest burden? Forever more? Oh, yes, she was. I wanted to break loose from my plight in life. I wanted to shout like Miriam. I wanted to dance. Yes, I did. So, by the time the children of Israel were on the other side of that Red Sea, I was crying and patting my feet. I was mumbling amen too. Yes, I was. Donna took it upon herself (yes, she did) to whisper in my mama's ear.

"Katie's playing with Jesus."

Mama looked over and saw me caught up in my moment. Anger poured out of her. She leaned across Donna and pinched me until a purple mark rose on my hand.

"You don't play with God, girl," she said. "You don't play with God."

I didn't know how to tell her that I wasn't playing. Donna looked down her long sloping nose at me. Smugness drew a tight smile on her lips. That was enough. My tears of pain changed to tears of rage. I vowed right then to bring down the plagues of Moses's on Donna's head.

"Miss Katie!" Tameka broke into my story.

"What?" I asked, licking icing from a spatula.

We had completely frosted the first layer of the wedding cake. White butter cream ruffles bordered the cake. A pale pink bow connected the ruffles. Clusters of Tameka's pale pink and deep pink roses bordered the top layer of the cake. My deep green leaves shot from her perfect buds.

"You didn't hurt Miss Donna, did you?" she asked.

I smiled my benign *I'm-so-innocent* smile. "You bet your HS diploma I got her and good. That's how she got the name."

"I'm afraid to ask, but I want to know," Tameka said. "How?"

I told her the rest of the story . . .

Mama knew I was spiteful. She knew I could hold a grudge longer than a mortgage company could hold the deeds on property. I did nothing while we were in the Delta. Our week ended, and we returned to Chicago. We frolicked about the city streets on our bikes. Back in those days, our parents allowed us to wander around our neighborhood. Occasionally, we hopped the CTA and rode across 59th Street to the Museum of Science and Industry. Nowadays, a child can't go to the park alone. Anyway, we enjoyed the activities afforded us by living on the South Side—the 57th Street Beach, the museum, and Funtown on Stoney Island. We licked snow balls and Popsicles. We jumped rope, played dodge ball, and yes, attended the annual Bud Biliken's parade. Every so often, I reminded Donna that I was going to get her.

"Girl, gone," she would say.

By the end of the summer, I knew she took it as a joke, so I didn't say it again. Always, I was thinking, *Get Donna. Get Donna.* Always.

There were about ten or twelve neighborhood children, not counting the millions of Jordans, that hung out together. Donna was the girl with her socks creeping into her shoes, and the girl with short nappy hair in haystack braids. Whatever problem a growing child could have, Donna had. She wore glasses, slobbered, and had a perpetual nose drip. Those problems we overlooked. However, Donna was a squealer, a whiner, and a braggart. Donna used every new item that her family acquired as an opportunity to remind us that our families were not as fortunate as her family.

"We went to Disneyland," she bragged. "Of course, we can afford it cause my daddy's a high school principal."

Her words just added bile to our envy. I was not the only who felt animosity toward Donna, but I was the only one brave enough to bring her down. My chance came right after Labor Day. As always, the temperature had changed, and we were back in school. Rain fell, and the streets were muddy. One morning, as we walked up Loomis, Miss Donna was in full bragging mode. Her mother had cut her nappy haystacks into a neat and trim Afro. She wore an Afro-centric dress to complement the hairdo. For once the girl looked decent.

"Mama said I'm from royal African blood," she bragged. "Mama said, our people can trace our roots back to the slave ship that our great-great-great-grandfather came over on. Mama said, most Black people can't even trace their roots back to Mississippi. Mama said . . ."

Oh! What to my grateful eyes did appear but the gray and blue Peoples Gas and Coke Truck. At the end of the block, a team of workmen slung muddy soil into mounds along the sidewalk. Quite by accident, I bumped into Donna. She went sprawling into a mound of gravel and mud, faced down with her dumb dress up around her white cotton panties. Our friends laughed while Regina helped her up. Donna stood wide-legged with her arms dangling in the air. Mud caked her hair, her face, and her royal dress.

"Poor Miss Prissy," I said, "Did you get dirty?"

The other kids (except Regina) joined in, "Poor Miss Prissy! Poor Miss Prissy!"

"Miss Katie!" Tameka exclaimed. She placed the last rose on the top layer of the cake.

"What?"

"That was malice."

"Yeah," I laughed. "I never claimed to be Miss Conge-niality or Miss Perfect. I was a ten-year-old girl tired of her friend squealing on her, lording over her, and bragging about everything in her life. I was a ten-year-old girl who wanted to humiliate Miss Prissy. I tell you the whopping I got after school was worth it."

"But you are still friends?" Tameka said. "I don't get it."

"Sometimes a tragedy will bind two people together," I said. "Donna and I had your Aunt Regina's death to bind us."

We packed the layers in separate boxes. A ten-inch round by two-inch high rose pattern separator would sit between the two layers and create the illusion of a large cake.

"This is one beautiful and delicious cake," Tameka said. She licked the remains of icing from her finger.

"Yeah," I agreed. "We outdid ourselves this time."

***

Donna arrived while Tameka was in the shower. She dumped her umbrella behind the door and slipped out of her jacket. Our plans were to drop Tameka off at the church and then continue to the banquet hall.

"Why didn't you tell me you lost your job?" Donna asked.

I didn't tell Donna about losing my job because she had a vision of us as business partners. She envisioned herself as marketing director and me as the kitchen scullion. *I'll sell and you'll cook* were her exact words to me. We both knew her limitations in the kitchen. Donna blundered through the simplest dishes. Her rice clumped like Playdough. Her boiled eggs solidified into rubber balls. The only thing she made successfully was instant oatmeal.

"I called your office yesterday," she said.

"Yeah?"

"Some woman answered your phone and told me you no longer worked there," Donna said, trailing behind me into the kitchen.

"You want coffee?" I asked and poured myself a cup.

"I want you to look at me."

Yes, she did talk to me in that tone of voice. I shook my head. Sometimes ignoring Donna was the best thing to do. I slowly returned the pot of scalding coffee back in its slot and turned to her. I lifted one eyebrow.

She frowned. Her perfectly shaped eyes lowered. I noticed her buttery pecan lipstick and smiled. Donna had learned how to maximize her toffee color. She wore a pair of fawn colored pants with a matching shirt and small amber studs in her ears. Gone was the scrawny friend of my youth. An elegant woman stood in my kitchen with disdain on her face. I had changed into a blue big-as-an-ox tunic and a pair of leggings. I wore a pair of dangling blue star earrings. Yet, even my deep plum lipstick paled before her.

"So, how's the job hunt coming along?" she asked.

"Not."

"Then we should look at catering as a full-fledge business opportunity for you," she said.

"I'm telling you again, Donna," I said. "I am not going into the cake baking, bread baking, catering business."

"You don't have many skills," she said. "It's not like you have an MBA or anything truly marketable."

The blood coursed through my body like lava. Donna was a master of the subtle put-down. I slipped into a chair and played with the string on one box.

"I have an MFA. Many local art museums need a woman with my talents," I said.

I looked at her. That MFA represented three dateless years, twenty-five thousand dollars in student loans, and two years of turning down job promotions. That MFA represented dreams and hopes, and something I accomplished without support or help. If I chose to weave it into a glittery nothingness, so be it.

Donna leaned against the doorpost. "You're right. I hear

that the Art Institute is looking for fund raisers. You could step right in and make those calls."

"You are coming dangerously close to an ass-whupping," I said.

"See, that's your problem," she said, folding her arms. "You don't think logically. You get all emotional. I'm only trying to get you to be practical."

"Tameka!" I shouted. "Are you ready?"

"Almost!" She shouted from my room.

"Hurry!" I shouted. "Or you're going to find Miss Donna dead on the kitchen floor!"

Tameka's laughter shot through the apartment loud as a rumbling el. Donna stood straight up.

"You told her the baby fight story," she accused.

I smiled my benign smile.

CHAPTER 5

MFA, indeed. The truth is I first went to college as a writing major because Jimmy Martin's exquisite fingers roamed across my breasts and kindled the most excruciating fire between my thighs. He spent hours caressing and sucking my large brown nipples. He respected me too much to do anything more, but that was enough. When he graduated from Parker High School and went to Washington State University in St. Louis, I followed the next year. I saw him a couple of times on campus, but his exquisite fingers were always interlocked with some dude's.

Well, there I was at Washington State enrolled in a terrific writing program, so why not try. I wasn't much into anything else. By the end of the first semester, it was painfully obvious, writing was not easy. However, Mama was back home saying *You need to give up that foolishness! Why don't you change majors! LaDell says computers are gonna be*

*big in ten years. Maybe you should use the practical side of your
head for a change.*

Mama never went to college or to high school. She barely
made it out of grammar school, but every day she read the
two major city newspapers, cover-to-cover. She read *Time,
Ebony, People, Jet, Essence,* and *Cosmopolitan* magazine. She
also read all novels and short stories from the Harlem Re-
naissance that she could find. Mama could discuss anything
from evolution and creationism, to the splitting of the atom,
to why America needed to stay out of the Middle East. She
knew every stitch of gossip on the rich and famous. Whatever Mama believed, you best agree with her or keep your
mouth shut. I kept my mouth shut around her and I smiled
a lot. That was easier and it drove her batty.

I would have completed my degree at Washington State
if I had not gotten pregnant by a teaching assistant. When I
told my sweetheart I was pregnant, he looked at me as if I
had just destroyed years of Einstein's work, shook his head,
and walked away. Yup. Just walked away. So, at the end of
my second year, I packed up, seven-months pregnant, and
went home.

LaDell and Georgie were sitting at the kitchen table
when I walked through the backdoor. They were poring
over bridal catalogs and house plans and all the crap people
who are planning a life together pored over. Mama was upstairs, in the attic/sewing room, singing, *He looked beyond my
faults and saw my need.*

"Katie! You're pregnant!" LaDell exclaimed.

"Mama Jeffries hasn't mentioned it," Georgie said.

"Mama doesn't know," I said.

LaDell and Georgie looked at each other. Their mouths
dropped. Their eyes widened. They looked at me and, like
syncopated performers, they shook their heads.

"Let's go, Baby," Georgie said and began gathering their brochures and magazines together.

LaDell leaped from the table like somebody had placed pagan food before him. They held their brochures to their chests, rushed passed me, and flew out the backdoor. A moment later, LaDell's Mustang roared, then zoomed away. I stood in Mama's kitchen and looked up the long hall to the living room where Daddy once sat. From that green chair, Daddy watched the whole house. After school, I rushed through the back door, up the narrow hall, and jumped into his lap. He tickled me until I begged for mercy. Then we sat and chatted like best friends. He listened as I poured out my day and my dreams.

"Here, Kitten," he said and held out his hand

A gold star, the kind the teachers used on excellent papers, glittered in his hand. I grabbed that star. Next, Daddy kissed me on my forehead, set me on my feet, and gently shoved me into my future. Then he turned his full attention to LaDell who was impatiently waiting for his *daddy time*. What transpired between Daddy and LaDell, I didn't know. I went into my room, did my homework until supper, and then watched whatever television program Daddy chose. Right after dinner, Daddy went to bed, rising later for his job on the night shift at a South Chicago auto plant. Day after day, my daddy gave me a star, and each star I placed in a small Welch's jelly glass. At night I put that jar under my pillow and dreamed of moonbeams.

When I was twelve, Daddy sat in that chair and only rose to walk to the bathroom and the bedroom. His hard hands hung over the arms of the chair like loose appendages. His eyes stared over our heads, into the past. At mealtimes, Daddy dragged from that chair to the table. One day, Mama placed a TV tray before him, and that became his permanent table. Daddy's breathing became deep and ragged.

LaDell, always wiser and always sensing the rightness of things, set a chair next to Daddy's chair. We alternated sitting there. We read and talked to Daddy. As Daddy got weaker and weaker, LaDell sat less and less. At times, daddy laid his head back, closed his eyes, and sang . . .

"Would you like to swing on a star?
Carry moonbeams home in a jar . . ."

Then, he opened his eyes and smiled, not at me or LaDell but at some distant memory.

"You can be better off then you are . . ."

At that point he always stopped singing and those loose hands gathered strength from those memories and tightened on the arms of the chair.

"Have no regrets, LaDell, Katie," he said to us, "swing on stars."

Sometimes, he wore a quirky smile for a few seconds then he leaned forward, and, in a tenor voice as sweet and poignant as any popular love ballad, he sang . . .

"Tempted and tried, we're oft made to wonder,
why it should be dost; all the day long . . ."

Although his voice was beautiful, rich, and filled with the awe of God, I hated for Daddy to sing that song. It meant that he had to rise from that chair, and, with Mama, LaDell, and my help, move out of the living room into the bedroom. There he spent two to three days in misery moaning and groaning and yes, crying. Six months passed with Daddy moving between the chair and bed. Finally, the day came when Daddy was too weak to rise from his bed. If Mama was around, I stood in the doorway, too afraid to enter. When she turned her back, he beckoned to me, and I went. Mama frowned but said nothing until I came out of the room.

"Why are you disturbing your daddy?" She jerked my arm. "You know he's sick, and there you are hanging around like a puppy dog."

I didn't care if her fingernails dug into my arms. I didn't care if she punished me for disobeying her. I defied her and sat with my daddy as often as I dared. She whupped me once because of my disobedience. I screamed so loudly that Daddy had a coughing fit. Mama dared not whop me again while he was alive. Although she begged and begged him to go to the hospital, he refused.

"I'm gonna die at home," he said to Mama. "That hospital will never suck my savings away. That money is for you and the children."

Once, I had the privilege of being alone with Daddy. Mama Verna and Mr. Pete, who usually took turns nursing him when Mama was exhausted beyond belief or had errands to run, were not available.

"Katie, you sit quietly by your daddy," Mama said, "And don't disturb him."

"Yes, ma'am," I said.

I sat beside my daddy's bed and watched him sleep. His dark face glistened with sweat until the blue, rose, and yellow undertones of his complexion twinkled. In his sleep, my daddy's face went through an array of expressions: Pain, peace, and a soft smile. He finally opened his eyes and saw me studying his face.

"Kitten," he said, trying to lift his hand.

"Daddy, don't talk," I said and held his hand. "Mama wants you quiet."

"Listen, baby girl," he said. "I'm trying to tell you . . ."

"What, Daddy?" I asked. "Do you want water or something?"

"Sh-sh," he said. "Listen. You and your brother and your mama ain't gotta worry. Everything is taken care of. The house will be paid . . ."

Daddy, with all the strength he could muster, held my

hand tightly. He told me about the arrangements he had made. He told me about his dreams for LaDell and his dreams for me. He even spoke of his hope for Mama's future happiness. Often he stopped and took big gulping breaths of air. I tried to get him to be quiet, to rest. Daddy ignored my requests.

"I want you to promise me Kitten, promise me . . ." He said at last. "You'll swing on stars."

"I promise," I said.

"Always."

"Always, Daddy."

He laid back and slept. When Mama came home, he was breathing peacefully. She looked at his hand in mine and snapped.

"I told you not to disturb him."

"He's okay, Mama," I said. "I didn't disturb him."

One night the ambulance came. A paramedic placed a mask over Daddy's face. She and her partner lifted him onto the gurney and wheeled him out. I tried to get to him, but Mama Verna held me back. Mama followed that gurney out the house and climbed into the back of the ambulance. Each day I asked Mama about him, and each day she snapped.

"How do you think he's doing? He's sick!"

Each day I asked if I could visit him.

"You're a child. They don't allow children in the hospital."

Each night I looked at that jar of stars, cried, and prayed that my daddy would come home and sit in his green chair again. He never did.

I shall forever lift my eyes to Calvary . . .

Mama's deep contralto voice broke into my thoughts and dragged me from memories of my daddy to that moment when I stood pregnant in her kitchen. I looked at that chair, the same dull green chair, and wished that Daddy were there, so I could wobble up the hall and fall into his lap.

"LaDell," Mama called. "Y'all run to Dominick's and get some of that Haagen Das cream."

Mama called ice cream, cream. Mama was country. She was born in the Mississippi Delta. She was proud to be from Mound Bayou. For years, she traipsed to the Delta for the Hill family reunion, dragging LaDell and me along. She, LaDell, and his family still make that yearly trip.

"They're gone, Mama," I called. I heard her chair scrape across the floor, followed by her heavy footsteps. I quickly wobbled down the hall to my room and managed to get my belly through my bedroom door before she stepped into the kitchen. Mama's house was one of many bungalows in Englewood. Back then, in the early 1980's, decay was rapidly taking over. Anyway, I had my belly through the doorway of my bedroom, so Mama saw only my backside.

"Gal, what are you doing home?" she asked. "Isn't this the summer you were going to spend in England looking at those dead writers' graves?"

"Tomes, Mama, not Tombs."

"Whatever."

Mama was quick. You could not put anything over on her. I think that's true of all mamas. They have ten pairs of eyes. They have noses like bloodhounds, feet like cheetahs, and hands like grizzly bears. Mamas are some mean, dangerous animals. Mama looked at me in that dim hall. From twenty feet away, she assessed the sway of my back and threw up her hands.

"Lord, Jesus!" she cried. "This girl done thrown all my teachings out the window."

"Mama," I whispered, "it was an accident."

Okay, by now it's obvious that I'm not the brightest light

on the street. Calling my condition an accident was the worst thing I could have done. Mama lit into me like a match to a cigarette.

"Accident! How, in all creation, is opening your legs an accident? And where is this fine specimen of a man who talked you into bringing shame on your daddy's home?"

Now, why did the lady have to bring my daddy into the picture? The man died when I was thirteen. She knew how much that had hurt me. He was the only one who ever said I was beautiful. I stood there, ashamed, deeply ashamed. It was 1981, and black girls, white girls, Chinese girls, girls all around the world were having babies without husbands. It wasn't a taboo thing anymore, but there I was, ashamed.

"Mama," I whispered again. "I'm sorry."

"Don't say sorry to me," Mama said. "You gonna spend the rest of your days apologizing to this child. When he asks about his daddy, *you gotta say I'm sorry honey, I don't know where your daddy is.* When other children tease him cause he ain't got a daddy, you gotta hold him and say *I'm sorry, baby. I'm so sorry.* So, just take your sorry tail into your room, and don't bother me until I make my peace with Jesus about this matter."

Mama was always making peace with Jesus. When she got upset, she prayed in her room, sometimes for days, until she made peace with Jesus. Mama stayed in her room for three days. The only sounds from her room were her prayers. Sometimes she entreated the Lord loudly. Sometimes she prayed softly. Once she broke down and cried, *The gal done brought shame on her father's house.* Once I heard her fussing about the wickedness of loose women. At the end of three days she emerged from her room and made an appointment for me with an ob-gyn.

When Alex Jeffries Jr. was born, Mama latched on to my

child and I became the surrogate mama. She named him after my daddy. Although I told her he wasn't really a junior, she insisted that Junior be included on the birth certificate. I always felt more like Alex's sister than his mother. He called me Katie like everybody else, although he knew I was his mother. If he needed something, then I became mom.

CHAPTER 6

Whoosh! The holidays were gone. Happy New Year! As I predicted, Roberta's boyfriend disappeared sometime around Christmas. Heartbroken and disillusioned, Clarence found a job in January—January 5 to be exact. His call came while I was making a banana pudding, and the boys were building a miniature snow man on the back porch. Chicago's weather could get as mean as a drunk in a rage, but making a snowman on the back porch was not a common thing. A New Year's blizzard dumped a whopping twenty-one inches of snow across Chicagoland in forty-eight hours. The temperature plummeted to below zero figures. After four days stuck in the house with me, the boys whined and whined until I agreed to let them spend ten minutes on the back porch every hour. I cleared enough snow from the doorway to shove their bodies outside. Anyway, Clarence had a job and I was unemployed.

"Since you're working now, you could send me your

other check," I said. I stood at the counter slicing and layering the last banana in the casserole dish. I peeped out the back window. The boys wobbled back and forth, across the porch. They were dressed in a triple layer of clothes, down jackets, woolen hats, scarves, and thin gloves followed by thick down mittens. Their heavy Timberland boots were hidden in the snow. The base of the snowman stood in a corner of the porch waiting for the second segment. They were determined little men.

"I got to find an apartment for me and the boys," Clarence retorted. "And I got to buy a car."

"I got to feed the boys!" I snapped and popped a slice of banana in my mouth. "They need shoes. They need clothes. CJ needs to have his cavities taken care of and we don't have dental benefits anymore."

"Didn't you take COBRA?"

"That costs money," I said. I checked the clock on the stove. The boys had four more minutes to spend outside.

"I'll send you money for his cavities," he said.

"Thank you very much, Clarence," I said. I crowned the vanilla wafers with bananas.

"I'm trying to get things worked out, Kay-Jay."

"Okay," I said, sarcastically. "I understand."

"Bertie says five hundred dollars a month is enough child support for two children," Clarence said.

"You tell your skinny-ass sister that when she has a child, she can tell me how much it cost to take care of one!"

"You're so mean," he said.

"Clarence, you haven't seen me mean," I laughed. I really laughed. Imagine, someone calling me mean! If you provoke a saint, she will fall.

"Clarence, " I hissed, "I'm struggling to take care of the boys. I have no job, bills kicking my butt, and your sorry butt as a husband. And just what are you doing? Sunning in glorious California and sipping lime water at the side of Bertie's pool! You're one ungrateful bastard."

"See, I'm talking nicely," he said, "and you're going off again."

I screamed. I opened my mouth and screamed in his ear. I slammed the phone down, waited five seconds, and then took it off the hook. I poured a rich custard over the bananas and vanilla wafers. I stuffed a wafer in my mouth. I turned on the electric mixer and jammed it into a bowl of egg whites. I ignored the recording that said *If you would like to make a call, please hang up and try your number again.* I ignored the beepbeepbeepbeep and tried to beat the crap out of those egg whites. Honey, that was the highest, thickest meringue I've ever made. I slammed the pudding in the oven and called the boys into the apartment. I could only blame myself. Clarence could traipse through life like a carefree cad because I made it possible. I had supported his habit of irresponsibility for seven years. Why should he expect different behavior? Why should he step up to the plate? Why? Because I was graveyard tired. I could not carry the load any further. After years of saying "yes" the time had come to say "no, no, no! Hell no!"

Ten minutes later, when the golden brown banana pudding sat on the counter, I hung up the phone and went into the bedroom. I shoved the bills aside on my desk and signed online as Stepmom8945. I was determined to have one good chat experience, to get my mind off Clarence. I scanned the list of chat rooms. I went in and out of rooms until I got one titled *Making New Friends.*

Stepmom8945:	Hello, everyone. I'm new to chat rooms.
MyBaggage:	welcome to the room, Mom
DogAround:	how your legs Val?
Stepmom8945:	thanks so much, My Baggage.

Tamara:	hi looking for a man dark and lovely
MyBaggage:	if ya need anything, lemme know, Miss Mom
MyBaggage:	try DogAround, Tamara
MaryMacaroni:	Hi Mom, Tamara. Welcome.
JoyJoy4U:	hi Mom, Tam.
MyBaggage:	got wavs, links, tips, whatever ya' want, Mom.
DogAround:	woohoo
Stepmom8945:	What are wavs, links, tips?
DogAround:	but im light and ugly
MaryMacaroni:	Ms. Mom, you **are** brand new!
Stepmom8945:	Yes, I am.
MyBaggage:	yup . . . meet the gang, Mom. You'll lik'em
Tamara:	DogAround, are you what im looking for?

The conversation in that chat room was casual, funny, and flirtatious. I learned that wavs were music samples and links carried you directly to other web sites. I noticed that the grammar and spelling were not Standard English. Most of the people used abbreviations and symbols to convey their message. Overall, I felt better after my phone conversation with Clarence. Signing online each morning quickly became a ritual. By day four, I was convinced that chatting was fun, and that I could do it. But then Darius got the flu, then CJ had it, and finally I got so sick that I had to call Mama for help. That's when she discovered my plight.

Mama and I were like the Antarctic and a tropical island, two opposing ends of life. Mama had loving relationships with her church members, neighborhood children, and strangers. People loved her. They called her Mama Jeffries. When LaDell and I were children our house was the place to be. Mama Jeffries had candy bars, potato chips, and cookies. She bought the syrup that went on snow balls and made freeze pops. Neighborhood children had a standing credit limit of a quarter with Mama Jeffries. Every two weeks Mama collected the debts. If you didn't pay, she revoked your credit privileges with a stern lecture that went like this:

Honey, when somebody is kind enough to give you credit, you should be kind enough to repay them. It's called honesty, honey. If you're not honest, your name ain't worth nothing. How you gonna hold your head up around me, knowing you owe me a quarter? See, when you are a grown woman, you wanna to be able to walk around with your head up. You don't wanna to be afraid to answer your phone, or afraid your boss gonna call you into his office cause somebody you owe money is garnishing your wages. Now, what if I go to your mama and say, Regina owes me a quarter and won't pay. Your mama gonna be upset. Just like your boss will be upset if somebody comes to him about your debts. And honey, those creditors won't just tell the boss, they'll tell the whole world. Put a credit report out on you that says, "Regina Jordan is a poor risk. Don't give that woman anything on credit." Now, when you can see fit to pay me, I think you oughta, but remember you get no more credit from me. There ain't many second chances in life.

My brother, my friends, and I were good with money and with credit. But I didn't have a job and could not keep up with all my bills. So, there were all those telltale bills, and there was Mama.

I had allotted a corner of my bedroom as my office. A computer stand and one file cabinet represented the entire office. Helter-skelter, chaos, a corner of confusion, several titles came to mind when I looked at that work space. Papers, bills, junk mail, and coupons cascaded across the small work space. The papers concealed the combination fax, copier, scanner, and printer. Pencils, markers, pens, makeup, CDs, lotion, half-emptied water bottles, ponytail holders, notebooks, memo pads, a Rolodex, old one- and five-dollar silver certificates, several pairs of reading glasses, address books, and a worn pair of pantyhose covered the remaining space.

Although I had a Franklin Planner and a stack of books to help me organize my life including *First Things First, The Seven Principles of Highly Effective People, DO IT! Let's Get Off Our Buts, The Success Journey, Time Management,* and others; I was not an organized person. The books were only helpful, if I read them. Many were still unread.

In contrast to the office space, the rest of the bedroom was a vision of yellow flowers and light oak. I tried to remember to hang up my clothes. I tried to remember to put my shoes back in the plastic boxes. I did manage to keep my makeup in its case.

"Katie, how can you sleep with all this commotion flowing across your desk," Mama said.

She stood between my bed and the desk with a glass of orange juice. My bed was shoved against the wall to make room for the office space. A chest of drawers stood next to the sliding doors of the closet. I had no night stand or dresser. A black fabric office chair held a mound of dirty clothes in the seat. Mama pushed aside the papers and sat the orange juice down. Slowly, as if she were about to picking up a dead carcass, Mama moved her hand to the top bill on my desk. Mama had thick, powerful hands that she kept perfectly manicured. Years of domestic labor had etched wrinkles and scars into her hands.

"Katie Jeffries Cannon Smith Robinson Coomers!" She broke the spell. "Tell me this isn't a shut off notice from Peoples Gas!"

I scooted down in the bed and brought the quilt up to my neck. When Mama was angry with me, she did the Erica Kane name call thing. She remembered all my husbands and, I swear, if she had known my boyfriends, she would have thrown their names into the mix.

"And ComEd! You got bills everywhere!" Mama barked.

She sorted through my bills. She looked at me with a *V* puckered in the center of her brow. Her fudge brown eyes narrowed. I was reduced to a trembling mass of childhood fears.

"I know Clarence is sending you child support," she said, "Why are your bills behind?"

"I forgot to mail the payments," I lied. I pulled the comforter up to my nose. At that exact moment, the nosey woman was reading my bank statement.

"You're drawing from your savings account. What's going on here? I tried my best to raise you to be responsible and decent. I tried to keep you reigned in. I knew, I knew your life would be a disgrace if somebody didn't break your spirit."

"You break horses," I whispered, "not children."

We stared at each other. Mama holding my business in her hand while the pulp in the orange juice peered through the frosty condensation. I wanted that juice. My throat burned. Mama rambled on. I shut out her words. I thought about a navel orange covered with bumps and ridges. That bumpy shell hid the sweetness and natural goodness of juicy fruit.

"Girl!" Mama snapped me out of my reverie. "Are you listening to me? What's going on in that big head of yours?"

"I'm not working, Mama," I said.

"Not working," she said and looked at me. The glittering stars and bangles on her jogging suit glared at me. "Don't tell me you quit your job!"

"I got fired," I whispered. "Can I have the orange juice?"

"Mercy!" she exclaimed.

My throat was parched and I knew my torment had just begun. Mama took my illness as an opportunity to get into the main artery of my business, to float around in my life. She looked through more of my personal information.

"When did you get fired?" she asked. "In December? These are old bills."

"I got fired in October," I said and pulled the quilt up to my eyes.

Hallelujah! For the first time, my mama was floored. She sat on top of the clothes in the chair. The clothes swooshed around her hips. Her round moon face quivered. Her fudge brown eyes narrowed. A thin line of sweat formed over her top lips. She held the bills loosely in her hand.

"And you didn't tell me?"

I didn't answer.

"Do LaDell and Georgie know?"

I shook my head.

"Does Donna know?"

I nodded.

"You told some outsider this and not your own mama!"

That's Mama for you. At times, she talked about Donna as if she were a recent acquisition to my list of friends. At other times, she remembered every detail of our childhood together. The truth is Donna, Regina, and I probably sucked from the same bottle at some point of our infancy. She glanced down at the bank statement.

"Why is Clarence only sending you the Department of Defense check? What's about the VA check?"

My questions, exactly.

"I never would have believed this of him," she said. "He's usually back by now. I feel like calling him and telling him to get his tail home."

"No, Mama," I said because Mama Jeffries would do just that.

"He knows you lost your job?" she asked.

"Yes, ma'am."

"And he's not back."

I looked at her and said, "I told him not to come back, Mama."

Her jaws tightened with suppressed anger. A spark of fire twinkled in her dark eyes. She shook her head slowly and held me with those burning eyes.

"Katie," Mama said, "you were strange the day you were born. Most babies come out kicking and hollering, longing to stay where it's safe and warm. They know that a world of trouble awaits them. Not you. You came out all smiling and reaching for something only you could see. You even smiled at the doctor. I knew then that your brain was kinda addle. I could never figure you out, and now you are throwing away another marriage."

All marriages were good to Mama. She was convinced that there was something inherently wrong with me because my marriages always ended within a year.

"The thing is, girl," Mama said as she placed the bills on top of a dictionary. "You think too highly of yourself. Always putting on airs. Heaven help me, but I don't know why."

Mama shook her head, closed her eyes, and held her head toward heaven. I expected her to break out in a prayer or a hymn. After two minutes of silence she opened her eyes and shook her head.

"You ain't no beauty," she said. "We both know that. Your daddy ustah feed you that rot about the world being yours, about swinging on stars, and other such nonsense. I use to tell him, 'Alex, I know you love your child, but don't feed her that foolishness. Be honest with the girl,' I use to say. 'She needs to use her brain.' Alex never listened to me. Just kept filling your head with foolishness."

Yes. Those were my mother's words.

"Please, Mama," I whispered, hoping she would lighten up, hoping she would give me the orange juice before I died of thirst. My throat was scratchy with thirst. I lifted a weak hand and pointed to the orange juice.

Mama picked up the orange juice and then bent over me. She helped me rise. I greedily gulped down the juice. Mama continued to fuss.

"Now you need to work things out with Clarence."

"What?" I stopped gulping the juice. A stream of it ran down my chin. I wiped my chin with my hand. My head was woozy. Mama was pushing me back to a man that didn't care enough about me to work with me.

"Girl, don't throw this marriage away," Mama said.

"He's the one who left," I whispered. I was so thirsty.

"But he wants to come back. Give him another chance."

"How many chances, Mama?" I continued to whisper. My throat was really parched. I needed more orange juice.

"Oh, Katie, he's just having a mid-life crisis."

"How long does it last?" I asked, holding my hand to my throat, hoping she would take the hint. "I would rather be alone than with a man who would let me drown, Mama."

Maybe Mama saw the weariness in my eyes and remembered the reality of my marriage. She helped me drink more of the orange juice then set the glass on the one clean corner of the desk.

"I'll lend you money to get current," Mama said. "But I'm gonna sit down and put you on a budget."

That was another thing about Mama helping me: She had terms and conditions. Mama had a desire to control my life. She removed the clothes from the chair and dumped them on top of the chest.

"Mercy, Katie!" she exclaimed as she returned to the desk. "With Clarence gone, your place is a disgraceful mess. I'm scared to touch this stuff. A rat or snake could come crawling out!"

"Mama," I said. "If you want to lend me money, that's

fine. But you're not going to take over my life or put me on a budget. If those are your terms, I don't want the money. I'll work it out. I will."

I tell you. When you can floor my mama twice in a day, it's good. It's all good.

CHAPTER 7

It turned out that I had acquired pneumonia or, as the old folks say, walking pneumonia. When Mama finally made her way back to the South Side, I rejoiced. My illness had me too weak to do anything more than think. I didn't want Mama paying my bills. I didn't want Clarence. I didn't want to carry around sixty pounds of extra weight. What I wanted was Katie Jeffries. The Katie Jeffries before all of the marriage. The one hundred and thirty pound Katie Jeffries. The assertive Katie with dreams. There had to be a way to shed whomever that sick person was laying in a rumpled bed in a too small apartment with too many bills and a dead marriage. I had to find a way back to me.

Now, you are probably wondering why I didn't live out south in the house Mr. Pete left me. Our old neighborhood had gone to pots. In Englewood there were elegant brownstone and gray stone buildings in shambles or boarded up.

From the Dan Ryan Expressway, across 59th Street to Damen Avenue was girdled with condemned building with broken windows, burnt out shells, graffiti, and hopelessness in hungry eyes. A string of unsolved murders also plagued the area. All the victims were women. The police and media claimed that the women had shady pasts or drug connections. Yeah, right. A lot was going on in Englewood that I was too chicken-hearted to deal with it. What affected me the most were the men with missing limbs. Englewood had a high concentration of men with missing limbs. Men scooted in wheel chairs and walked on crutches. Empty sleeves dangled from shoulders. Men walked with the aid of stiff prostheses. In my mind, crime and a lack of money crippled Englewood. So, I ran far north, and ha ha ha, the joke was on me. It was crappy up there too.

Anyway, Alex came to visit me the day after Mama went home. When I looked at Alex's chocolate skin, his round face, and pug nose, I saw his father. I won't say his father's name since he is a very famous news reporter for a national television network. Once, during the Gulf Crisis, Alex and I were watching a special report. He was eight or nine years old at that time. I was at Mama's house to baby-sit, while she attended some church function. Anyway, the news reporter just happened to be Alex's dad. I inadvertently let that piece of information slipped. Alex swirled around on the floor and looked at me.

"That's my dad?"

Just then Mama walked out of her room, rolling the last curl in her head. (To this day, Mama twirls her hair around those pink sponge rollers.) "Who's your dad?" she asked.

Alex swirled back to the television. When his dad reappeared, he pointed. "Him! Katie said he's my dad."

"Katie, don't lie to the child."

I grimaced. I did lie. I'll admit that, but I desperately avoided two things: lying to children and breaking promises to them.

"How did you meet him, Katie?" he asked.

"We went to college together," I said.

Mama moseyed over to the sofa and sat next to me. She leaned into the television screen. Mama was one of those women who liked clutter: Doilies, bric-a-bracs, pictures, figurines, and plastic flowers from eons ago. That clutter smothered me as she and Alex leaned into the television and studied the man's face. Her living room shrunk to the size of a closet, at least that's how I felt, as if the walls were pushing in on me. I was hot and stuffy. I itched to get out of that clutter. There was a tapestry picture of the last supper above the television. John was at the Lord's feet, and Judas was heading out the door. Jesus held a cup of wine and a crust of bread in his hand. His eyes held my gaze. *This is my body given for you. Take eat.* I sent a silent entreaty to him, *help me out of this, and I promise to be good.*

"Does he know about me?" Alex asked. I could not open my mouth and give Alex the answer he needed.

"Well?" Mama snapped when I did not reply.

Alex scooted closer to the couch and waited for my words. His round face posed with expectation. I was trapped.

"You never told him you were having his baby?" Mama snapped. She turned her head and frowned at me. Her new glasses magnified her dark eyes. I didn't like those glasses. They reminded me of Mrs. Wilson, my third grade teacher. Mrs. Wilson didn't care for me any more than I cared for her. She thought I exaggerated too much.

"I told him, Mama," I said.

"And?"

"And nothing. He walked away."

"Humph!"

"Maybe I'll call him," Alex said.

I laughed a nervous laugh. I knew my son-brother was serious. If that germ stuck in Alex's mind, he would find a way to call.

"You'll do no such thing!" Mama interjected.

I breathed. Mama did everything and anything to protect Alex from the slings and arrows of an outrageous mother. Often, she blasted me about some asinine thing I had done to embarrass, shame, or humiliate Alex. Translation: *How could you embarrass me like that, Katie?* Remember those short dresses with matching panties? Mama blasted me for wearing those when Alex was four. Like a four-year-old boy could express shame over what his twenty-five-year-old mother wore. Remember Jell-O shots? Okay, so I came home tipsy once because I didn't understand the potency of those cute red squares made with vodka. Did my son-brother really understand me sleeping off a drunk? Anyway, you get the drift. Mama was very protective of Alex. She would knock the idea out of his head.

"I wanna talk to him," Alex whined. "Imma call him."

"No, you won't, young man," Mama said. "Katie will call him!"

"Me!" I exclaimed.

"It's the least you can do for your child."

"Oh, now you'll let me be the mother?"

"Watch how you talk around him," Mama snapped.

I leaned back on the sofa and watched the rest of the report. Alex leaned forward, twisted his small head back and forth, and examined his father's face.

"Is he smart like me, Katie?" he asked.

"Yes, Alex. He is smart like you."

Alex leaned forward and touched the screen.

"Is he tall?"

"Yes."

"What color are his eyes?"

"Brown, just like yours."

"Does he like Tootsie Rolls?"

"Actually, yes. He kept a package in his book satchel."

"Really?"

"Really."

"He seems like a decent man," Mama said. "Are you sure you told him?"

"I told him or somebody that looks like him," I cracked.

"This is no time for your foolishness," Mama said. "You call the network now, and leave a message for him."

"Mama!" I exclaimed.

"Do it."

"Yeah, Katie," Alex piped. "Do it now!"

I wish I could say that the man never returned my call. I didn't hate the man, but I didn't like the idea of going to him. I figured he knew I was pregnant. He should have looked me up. I used a contact that I had at the Chicago Police Department to track down his number. I made the call and left a message. Two months later, when he was back in the States, Alex's dad returned my call. He wanted to do lunch the next time he was in Chicago but I told him straightforwardly, "Your child wants to see you, not me."

I gave him Mama's address and telephone number. He and Alex developed this wonderful relationship. So, the day Alex paid me a visit, I was not surprised by his ultimate request. Alex was seventeen and headed for Penn State on an academic scholarship. I always thought that he should have played basketball, but Alex was a true egghead like his dad.

"Kay-Jay, are you better?"

He used Clarence's nickname for me and rubbed my head. I bumped my head against his hand like a cat would do. He ruffled my hair then sat on the love seat. His long legs stretched in front of him. The love seat and sofa were arranged in an "L" patterned with a wood and glass cocktail table in the center and the television sat against the wall. The entire room was the dot on the small *i*, so small that I could have stretched my leg and touched Alex's pants with my toe. Compared with Mama's living room, mine was sparse. My cocktail table held only my orange juice glass on a coaster, photo albums, and the remote control for the television. The room was too small for pictures, flowers, and artwork. Once I had a huge mirror over the television, to give the appearance of space. During a vicious argument with Clarence, I threw a coffee mug and shattered the glass.

"I want you to meet somebody," Alex said.

His brown eyes were full of merriment. A bright smile played across his face. I liked Alex's face. It was in contrast to itself, round with a squared chin, thick lips under a pug nose, and a deep crayon brown complexion."Who?" I asked.

"A girl."

"Girl?" I quipped. "What happened to Tameka?"

"Oh, Tameka's my friend. She's cool. But Max is da bomb!"

"Uh huh?" I said.

"You're gonna love her."

"Uh huh."

"Mama doesn't know her, really,"

"Uh huh."

If I let Alex talk long enough he would tell me everything in a few sentences. I analyzed what he was saying. Obviously, he had demoted Tameka down to a *friend*. Obviously that Max creature had sex appeal, and obviously Mama Jeffries didn't like her. Mama probably thought Max was some hoochie with her eyes set on Mr. Fine himself! Mama watched the girls, ever mindful of a particular kind of danger, baby machines. Those girls, mama thought, wanted to trap a young man in a bad situation. Alex needed me to validate his selection.

"So, you gonna help me or not?" he asked.

"Or not."

"Ah, mom!"

I leaned forward, held my hand to my mouth, and faked a cough. Alex and I had an easy relationship. Often we tried to outsmart each other either with words or some silly game, like that one. Would I help him get Mama's approval for that girlfriend? No. I trusted my mother's judgment when it came to male/female relationships. She matched LaDell with Georgie, Donna with Mike, and Regina, she always claimed, would be better off alone. That proved to be true. Mama's only mistake was my match with Clarence. Although, truthfully, she didn't make that match. I did.

"So, tell me," I said. "What's Mama got against her?"

"She says her dresses are too short and that her hair is butter-whipped."

"Butter-whipped?"

"You know. Her hair is piled high like whipped butter."

I laughed. Mama hated braids, dreds, fades, and what she considered *dos.* Mama also hated when I got my hair symmetrically cut. If it were left up to Mama, all African American women would wear relaxed hair or a press and curl done up in an old-fashioned hairstyle that required big pink sponge rollers to maintain. So, Mama was not going to like Max's hairstyle. Yet, Mama never judged people by hair alone. The problem was more than butter whipped hair and short dresses.

"So? What's the catch, Alex? You can't put one over on me."

Alex sighed and bent forward. I knew then it was deep.

"Is the girl pregnant?" I asked.

"Well, no," Alex said. "Although she does have one baby. Her sister keeps it."

"Are you crazy?" I shouted and sat up on the sofa. "You want me to get Mama Jeffries to approve of a girl with a baby. No way!"

"Katie," he whined. "I want to take her to the prom, not marry her."

"What about Tameka?"

"What?" he asked.

"Who's taking her?" I asked.

"She'll probably go with her cousin," he said. "Her senior prom is next year any way."

"Oh, no," I said. "There's no way I'm giving my approval. You have created some mess here. You know Mama loves Tameka."

Why did an eighteen-year-old boy need the approval of his mother and grandmother? He didn't. The whole thing wasn't about approval. Alex always built up to what he really wanted.

"Alex, I'm too sick for all this drama," I said and faked another cough. "Besides, you always do what you want anyway."

"Why is Mama old-fashioned?"

"And I hate to tell you this, Alex, but I'm with Mama on this one."

"I can't believe you gonna be a hypocrite about Max."

"Hypocrite?"

"Well, you never married Mr. *Tonight a special report from Hong Kong?*" Alex asked in a mocked announcer's voice.

"Well, it's not like he asked me!" I snapped.

"If he had asked you, would you have married him?"

I shifted on the sofa. I reached for the glass of orange juice on the table and took a sip. I lost my virginity to Alex's dad because he was older, and had the most gorgeous velvety chocolate skin. Yes, I dreamed of being his wife. Yes, I thought he would marry me when I told him I was pregnant. After he walked away from me, I erased him from my dreams. I reached for the remote control, but Alex beat me to it.

"Katie," he said. "You can't avoid the question."

"You know my history," I said.

"You would have married him?"

"Yeah, most likely. Anything to keep from facing Mama, alone and pregnant."

"So, what happened?" Alex asked.

Why can't other people have serious talks with their children? My three sons talked to me about anything and everything. Many times, my mama would say, *Katie, don't tell them that.* Or *Don't play with those kids. They won't respect you.* I never had any problems in that area. The boys came to me with their problems and their dreams. They knew, no matter how uncomfortable I was with a topic, I would answer their questions and give them my honest opinion.

"I told him . . ."

"Right before he graduated," he said.

"Yes."

"What happened next?" he asked.

"Nothing," I said. "He walked away. He graduated that January and I never heard from him again."

"Maybe he thought you were lying."

"Is that what he said?" I asked.

"Yeah," Alex nodded.

"Why would he think that?"

Alex cocked his head and looked at me. He shook it slowly and leaned forward. With a soft, kind paternal voice, Alex revealed his *mom* to me.

"I will tell anybody, anybody," he said. "Katie has never

lied to me, but the woman can tell other people the biggest whoppers you ever heard."

"What!" I exclaimed.

"Kate, nobody knows when you are serious or joking," he said and then counted off my habits on his fingers. "You tease, you lie, you exaggerate, and you do anything and everything to avoid situations."

I squirmed. He had the remote control. I look for the latest copy of *Essence* magazine, but it wasn't around. The book I was reading, *Philadelphia Fire* by John Wideman, lay on the couch next to me. It required too much attention, too much dedication. It was not a book to read lightly.

"Look at you," Alex read my movement. "Right now, if I wasn't your son, you would begin one of your wild tales to change the conversation."

"So," I said and lay back. I had to end the conversation quickly. "The man has made me out to be the bad guy."

"No, actually, he thinks or thought, you were a beautiful young woman, just batty as hell. He didn't know you were pregnant. He didn't believe it."

"And now you are blaming me for . . . ?"

"I'm not blaming you for anything," Alex said.

I arched one eyebrow and looked into his soft brown eyes until he dropped his own. You can't fool a jester.

"Okay," he said. His eyes misted. "Maybe I have thought 'if Katie had been a little more serious, I would have had a dad.'"

There he said it. It was out. He looked toward the TV and flipped it on. I gripped Wideman's book. My hands were warm. My face was flushed. My son-brother sat in my cramped apartment, upset because I had not given him a dad. Hell, to be honest, I hadn't given him a mom either. All of Mama's words came back. *You gonna spend the rest of your days apologizing to this child. When he asks about his daddy, you gotta say I'm sorry honey, I don't know where your daddy is.*

"We can't go back," I said.

"No, we can't," he agreed and dropped his head. His clasped hands dangled between his legs. His conversation about Tameka and Max was a put on. Alex had a bigger thing that he wanted. A serious thing.

"What is it Alex?"

He turned his soft eyes on me and I caught my breath. There was an entreaty for help.

"I've told Mama that I'm not going to college this year."

"What!" I exclaimed.

"She won't listen to me. She says I'm throwing my opportunities away."

"You're going to pass up your scholarships?" I asked. "Why?"

"I want to spend the year in the Middle East."

"Are you crazy?" I screamed. "You know how Mama feels about the Middle East. You know she expects those countries to unite and rise against the United States."

"Her beliefs are more biblical then reality, Katie."

"The Bible and reality are the same to Mama, Alex. You can't get around that," I said. "You best grab that scholarship . . ." I clamped my mouth shut. Realization dawned on me. "You want to spend the year with your father?"

He nodded.

"But the Middle East, Alex," I whispered.

"If you talk to her," he pleaded. "If you tell her I need to spend time with him, she'll listen."

"When does Mama Jeffries ever listen to me?"

"Whenever you take up for me," he said.

I knew he spoke the truth.

CHAPTER 8

Donna came through my door with "Are you better?"

She wore a winter white cashmere coat with the softest pair of brown leather boots I'd ever seen. A large gold peacock broach with gems in its tail feathers perched on the lapel of her coat. Everything about Donna was always well pulled together. There was not a missed step anywhere in her life, except me as her friend.

"Yeah," I said and walked back to the sofa where I had camped out for the past two weeks. I eased beneath my quilt.

Donna removed her gloves and stuffed them in her pocket. By the time she placed her coat on the back of the love seat, I was enthralled with the Disney Channel. Donna stared at me. I could see the words forming in her head. She had some scheme up her sleeve. She rambled on and on, about work and Mike. Finally, she arrived at her destination, my cakes.

"Are you interested in going full time with the business or not?" she asked.

"Not," I answered.

We glared at each other. Outside the apartment children's voices swelled as they made their way home from school. Soon CJ and Darius' voices and footsteps thundered in the hallway. When they crashed through the door, Donna and I were still glaring at each other.

"Hi, Aunt Donna," CJ and Darius said.

"Mom, tell CJ it doesn't snow in California," Darius said as he slung his backpack onto the kitchen table.

The boys were identical in face, wild jungle eyebrows, wide noses, small mouths, and the brown of corrugated boxes. That's where the similarities ended. They stood next to each other like the characters in the old comic strip *Mutt and Jeff.* Darius, a short eight years old, was the clown, always laughing and causing a ruckus. Nine-year-old CJ, as tall as most eleven-year-old boys, was quiet. Husky boys with athletic bodies, they were sweethearts, dears, loving, and . . . leaving.

"Yes, it does snow in California," CJ asserted.

"Only in the mountains," Donna said. I think she saw a look on my face, a look of sorrow, and decided to call a truce. The closer the time came for the boys to leave, the more despondent I've become.

"See, there, I was right," CJ and Darius said simultaneously.

Donna laughed.

"You have homework?" I asked. I sat up and tugged the quilt around my legs. "There's a plate of Lemon Squares on the sink."

"I'm out of here," Donna said.

"Mom, tell Darius you're not coming with us," CJ called as he walked to his bedroom.

"I'm not going with you," I said woodenly.

"Why not," Darius asked. He stood directly behind Donna. He snatched the lapel of his jacket apart and I heard the distinct popping of the snaps.

"Everything I am is right here," I said.

"Maybe you should think about that," Donna said. "The man is working now."

"Maybe you should think about finding yourself another business partner!" I snapped.

"Oops," Darius said and hurriedly left the room.

"You're a stubborn cow," Donna said.

"Moo-o-o-o-o," I said.

She rolled her eyes at me and called to the boys, "You boys wanna catch a movie tomorrow night while your mom goes to the opera with Uncle Mike?"

"We can't," CJ said. "We're spending the night with Alex."

"I have nothing to wear to the opera," I said.

"If you had a regular full-time business, you could buy a decent dress."

***

Those boys were perfect kids. I never had to tell them to do homework, to go to bed, or to do their chores like wash dishes or empty the garbage. Occasionally, I had to tell CJ to bathe or to tell Darius to rest his mouth. Their bedtime was eight-thirty, Sunday through Thursday. Friday and Saturday nights I allowed them to stay up late. Usually they drifted to bed by ten o'clock on the weekend. That Friday, the sugar in the lemon squares had them wired. They stayed up until the midnight, yakking about California.

"Dad said he's gonna buy us new bikes and a Play-station."

Clarence always promised us the moon. I was still waiting for wedding rings. I never got the marquis of my dream. By the time the little darlings were in bed, I was ready to chat my night away. I signed online as Stepmom8945. When I entered my regular room, it was empty. Disappointed, I tried another room, and another room. The rooms were fast and asinine. The conversation was as jumbled and silly as a bad elephant joke. I popped into a room called CyberGames99 and flushed when I realized that the chat was all sexual. I popped out the room. Before I could pop into another room, I received an instant message from some guy. An instant message is a window where two people can hold a private conversation outside the chat room. In other words, it's a one-on-one chat room.

HumpinMan:	hello, Stepmom.
Stepmom8945:	Hello.
HumpinMan:	are you up for a little cyber fun?
Stepmom8945:	Cyber fun? What's that?
HumpinMan:	you've never cybered before?
Stepmom8945:	No. I'm new to chat rooms. What is it?
HumpinMan:	it's making love online.
Stepmom8945:	What?
HumpinMan:	you kinda like describe a scene
Stepmom8945:	Like a romantic scene
HumpinMan:	romantic/sexual, can be either, or both
HumpinMan:	it starts romantically but gets graphically sexual
HumpinMan:	wanna try.
Stepmom8945:	Sure
HumpinMan:	tell me about you. what do you look like?

Okay, you know I was going to lie. There was no way I would tell him I looked like a walrus. I was alone in my room. I could be anyone, Miss America, Miss Universe, or Miss Piggy. I decided to be Miss Universe.

| Stepmom8945: | I am 36C 25 38 |
| HumpinMan: | hmmm do you want to know the size of my, uh, equipment? |

No, he was not going to tell me about his member! Was he? I wondered how far cybering went. I wondered if it was like a super romance novel, spicy with no meat.

HumpinMan:	i told you it gets, uh, well ya know
Stepmom8945:	Tell me the size of your equipment
HumpinMan:	7½ inches
HumpinMan:	very thick
HumpinMan:	i love to suck a woman's breasts
Stepmom8945:	That's nice.

Cybering bored me. It reminded me of my first kiss with George Hartman. When George closed his eyes and leaned in, nervous anticipation swept through me. I expected Sousa's 1812 Overture to burst forth, Forest Preston to march through the door with thirty-six trombones and a big parade. Instead, George landed a wet slobbering mess on my lips and my nose. His breath smelled like sour toes. His slimy mouth tasted salty. Like that first kiss, cybering created a slimy, sour feeling. Obviously HumpinMan was not clueless to how I felt.

HumpinMan:	am i boring you?
Stepmom8945:	I got to say, I don't find this stimulating
HumpinMan:	well, we haven't gotten to the cyber part, i was trying to ease into it slowly.
Stepmom8945:	Oh.
HumpinMan:	do you want to try the real thing?
Stepmom8945:	Yeah, why not.

HumpinMan:	most people on here tell me they get off, so here goes
HumpinMan:	i'm wearing boxers and T-shirt. you can see a bulge growing underneath my shorts

I imagined a potbelly man in pale blue shorts and a tee shirt that curled across the shelf of his beer belly. The image was too funny.

Stepmom8945:	ok
HumpinMan:	I come sit next to you on the bed and start kissing the nape of your neck
HumpinMan:	I work my tongue up to your ear
HumpinMan:	sucking on your lobe
Stepmom8945:	uh huh.
HumpinMan:	my hands are running through your hair
HumpinMan:	I start to kiss your cheek and work my way to your mouth
HumpinMan:	I partly open my mouth and my tongue slips over your lips
HumpinMan:	intertwining with your tongue
HumpinMan:	I kiss your neck and slide my tongue down and back up again kissing you just behind the ear

HumpinMan kissing me in cyberspace was unnerving. The man was too wet and oral. I did not want to continue with the game. I know. I know. You see it all the time on television. People, with their tongues down each other's throats, moaning and grasping at each other with raw lust. I remember the old days when kissing in the movies meant two people pressing closed lips together. That was romance. I was about to end the session when the man changed the game.

HumpinMan:	now taking your left nipple into my mouth and gently sucking
HumpinMan:	taking the other nipple between my fingers and rubbing until it's hard
Stepmom8945:	oh, my!

See, we all have our sexual weaknesses. Mine just happened to be my breasts. Show me a man who can fondle my nipples until unbridle passion overwhelms me, I'll show you husband number five.

HumpinMan:	rub yourself as we go ok?
Stepmom8945:	yes. I will.
HumpinMan:	laying you down now and sliding my tongue down and across your tummy
HumpinMan:	sliding my tongue down your leg
HumpinMan:	coming back up now, on the inside of your thigh
HumpinMan:	still rubbing your nipples as I go
HumpinMan:	sliding tongue deeper and deeper inside

Ah, the man was good. Using one hand, I typed. My other hand parted my robe and slipped into my panties. It had been months since I had been touched. I slipped over the rolls that composed my stomach. A moan slipped from my lips.

HumpinMan:	taking it into my mouth now
HumpinMan:	gently sucking harder and harder
HumpinMan:	sliding one finger down just between your wet lips now
HumpinMan:	gently parting your lips as I begin to suck harder and harder
Stepmom8945:	uh-huh

HumpinMan:	finger sliding inside now slowly
HumpinMan:	deeper and deeper and still sucking
Stepmom8945:	uhmm
HumpinMan:	finger slides out now and tongue slides inside

Waves of pleasure coursed through my body and I shuddered. A hot flush rushed through my stomach. My vision blurred. I bit my lip to keep from screaming. My head fell forward. I could not believe it. I had an orgasm with my computer. Man! That orgasm reminded me of James, my first husband. I always stood with my nose on his naked chest and sniffed his aroma hungrily. One look across a crowded room, one nod of his head, and I would follow James into a closet and surrender to white-hot lust. I lusted for and loved that man. Unfortunately, I was not woman enough for him. James needed three or four women to drench him with constant attention. I probably would have stayed with him anyway if he had not wanted a baby. I mean I had been through childbirth. It hurt. The pain was like pressing an elephant through a keyhole. Once was more than enough. James had an agenda. Fill the Mrs. with babies, then he could play the field. It's true. When James began stroking my belly like it was a shrine, I knew *babies* were on his mind. One morning, my birth control pills disappeared from the medicine cabinet.

Hmph. We broke up soon after that. I sat, in front of my computer, in the afterglow of cyber sex with those thoughts running through my mind. My body was still flushed but my breathing was steady.

| HumpinMan: | are you there? |

The first wave of shame washed over me—overwhelming disgust and self-loathing smothered me. I was a sick chick, a cyber hoochie. I had shared an intimate moment with a stranger. He could have been anyone. Anything! He could have been sixteen or ninety-six. He could have herpes, a hairy back, or no teeth. WHAT HAVE I DONE? I hit the X in the upper right-hand corner of the screen and immediately signed offline. I shuddered and pushed away from the desk. Oh, I was a cyber hoochie. I might as well post my name on a bulletin board, call 1-800-cybergal. Worse yet, suppose I went into a chat room and he was there. I could not remember his complete screen name. I had spent an hour cybering and could not remember his name. I could never go back on line as Stepmom8945. I signed on as KatieJffries. I deleted Stepmom8945. Immediately I realized that all my new buddies and favorite places were under Stepmom8945. I had lost all my new friends for one careless act of passion.

***

I stayed off line and threw myself into baking. My unemployment was coming in steadily but it was less than half my regular salary. So, it was a good thing that Donna was marketing the baked goods. I worried about licensing and the Chicago Board of Health but Donna had her own agenda for me. We sat at the kitchen table poring over cookbooks, searching for a Mississippi chocolate bourbon cake. Donna had on an off-white business suit, strands of cultured pearls, and cultured pearl earrings. I had on a pair of black leggings and a big flower tunic that dropped to my knees. We were as coordinated as lava and ice. I couldn't stand her. All the jewelry I own in the world came from Mama Verna who had been the neighborhood policy queen. In Chicago, those cream color policy papers with the blue ink were as familiar to my childhood friends as the blue and white Jays Potato Chips bag. I will admit that Mama Verna had a few attractive, genuine pieces. She had a thing for white gold.

Most of it was heavy and ornate and encrusted with gems. I had no choice but to lock the small collection away, especially after I found a pawn slip for a beautiful emerald ring. Joe (husband number three) had pawned it. Anyway, Donna sat at my table with a new green rock on her right hand the size of a nutmeg. The clarity of that emerald boasted of a worth more than my house in Englewood. Old WhiskyLips had done right by Donna. She was discussing the possibility of me starting a full-fledged catering business. That was her favorite subject of the day. Every time she came over she had another scheme. Today it was the house in Englewood.

"If you're so worried about the Board of Health," she said, "you could throw out the Gordons and move into Mr. Pete's house. You could convert the basement into a commercial kitchen."

I rolled my eyes toward the ceiling. The cake baking business and Donna were getting on my nerves.

"Just where do I get the money for the renovations?" I asked.

"Mike and I talked about it, we could back you. You are one of the best cooks I know."

"What makes you think I want to be a damn baker? I'm an artist."

"You're not practical," she shook her head.

"You never supported my art," I said. "Not my writing, not my painting. Regina was the only one who believed in me."

Donna slammed the cookbook on the table and said, "Then why are we looking for a cake recipe? Why am I asking people to buy your cakes and breads?"

"This was your idea," I said, looking down at the tiny stone in my class ring. "I wanted, want to concentrate on my art."

"Oh, don't start that again," Donna sneered. "What art?

You have never completed any of those paintings in Mama Jeffries's basement."

"Regina knew what my art meant to me," I whispered to the air.

"Regina filled your head with a lot of nonsense," Donna snapped. "She was a bigger dreamer than you."

"Oh?" I smiled. I looked at Donna. Although Regina had been dead for ten years, I knew that the rivalry between her and Donna still existed. Donna sat at my table in her business suit, playing hooky from a seminar. She picked at a pimple on her face. Underneath the layer of creme foundation were the telltale signs of pockmarked skin.

"What's wrong with dreams?" I asked.

"They are not practical."

"Hmmm, practical," I hissed. "Like refusing to give Mike a child because it would ruin your figure."

"You're mean."

Do you see? Do you see? Everyone I knew could say what they wanted about me, to me, and against me, but I could not retaliate.

"Oh, and you're a regular Pollyanna," I said.

"Sometimes I think you wish I were Regina."

"There was one Regina, Donna, and you are nothing like her," I said. "You are always pushing me to be what I'm not."

"I'm just saying you need to be practical," she snapped. "Maybe if Regina had been more practical, she would be alive."

"What?"

"I'm just saying . . ."

"Go home," I smiled, but my tiny eyes were tight. She saw that. She had made her mistake by criticizing Regina. There had been three of us: Regina, Donna, and I. Regina and I had been inseparable, more like sisters than friends. Even as children, we sometimes hid from Donna. She searched the neighborhood for us. We snickered and watched her from our hiding places: the second floor window of Regina's apartment building, the crawl space of my back porch, behind cars, trees, and once in Donna's own hallway. We listened to her high-pitched whine; *I know y'all hiding from me.* It was thirty years later, and Donna was still on the outside.

"I'm just trying to help you," she said.

"I don't remember asking for help."

"You're not doing much to help yourself," Donna snapped. "Just look at you. No job, sitting in a dark apartment gorging on cakes and pies, letting yourself get as big as a blimp, and letting your hair get scraggly and nappy. You've got problems, Katie Coomers. Big problems."

"Thank you, Dr. Sigmund," I said. "With friends like you, it's a good thing I'm not suicidal. What would you do then? Push me off a cliff and say, *It's for your own good, Katie.* Or maybe just take me to a slaughter house."

She gasped. I mean girlfriend sucked in so much air, her head jerked back. She snatched her purse from the table, grabbed her coat from the love seat, and was out the door. I never looked around. I felt the smile slide down my face. I was tired of everybody helping me like I was some weak woman, tired of everybody telling me to be practical.

I heard the door in the vestibule close behind Donna. I closed and stacked all the cookbooks. The itching started behind my eyes, the itching that comes right before a good long bawl. I'd be damn if I cried! I pushed myself away from the table, locked the front door, and walked to the bathroom.

Big as a blimp, she had said. *Gorging on cakes and pies.*

In the bathroom, I used my foot to drag Clarence's scale from between the sink and tub. If the pointer went beyond two hundred pounds, out the window it would go. I climbed on and the thing creaked and groaned. I ignored its pain. I held my stomach in, and looked down. My plump toes pointed to the shameful numbers 1-9-5. I groaned and stepped off the scale. I had lost two pounds.

After seven years with Clarence I had scaled the mountain of weight from a pleasing one hundred and thirty pounds to a whopping one hundred and ninety-three pounds. At five feet four inches and possessing bones like a Barbie doll, the unmitigated truth slapped me in the face— I was a candidate for a fat farm or at the very least, a heart attack. I closed my eyes and there was Robert Preston in white pants and a red jacket with brass buttons and gold braids. He leaned toward me and said:

"There's Trouble, with a capital T."

I opened my eyes before twenty-six trombones burst through my door. I went into my bedroom. I wanted to fling myself on my bed and cry but instead I flopped down in the office chair. Why cry? I could not cry away fifty pounds. When the tears dried I would still be Donna's blimp of a friend, Clarence's rejected wife, Mama Jeffries's wayward daughter, and Alex's batty mom. Instead of crying, I signed online.

It had been two weeks since my cybering experience. I thought long and hard about a new screen name. I thought about my daddy and my jar of stars. I thought about Regina and Broadway. I thought about my dreams, impractical dreams.

I signed on as SilkyDreamGirl and immediately began popping in and out of rooms. I found my old room. JoyJoy4U, TereseSpin, DogAround, MaryMacaroni, and the whole crew were there. I immediately sent a hug to everyone.

SilkyDreamGirl:	(((((((Everyone)))))
DogAround:	Thats so cool
Chuckles76142:	hello ladies
SilkyDreamGirl:	(((((JoyJoy)))))
JoyJoy4U:	Who is SilkyDreamGirl?
SilkyDreamGirl:	<~~~Stepmom9845
MaryMacaroni:	Why the name change, Silky.
SilkyDreamGirl:	Just learning my way around.
DogAround:	Hmmmmmmmmmm
DaJudge:	Ok, Silky
SilkyDreamGirl:	DogAround, have you been good?
Chuckles76142:	lookin for sweet babe any replies
JoyJoy4U:	QQ
DogAround:	Yes . . .
MaryMacaroni:	babe??
Chuckles76142:	im me please
MaryMacaroni:	you pig . . . "babe" . . . ROFL
TereseSpin:	hi Chuckles
Chuckles76142:	TereseSpin, hello
Babe 42:	what Mary??
TheWildJoker:	37/m/chicago area looking for a fine ebony lady

I felt good in that room with all my buddies. The conversation was very decent and had nothing to do with cybering. True, they were a flirtatious bunch. Sexual innuendoes filled their chats, but that room became my base. Every night, after the boys were in bed, I was there. I went to my profile and made a special note: No cybering. I quickly learned the chat room lingo:

bbl—be back later
brb—be right back
LMAO—laughing my ass off
LOL—laugh out loud

OIC—oh, I see

OMG—Oh my God

QQ—looking

ROFL—rolling on the floor laughing

IM—instant message

:-) a smiling face.

I tell you, by the end of the month I was laughing out loud all the time. I developed a relationship with MaryMacaroni and DogAround whose real name was Louis. He was a sweetheart who had caught one wife in bed with his best friend, and another wife with a crack pipe. Wife number three dumped him after he injured his back and could not keep her in a high-price lifestyle. Two or three online women had also dumped Louis. I teased him about his name.

SilkyDreamGirl:	I thought your screen name meant player
DogAround:	LOL.
SilkyDreamGirl:	Your name is deceiving. You should change it to NiceGuy4U2Abuse.
DogAround:	See, you ain't right.
SilkyDreamGirl:	LOL. Never said I was.

I told Mary, her honest-to-goodness real name, about my marital woes and about Donna. I told her how helpless I felt in my present situation, like there was nothing I could do to change my plight. I even told her of my weight problem. She had one too. We swapped telephone numbers and she called.

"Whatever you do," Mary said in her first phone call. "Stay away from health clubs."

"Why, Mary?" I asked.

I was sipping black coffee and trying to stay away from the coconut cream pie in my refrigerator. Victor Newman was sitting before Nicky's hospital bed on *The Young and the Restless*. The volume was down because I knew the writers planned to put Victor and Nicky together again.

"Men who hate their fat mamas designed those places," she said.

I laughed. Mary was a woman after my own heart. She had a great sense of humor and a quick tongue. Mary's husband had died a year before and left her with three babies to raise.

"Why do you say that?" I asked.

"I tell you why," Mary said. "Imagine yourself walking into a torture chamber. It's a massive room with gleaming chrome and black leather. It's a sadist dream world. You straddle a black leather seat and drape your arms over cold levers. Now the machine compels you to twist to the left and then to the right while moving twenty pounds of pressure. You gotta do this until your arms are bone-weary."

I clicked off the television and laughed, "Mary, you gotta exercise to lose weight."

"Listen to me, Katie," she said. "Those places take your money and torture you. One day you can't make the gym. That day turns into a week and that week turns into a month, but you signed a contract. You still have to pay that bill."

I laughed, "sounds like you have experience."

"Girl, five hundred and sixty dollars later and I'm still battling a midriff bulge. I had three babies in four years and gained sixty-five pounds. I got so big with my last child that the doctor did two ultra sounds. He thought another baby or two was hiding. It's been hell, Katie, hell, trying to lose sixty-five pounds."

"Have you lost any of it?" I asked.

"Yeah, girl," she said. "I've lost thirty pounds."

"How?"

"Walking," she whispered like it was some big secret. "And I cut out pork and butter."

"Really. Butter."

"And fatty pork like bacon, pork chops, and gravy."

"Well, pork is not a problem," I said. "I don't eat it."

"Are you Muslim?"

I laughed. "No, and I'm not Jewish either. Ninth grade health class and Mrs. Pritchard's lecture on pork and trichinosis cured my cravings for bacon."

Mary laughed, "You can do it, Katie, if you're doing it for yourself and not to get your husband back or to please your tight-ass girlfriend. You gotta do it for you."

"I want me back, Mary," I told her. "I could not care less about Clarence. And Donna's head is lopsided. She needs an attitude adjustment. I want to do it for me."

Mary gave me her weight-lost program that included Müeslix and a vigorous walk. In my mind's eye, I did a perfect trek up Clark Street, to South Boulevard, to the lake, and finally back home, a brisk hour walk. In reality, I huffed and puffed from my apartment through Touhy Park over to Clark Street that always steamed with too much traffic and too many people. I crossed Howard Street that divided Chicago from Evanston. There Clark Street changed to Chicago Avenue. I dragged my large butt past the El terminal, past the empty trains in the dead train yard. Once passed the viaduct the quietness of the cemetery to my right, and the slow traffic on the street made my trek even more strenuous. I read the tombstone of three sisters who died within a year of each other. I wondered about the deaths of a young baby. I plodded on toward my goal but barely made it through the doors of Dominick's, where I plopped on the thin window ledge and caught my breath. It was weeks before I could make it over to Lake Michigan, but determination forced me onward.

Each night, I soaked uncooked oatmeal (old-fashioned rolled oats), dried fruits, and nuts. Each morning, I sliced half a banana into the mixture, sprinkled a little coconut on top, and ate. I spent the afternoon in front of the computer typing on *Jerissa's Journey* or baking cakes that I no longer taste tested. I was online every night and at least two hours during the day between *The Young and the Restless* and General Hospital. Luke and Laura broke up on *General Hospital* so I stopped watching that soap opera. Later, the whole Victor-Nicky romance sickened me, so I gave up on *The Young and the Restless* too. Only the baking saved me from being a total online junkie.

CHAPTER 9

I was practical when I married Mr. Pete, or rather, I felt obligated to marry him. Mr. Pete first broached the subject of marriage, the summer of Alex's fourth year. We lazed in Mama's backyard on Loomis Avenue. It was too hot to do anything but sip lemonade and watch Alex play with Paris, Mama's cocker spaniel. Mr. Pete and Mama yakked about the good old days when he and my daddy ran the streets.

"Now, Helen, you know Alex never cheated," Mr. Pete reassured Mama.

"Humph, show me a man that doesn't cheat, and I'll show you a dead man," Mama said.

Mr. Pete laughed, low chuckles that sound sinister. The shrill of the phone disturbed our tranquility.

"I'll get it." I rose, but Mama flagged me down.

"It's cranky old Pat," Mama said. "I told her I was coming over."

While Mama was in the house, Mr. Pete and I laughed at

Alex and Paris's antics. Paris was so old that he limped as he tried to escape Alex's grasping hands.

"You know, I always wanted a son," Mr. Pete said.

"You and Miss Verna never had any children?" I knew the answer before I asked the question.

"No, Verna could not have children."

"Uhmm hmm," I said. I was not good company for old folks like Mr. Pete and Mama. The past lived in their heads like old sitcoms, same stories told and retold. Their conversations revolved around things that happened or should have happened or shouldn't have happened.

"Here I am, seventy-three, and still wanting a child," Mr. Pete said. "A son from my blood."

"Well, Mr. Pete," I said brazenly, "You need a woman for that."

He looked at me and laughed, "Maybe you could be that woman? Ain't nobody in the world but me. The house is paid for. Got a few dollars saved, and there's my retirement annuity from the railroad. You'll get that forever."

"Mr. Pete, I'm only twenty-four!" I exclaimed. The last image I wanted in my head was that old man humping on top of me.

"Twenty-four with proof that you can give birth," he said. He nodded to Alex who chose that moment to look at us with an angelic face.

"Katie!" he shouted and ran toward us.

It was one of those storybook moments. He ran straight into my arms with Paris yelping at his heels. Mr. Pete chuckled, and I felt absolutely trapped. Just then Mama came out the house, and I used her entrance to escape.

Mr. Pete was on a mission. He wanted a child. After that encounter, I saw him with a few of my high school classmates. The girls always dressed to the nines and had jewelry galore. Fine and dandy. I met James and married him. James and I got a divorce just when LaWanna Jordan, Regina's baby sister, announced her pregnancy by Mr. Pete. She planned a huge wedding with fifteen bridesmaids, two flower girls, and a white limousine. Her wedding plans were as grand as the plans for the royal wedding. Donna was one of the bridesmaids. Regina was given the dubious role of maid-of-honor. LaWanna did not ask me to join the group. We did not get along. Mama talked about the affair with distaste and disbelief.

"Can't believe Pete's letting some twenty-year-old child trick him into marriage. Everybody knows she ain't pregnant by him. Old goat! Thinks he gonna leave a string of children behind. Married to Verna for forty years and never a hint of a baby. Of course, he blames her. Go around saying she couldn't have any children but the man cheated on her left and right, where're the babies from all those affairs. And Verna? Heaven knows I loved that woman, but why she spent most of her life crying over that dog, I don't know. Like it was her fault, that the good Lord saw fit not to bless them with a baby. And didn't Verna coo over you like you were her own. Never saw a woman so taken with another woman's brat. I tell you. Verna was a saint, a saint married to a low-down dog."

"Woof-woof," Alex said from the floor. "Woof-woof."

"Stop that boy!" Mama snapped.

He and I were watching our Thursday night television lineup, *The Cosbys, A Different World,* and everything else that NBC had to offer. Back then I spent Thursday evenings at Mama's house. Every other Saturday, I picked Alex up for a movie and dinner date. Sometimes he spent the night with me. Most of the time he didn't. I was in school at the time, trying to get my master's. It was so much easier for Alex to stay with Mama. I didn't have to hear how I wasn't taking care of the boy properly.

"You said he was a dog," Alex pushed his luck.

"You keep on, and you won't see another episode of *The Cosbys* this year," Mama warned.

I guess LaWanna would have married Mr. Pete and gone to Vegas for the honeymoon if she hadn't been spooked out of her plans. A week before the wedding, the story goes, LaWanna and Mr. Pete did a walk through his home. She wanted all of Mama Verna's things gone. LaWanna planned to redo the house in soft lavender and blue with sprinkles of yellow. On the second floor Mr. Pete walked past a closed door like it didn't exist. LaWanna insisted on going into that room.

"Pete, honey, I need to look in this room," she said.

"That there is gonna be the nursery," Mr. Pete said.

"Well, don't you think I should look inside and make some plans?" she asked.

He reluctantly took out an old-fashioned skeleton key and unlocked the door. The room was large and bright. The cream wallpaper had teddy bears holding colorful balloons. There was a beautiful hand-carved oak crib against one wall. A white wicker bassinet, draped with netting, stood against another wall. The bassinet and netting were yellowed with age. The third wall supported a changing station and small white dresser. A bamboo rocker sat by a window that over-looked the neighborhood. Scattered around the room were toys. GI Joes marched across the tiny window sills. A Chatty Cathy doll and several Barbie dolls crawled across the lap of a huge panda bear. There were toys out of Burger King and McDonald gift packs. A family of dead sea monkeys floated in a dirty fish tank. Winnie the Pooh rode a tricycle. Quick Draw McDraw sat on a bicycle. Fred Flintstone and Barney Rubble sat on a Big Wheel. A scale model Lionel train set, a go-cart, three racing tracks, and thousands of Matchbox cars ran around the room. There were Raggedy Ann and Andy,

Winnie the Pooh, and Barney Rubbles stuffed dolls. Posters of Mickey Mouse, Minnie Mouse, Underdog, and a rare one of the Little Rascals looked down from the wall. Model airplanes, ships, and a model of the U.S.S. *Enterprise* from *Star Trek* dangled from the ceiling on thin wires. There were smaller things like crayons, coloring books, bolo bats, jacks, marbles, a slinky, and a Rubik's cube. Mr. Pete had added to that collection of toys year after year.

Some said it was that rocker moving slowly back and forth that tipped the scale. Others swear that LaWanna heard Mama Verna humming a lullaby. Still others testified that it was the ghost of Mama Verna that made LaWanna back out that room, until she hit the wall in the hallway. LaWanna swore that she felt something tap her on the shoulder. When she turned, Mama Verna scowled down at her from a huge picture. I knew that picture well. Mama Verna was not happy that day. In that picture, her eyes were narrow, tight slits. Her mouth was a wrinkled pucker. Mama Verna had been a thin, pointy looking woman. Anyway, LaWanna ran down the stairs, screaming at the top of her lungs, and Mr. Pete was behind her calling:

"Girl, girl, What's the matter with you, girl?"

Mr. Pete was old and LaWanna was fast. She was outside the house running up Loomis Avenue before Mr. Pete could get to the first floor. To this day, LaWanna swears Mama Verna followed her around that house and whispered, *don't touch nothing here.* LaWanna called the wedding off. She claimed she lost the baby in the flight. In less than a month, Mr. Pete was back to begging me to marry him. I married Mr. Pete for one reason only. He saved my son-brother's life.

I don't know about other cities, but in Chicago, the children will get in the middle of the street and play ball—football, dodge ball, baseball, and soccer—ball. Drivers tooted their horns and the kids scattered. The drivers never, ever rolled their cars over the children like a ball over bowling pins. The day Alex was mowed down, we sat on our stoops, up and down the street, and watched the kids play dodge ball. An ice cream truck had passed, so almost everybody was munching on something. A few of the boys had wolfed down their treats and were back in the street. Alex, who was not allowed to play in the streets, was with them. He had a way of blending into a group of kids so Mama and I could not see him.

Along came a yellow Pontiac Firebird. It was a beauty. As it passed our house at top speed, I saw the red emblem on the back. I saw my child in its path. I leaped up and screamed. I heard the screeching of tires. The car swerved. I heard the grind of metal against metal. I fainted. I regained consciousness as the ambulance wailed down our street. Mr. Pete kneeled by Alex. The Fire Bird had careened into a park car but still managed to hit Alex on his side. Mr. Pete administered CPR. He breathed into Alex's mouth and pumped his tiny chest. Mama and all the other mamas were praying, "Dear Lord, oh, Jesus, save this child." By the time the ambulance made it way down our street, Alex was breathing. I vowed then to take CPR, which I later did.

Mr. Pete drove Mama to the hospital, while I rode in the ambulance. He handled the doctors because Mama and I were in shock. I was still in shock when he asked me to marry him. I was half comatose with thoughts of losing my only son-brother. I said yeah and Mr. Pete didn't allow time for me to change my mind. He raced me from Mercy Hospital to city hall. We were married that day. Mama never spoke about that marriage. LaDell laughed up and down the hospital hall. He stopped because a nurse threatened to kick him out. Poor Georgie shuddered and looked at me as if I were the most addlebrained woman on earth. Naturally, Regina and Donna disagreed about my decision.

"Smart move," Regina said sarcastically. Her short rotund body drew away from me.

"Girl." Donna grabbed me. "It's about time that you used your big head."

"Are you stupid, Donna? Katie had no business marrying that old fart!" Regina barked. Regina had been a dyed red-head with the biggest pair of breasts you could get on a short woman. Despite being plump, Regina was spandex queen—anything short, tight, and clingy—anything that accentuated her wide load. Donna always cracked on her with *girl, why don't you cover up that stuff?*

By time Alex got out the hospital and I realized my mistake, I was firmly ensconced in Mr. Pete's house. Mama Verna never frowned at me or made any type of appearance. I thought, *Well hell, the man does think I'm pretty. He's nice, and he did say he would wait until I was comfortable being Mrs. Peter Smith, before we attempted to make his son.* It must have been my hips. I have those child bearing hips—wide and ample.

I reminded him of his promise to set up a trust fund for Alex's education and to change his will so I could get the house. I really didn't expect the old geezer to do it. Mama said that a distant cousin of Mama Verna would inherit everything. I could not see him changing his will but he did. One morning, he placed a manila envelope in my hands with all the appropriate paper work. What else could I do but keep my part of the bargain? I am a woman of my word.

On our official wedding night, the man was anxious. Vile sloshed in my stomach. Every time I looked at the old geezer, I shuddered. When I was a child, Mr. Pete wasn't bad looking but on our wedding night old age had twisted all his good looks into a comedic nightmare. His pink lips were simply cups to hold saliva. He had the fragility that comes with old age. His skin was thin, dry parchment with liver spots. He moved as if every bone in his body was on the verge of breaking. His soft curly hair had yellowed with age. His eyes were huge behind his triple thick eyeglasses.

I figured that Mr. Pete had one good go in him. He would hump me, roll over, and wait for the baby to grow in my stomach. I bought a black gown that splurged so far down in the back that the crack of my butt gulped air. A thin spaghetti strap criss-crossed my back. A slit ran up the front and the bosom plunged down to the navel. I figured that would excite Mr. Pete so much that the whole sordid act would be over in, say, five minutes.

To guarantee that the old geezer would not have enough energy to last past a hit and a miss, I cooked a huge dinner; oxtails in speckled butter beans, candied yams, fried chicken, macaroni and cheese, fried okra, sliced tomatoes with mayonnaise, and a peach cobbler with so much butter and sugar in it that the crust glittered. Hell, that meal would have put the strongest man to sleep. I put on Isaac Hayes' *Hot Butter Soul* LP, and prayed that the man would be finished with my body before the long version of *Walk on By* was completed.

Mr. Pete started at my toes, licking and sucking them like candy, while his fingers played my satin hips like a fine harp. He nibbled my calves while he massaged my ankles and I felt the first stirring, the first quivering of excitement. He nibbled up my body to my navel. His tongue darted in and circled slowly, almost ticklishly. An ancient core of lust burned inside my stomach. Did it matter that his body was as wrinkled as an old cotton sheet? No. When he took one of my nipples into his mouth, and rolled his tongue around it, I heard myself groan from some hot orange place where desire controlled my mind and body. I clawed the bed and pulled the sheets up as my hips rose. By the time that old man released my hardened and wet nipple from his mouth,

I was begging him for more. I hated him for that. I tell you, I despised him. I did not want to want him but there I was writhing on his bed underneath the watchful eyes of Mama Verna, writhing and saying *please* like some young girl who didn't know any better. And Mr. Pete, you could tell was a master, he nursed at my breasts softly. Notice I said nursed, not lick or nibble, but nursed one after the other. Long before we consummated our marriage, I had orgasms. I had many mini orgasms. When he finally entered me, I could only scream as flashes of light, so intensely bright, filled my sight. Little did I know that was only a mid-size orgasm under his masterful hands. I thought it was a major thing but Mr. Pete proved to me that I knew nothing about sex, about making love, or about the male-female mating ritual. That man took me on one roller coaster ride after another. At one point, I thought my heart would explode. I felt such an overwhelming need to strangle him. He moved slowly, like honey coming out of a jar, like he had a lifetime to consummate our marriage. There was no rush, no hurry. When I thought the old geezer was at the point of orgasm, he stopped, just stopped and breathed. Obviously, he intended to go on and on forever. I would have to smell the pissy-age of his skin forever. When the man finally ejaculated—no, wrong word—unloaded all that was in him, I was weak and angry. I curled away from him, ashamed of my body's betrayal. His hand rested on my belly. I lay in the darkened bedroom. I wanted to scream. I had married a man who expected a baby and who had the stamina to work diligently toward that goal.

When Mr. Pete died a couple of months later, I had the house and his retirement. Alex had what was in Mr. Pete's bank account in a nifty little trust fund, but I was not pregnant. After Mr. Pete's funeral, I donated the toys (except a few collectible items) to LaRabida Children's Research

Hospital. I gave all the furniture away to Goodwill Indus-
tries. I painted the house and rented it to the Gordons, a
couple with life. I moved to the North Side, far away from
Englewood. Folks looked at that house on Loomis and
*thought if that old goat hadn't tried to make a baby he would
have lived much longer.* But, if that old goat had lived longer,
he would have worn my young body out.

CHAPTER 10

The shattering of glass woke me from a deep sleep. The sound came from the kitchen. I sat up in bed and held the comforter against my chest. I reached between the wall and the bed for the billy club, a memento from a security job Clarence held for two months. I eased out the bed. I found CJ and Darius bunched together in the hallway. Darius gripped his Buzz Lightyear figurine while CJ clutched his scale model of Godzilla. Our Dr. Denton's barely protected us from the arctic air that blasted through the apartment. In the dim overhead light of the hall, CJ's huge eyes took on a ghastly appearance, fear. A twitching grimace played on Darius's face.

I pressed my finger to my lips and eased into the living room. I could not believe some fool broke into a poor woman's apartment. Hell, what was he gonna steal, the KitchenAid mixer that Donna gave me for Christmas. I didn't have a wide screen TV or a DVD or any other new-fangled gadget. The only jewelry in the apartment came from those trinket shops in every mall.

He wants your body, a voice whispered. I pressed against the wall, all one hundred and eighty-one pounds of me. (Yes, I had lost fourteen pounds on Mary's plan). I tightened my grip on the billy club and jumped my heavy butt into the kitchen. I swung the billy club. The glass in the cupboard shattered. I swung again and the flower arrangement skittered off the table. Darius flipped on the light before I could do more damage. The kitchen was empty. An icicle about two feet wide and one foot deep bulged through the kitchen window.

"Dang!" CJ and Darius exclaimed.

"Look at that icicle!" Darius said.

We all shivered and hugged ourselves. I looked at the window and knew I could do nothing about it tonight.

"Guys, you need to go back to bed," I said.

"We'll freeze," Darius said. Darius was smart like that. He could assess a situation and cut to the chase in a heart beat.

"I'll figure something out," I said. "You go back to bed."

"Man, it's coooold," CJ said through chattering teeth. His eyes were back to their normal, wonderful natural bright-ness.

"I'll help you think, Mom," Darius said. "Dad said we had to help you think."

"Boy, take your butt to bed," I snapped. "You do not need to help me think."

"First thing, Mom," he said, ignoring me and pointing to all the glass on the floor, "you need to get this glass up."

I could tell right then, that Darius would make an ex-cellent, chauvinist husband.

Working in coats and gloves, we cleaned up the glass. We used two old quilts to cover the window and block as much air as possible. I called the landlord service and left an emergency message. My room had no radiator, so I closed up in the boys room. The boys and I burrowed under mounds of coats and quilts. We slept until the landlord rang the door bell. They would be really late for school but decided late was better than freezing.

The landlord cut the icicle with a chainsaw. It shattered into thousands of shards and chunks on the ground below. Next he removed the broken glass from the window and boarded it up. After the landlord left, I made a pot of homemade tomato soup. The boys and I ate grilled cheese and tomato soup for dinner and laughed about the incident.

"Mom was swinging that billy club like crazy!" Darius laughed as he pulled his grilled cheese sandwich apart.

"I thought she was gonna do karate on that icicle!" CJ joked. He had both arms around his bowl of soup as if to protect it from us.

That was the good thing about my small cramped kitchen; it created a feeling of closeness and encouraged us to talk to each other. We sat at the table joking about icicles and the imagined burglar.

"Who were you gonna kill with Godzilla?" I asked CJ.

"Well, Darius had lame old Buzz Lightyear."

"Buzz Lightyear isn't lame," Darius said.

I realized, for the thousandth time, how much I will miss the boys. I didn't like it. I nursed those boys through chicken pox, flu, a broken finger, a cut foot, black eyes, and the loss of a bird. I taught them to respect other people's property, a pet peeve of mine. They, in turn, improved my *your mama jokes* and taught me the value of human souls. Now in four months they would be out of my life. My heart tightened and I smiled.

"What's wrong, mom?" CJ asked.

"I love you, guys," I said.

"I love you too, mom," CJ said.

"All shucks," Darius said. "Just don't start with the kissing stuff."

When the boys went to bed that night, I was in a funky spirit. I worked a little on *Jerissa's Journey*. The cow was not finding her leading man appealing. I shut down the program and immediately signed online.

***

March pounced and I was in full swing with cakes. Yet, no matter how much I cranked out, Donna wanted more. I was also busy packing up the boys' belongings and tossing out Clarence's belongings. Clarence had left things behind to stay anchored in my life. He refused to send money so that I could ship his stuff. We were not on friendly terms at all. He considered me a money hungry cow and I considered him a donkey, mule, ass.

Depression was sinking in. Every time I packed a box of the boys' belongings, I got misty-eyed. Insomnia also crept in. The more depressed I became, the less I could sleep. I was down to four hours a night. Some nights I signed online and watched all my buddies drift off to bed.

> JoyJoy4U: Good night, bed is calling.

One after the other they signed off . . .

> MaryMacaroni: I'm outta here.
> DaJudge: So am I.

. . . until there was only one . . .

SilkyDreamGirl:	Good night all.

. . . me, sitting alone in an empty chat room. Most nights I room hopped. Yet, no matter how friendly others greeted me, I could not find a second online home. I surfed from one room to another. One night, I went through all the rooms under FRIENDS and finally, after a third shot of tequila, began looking under ROMANCE. I was determined. I quickly scanned the topics and found a room that seemed sane and there he was, MastrThief, crooning *Let's Stay Together* by Al Green.

MastrThief:	whatever you want to dooo
GirlyGirlOK:	Hello Silky
SilkyDreamGirl:	Hello
MastrThief:	is all right with meeeeeeee
ManGoneWild:	Welcome Silky. Are you really Silky?
MastrThief:	You make me feeel
Silky:	LOL. Who's the man with Al Green's voice?
MastrThief:	Hello Silky
MastrThief:	so brand neeeewwwww

He crooned. I swear I could hear a rich voice speaking to me. Then right in the middle of my fantasy, he began to sing an old Jerry Butler song, *I Stand Accused*.

SilkyDreamGirl:	MastrThief, I love your voice. LOL.

His songs and his words keep me so enthralled that minutes passed before I realized that the entire context of the room's chat was sexual.

SilkyDreamGirl:	Why are people talking about sex?
MastrThief:	Look at the names, Sweetie.

I blushed. The names were erotic: hotbod4u, wetonehere, getdownNnasty. I wanted to watch him type songs but I didn't want to get caught up in another cyber affair.

MastrThief:	Silkieeee, Silkieeeee, are you there?
SilkyDreamGirl:	I'm here, MastrThief.
MastrThief:	Why so quiet?
SilkyDreamGirl:	I'm not into this type of chat, MastrThief.
MastrThief:	How old are you?
SilkyDreamGirl:	I'm a woman . . . I don't tell my age.
MastrThief:	You have a pic? You wanna trade.
SilkyDreamGirl:	No. I don't have a picture. I'm new to chatting.

I was not sending him an ugly butt picture of me. I mean the man was singing Al Green, Curtis Mayfield, The Temptations. How romantic could he be?

MastrThief:	So, how tall are you?
SilkyDreamGirl:	I'm short. 5'4".
MastrThief:	I'm 6'2, 220 lbs, deep blue-green eyes.

Oh, my! I never thought about race before until he mentioned his eyes. Here I was chatting with a blue-green-eyed man who could be a racist. I decided to end the conversation quickly by letting him know I was black.

SilkyDreamGirl:	That's nice. I have dark brown eyes and dark brown hair and a Deep, Deep brown complexion.

I scanned each line of text in the room, waiting for his comment. Instead he sent an instant message.

MastrThief:	uhmmm, that sounds lovely.

Okay. Maybe the man wasn't a racist. We could talk.

MastrThief:	Too bad you don't have a pic. Love to see that loveliness.

I thought about a picture that Clarence had taken once of my legs. Clarence always said I had the finest legs that he'd ever seen on any woman except Tina Turner, of course.

SilkyDreamGirl:	I have a picture of my legs that I could scan.
MastrThief:	Really? Well send it on.
SilkyDreamGirl:	Wait. BRB

Clarence had snapped the picture as I did a runner's stretch against a tree. I wore a pair of tight black capri pants and a skimpy tee-shirt. I quickly scanned the picture of my legs and sent it. I waited until he opened his mail.

MastrThief:	LOL, Sweetie.
MastrThief:	I expected a different picture.
SilkyDreamGirl:	What?
MastrThief:	Cheesecake.
SilkyDreamGirl:	Oh! I wouldn't send a picture like that.
MastrThief:	I like your legs. When can I see the rest of you?
SilkyDreamGirl:	That's presumptuous. We've just met. LOL.
MastrThief:	LOL. I like your wit.
SilkyDreamGirl:	Thank you.
MastrThief:	So tell me about you.
SilkyDreamGirl:	Nothing to tell. I bake cakes, and I'm taking care of my stepsons for my husband.
MastrThief:	Oh, you're married.
SilkyDreamGirl:	No, separated headed for a divorce.
MastrThief:	Is that good for you?

Finally, someone was asking me if the separation were good for me, not for the family, not for Clarence, but me, Katie Jeffries Cannon Smith Robinson Coomers. My seven-year marriage was down the drain; seven years of begging, pleading and feeling like an idiot, seven years, gone.

| MastrThief: | Did I ask the wrong question? |
| SilkyDreamGirl: | No. You didn't. It's good. It's good for me. |

There I said it. The whole separation thing was good for me. Clarence didn't love me. He would never love me. I could do nothing about that.

MastrThief:	Why do you have his sons?
SilkyDreamGirl:	He moved to California. He wanted to get himself straight before sending for them.
MastrThief:	Tell me something else about you. What do you do for fun?

When I thought about fun, I thought about Regina. We took excursions to different cities: four days, three nights in Cancun, three days and four nights in Vegas, or five days, four nights in beautiful St. Thomas. We stumbled half drunk along Lake Michigan until cops escorted us out of the park. We milled through the crowd at the Chicago Jazz Fest and pinched the bottom of every fine man we passed. Fun was part of another lifetime. Then, I thought about the opera.

| SilkyDreamGirl: | I attend the opera with a friend's husband. |
| MastrThief: | WHAT??? |

I explained my arrangement with Mike. Immediately, MastrThief asked if there was somebody special in my life. I wanted to say you, man. I don't know anything about you but you are special to me. This moment is so crucial to my existence. Instead I told him no. Next he wanted to know how long Clarence had been gone.

SilkyDreamGirl:	Since September.
MastrThief:	And you haven't dated.
SilkyDreamGirl:	No.
MastrThief:	Why?

Why? I was a married woman. No. That wasn't true. Because I'm fat. That wasn't true either. I knew plenty of large women with intelligent, fine men on their arms. MastrThief was probing inside me. I felt uncomfortable, yet I wanted to stay in his presence.

SilkyDreamGirl:	Cause all I do is stay home and take care of the boys and bake cakes and listen to everybody complain about my life and tell me how I've messed it up and most of the time I feel worthless.

I typed all that and sent it without thinking, like I was speaking to another part of myself. I sat back in the chair and waited for his response. It wasn't long in coming.

MastrThief:	I want you to get up right now and go look in the mirror.
SilkyDreamGirl:	Why?
MastrThief:	Just do it, and really look at you. Okay?
SilkyDreamGirl:	Okay.

I got up from the computer and went into the bathroom. I looked at myself in the mirror. My hair was all over my head. My skin was splotchy. The frayed collar of my robe was bleached from navy to gray. Large fudge-brown orbs stared from a fat brown face. Since I was drinking more water than Pepsi, my skin was clearer. (Part of Mary's weight loss plan included cutting out the sodas.) He said to look at me, to really look. I was drawn into the eyes of a woman possessing a great sense of humor, and who used that humor to smother her pain. I saw an unconventional woman stuck in a conventional world, a woman whirling like crazy while the world played a sedate melody to calm her down. There stood a loyal, devoted, and indefatigable woman who climbed mountain after mountain. Me. It was me. I returned to the computer.

SilkyDreamGirl:	Back.
MastrThief:	Tell me, what did you see?

I flushed with embarrassment but felt compelled to be truthful with him. I even mentioned my eyes and dewy skin, but skipped over my weight. Why bother the man with that detail?

MastrThief:	Why are you putting yourself down? If others don't appreciate you, that's their problem not yours. Everyday, Sweetie, you need to do something for yourself.
SilkyDreamGirl:	OK
MastrThief:	Promise?
SilkyDreamGirl:	I promise.
MastrThief:	Silky . . .
SilkyDreamGirl:	Huh
MastrThief:	I like you.
SilkyDreamGirl:	Thank you.
MastrThief:	By the way, my name is Matt.
SilkyDreamGirl:	Hi Matt, I'm Katie.

I didn't panic when I told him. Soon, my fingers were flying across the keyboard as I answered his questions and asked questions of my own. He was a consultant for an international security firm who traveled and checked security procedures for both domestic and foreign companies. He had been married twice and had two children by each wife. He played golf, drank wine, loved women, and would never marry again. He also had a brother who thought he should move back to North Carolina and help in the family furniture business. More important, Matt's wit was sharp and he could type just as fast as I could. Finally, he ended the conversation.

MastrThief:	I hope we can talk again, Katie.
SilkyDreamGirl:	That would be nice.
MastrThief:	Now, I have to sleep. LOL.

I looked at the clock it said 3:45 A.M.

SilkyDreamGirl:	Oh my, the time got away.
MastrThief:	It's like that with good company, and sweetie, you are good company.
SilkyDreamGirl:	Thank you.
MastrThief:	Nite.
SilkyDreamGirl:	Nite.

You ever had a good date? I mean the kind of date where afterward you floated for days? That was a good date.

The next day I had energy. I cleaned the apartment, baked a cake, made yeast dough, and assembled the rolls for two bread baskets. I took a bubble bath, gave myself a manicure and pedicure, rewrote chapter nine of *Jerissa's Journey*, and had tacos on the table when the boys walked in the door. We spent the evening trying to help CJ understand multiplication. Math was not his favorite subject. I told him that the numbers were jumbling up in his mind so he had to push them aside and do something else. So, we played a game of Sorry. Guess what? In the middle of the game CJ yelled *I got it* and went back to his homework. By 8:45 the boys were asleep. I did a complete make-over. I washed and blow-dried my hair. I caked mascara on my lashes until they were thick and heavy. I smeared on deep purple eye shadow. By the time I put on the finishing stroke of fuchsia lipstick, I was a bad imitation of Jezebel. I squirted Anais, Anais behind my ear.

"Silly goose," I said to myself in the mirror. "He's not going to smell you."

I signed online and scanned my buddy list. He was not online. What? Did I expect him to be there with flowers and candy, waiting for me to sign on? Well, yeah.

I went to my regular room and sat quietly. Everyone typed hello or sent me hugs and kisses.

JoyJoy4U:	Hi Silky, did you get my wavs.
Silky:	yeah. I downloaded it.

JoyJoy helped me download an add-on program. The program allowed me to organize, play, and create wav. She spent an hour teaching me how to create and send wavs. I spent another half hour chatting and still no MastrThief. *I'm waiting around for him like a fool*, I thought. *I'm just another stranger to him*. I flushed with embarrassment. I said goodnight to the room and received their goodnights in return. I signed off at 10:47. I was embarrassed, humiliated. I went looking for MastrThief like some silly school girl. What if he had a different name and saw me waiting for him? What if he changed his name to avoid me? I crawled into bed and had a miserable night. It was 3:30 a.m. when I finally fell asleep.

***

"Mom, Mom," CJ shook me.

"I'm awake," I said and stretched.

"Aunt Donna's on the phone. She says she's on her way for the bread baskets?"

"What time is it?"

"Seven o'clock."

"Geez!" I said and leaped from the bed. I was supposed to have everything ready for Donna.

CJ shook his head and walked out the room. "Darius, tell Aunt Donna that Mom overslept again."

"Darius, don't you dare!" I yelled. "Tell her everything will be ready for her."

I rushed into the bathroom. I washed my hands and half-washed my face. In the kitchen, I removed three trays of rolls and mini loaves of bread from the refrigerator. I slammed the first tray of rolls into the oven. By the time Donna waltzed through the door in her fabulous silver fox, the rolls and loaves of bread were done. The apartment had that wonderful yeasty smell of a bakery. I emphasized it by putting on a pot of coffee. I knew the weather was bitter cold outside. Donna did not wear her fur for show. She hated to see women in fur when the temperature was in the 40's or 50's.

"You have to stop cutting it so close, Katie," she said and slipped out of that coat.

She casually dropped the coat on my love-seat. I swear it drifted down as gently as a silk scarf. She had on a taupe pant suit with a pale cream blouse. On the lapel was a cluster of camels and monkeys with amber eyes. She followed me into the kitchen and squeezed passed me to the coffee pot.

"I have to be at work by ten o'clock today," she said. "When you want me to make your loop deliveries, you should have the products ready by seven thirty."

"Yeah, yeah," I snapped. "Products. You make this sound like big business."

She looked at me and shook her head. She had butchered one of her eyebrows then tried to correct her mistake with a black eyebrow pencil. Her correction stood out against her dark brown eyebrows. Donna spent a fortune on clothes and jewels but not one dime on a wax job or a good hair stylist. She relaxed her own hair and wrapped it in a chignon.

"Were you online all night?" she asked.

"No, I was not online all night."

She looked at my polished fingernails. She took a whiff of me.

"Katie, you had a man here!" she hissed.

"What?" I asked.

At that moment, CJ and Darius wobbled out of their rooms with their heaviest down coats, gloves, and scarves wrapped around half their faces. Those boys were scary perfect. They watched the news faithfully each morning for the weather report and sports update and then turned to PokeMon.

"Bye, Mom." CJ shifted his book bag, stepped into the kitchen, stood on his toes, and gave me a peck on the check. Darius dismissed me with a wave of his hand. Donna waited patiently and quietly until the boys had left the apartment, and I had locked the door behind them.

"Look at you!" she said when I reentered the kitchen. "All gussied up. Your makeup is smeared."

"I didn't have a man here. I wouldn't have a man here while the boys are still under my roof."

"Why are you gussied up?" she asked. Her crooked, badly colored eyebrow shot up.

"You sound like an old woman, Donna," I snapped. I moved around the table until we were facing each other. "Gussied up? Who uses that kind of language?"

"I know you, Katie Coomers."

Donna took a roll from a bread basket. She bit into it, closed her eyes and chewed.

"Delicious," she muttered.

"Don't eat the products," I mocked.

"Who is he?" she asked. "Did he stand you up?"

"Help me wrap the baskets," I said and pointed to the large sheets of cellophane on the table. The bread baskets, two flattened boxes, and two ribbons were also on the table.

"He did!" she exclaimed, almost joyously. "Who is he?"

"Nobody," I said. "Will you tie this, please?" I set a bread basket in the center of the cellophane.

"Tell me," she said.

Donna took one ribbon and wrapped it around the top of the cellophane. In the middle of tying the bow, she stopped and looked at me. I heard her brain ticking.

"No! Katie! You met some guy online."

I lowered my eyes.

"You invited some strange guy to your home!" she exclaimed.

"No, I did not invite anybody to my home," I said the words slowly. My fingers adeptly finished the bow that Donna had started.

"You met him!"

"No, I didn't meet him," I said.

I set the basket aside and moved the second basket in its place. Again, I brought the cellophane paper up over the baskets. Again, Donna wrapped the ribbon close to the top and half tied a bow. All the time she looked at me quizzically. Finally, she shook her head.

"So how did he stand you up?" she asked.

"He didn't stand me up," I said. "We didn't really have a date. I just thought he would be online last night but he wasn't."

"Wait! Wait!" She laughed and threw up her hands. "You gussied up for some online guy?"

I didn't say anything. I folded the corners up on the flatted box and inserted the tabs into each other. Stenciled in Fuchsia lettering on the pale pink boxes were the words, *another SWEET SUCCESS.* Sweet Success was the name Donna gave our imaginary baking business. I hated the name. I hated the business, and I was close to hating Donna.

"No, you didn't!" she exclaimed. Her laughter rang and bounced around that tiny room. "You got all dolled up for some online guy who probably looks like a reject from the *Texas Chainsaw Massacre.* "

Donna fell into a fit of laughter. She held her stomach and laughed. She laughed until tears streamed down her eyes. It wasn't funny, not funny at all.

"You will be late for work," I said dryly.

"Who is this Romeo?" she asked as she dabbed the tears from her eyes with a perfect linen handkerchief. She always carried one in her pocket. Donna was a throwback to the 50's with her handkerchief sprinkled with perfume, her garter belts and stockings, and those exquisite brooches she wore on her jackets and coats.

"I'm not telling you anything," I said. "It doesn't matter. I'll probably never chat with him again."

"Girl, you're becoming a junkie."

"I'm not."

"Right. You're all dolled up for some guy, who you don't

know, never met, will never see." She shook her head. "You're strange, Katie. Strange."

***

After Donna left, I went into the bath room and showered. I washed all the make-up away. I washed the stiff gel out of my hair. I dried my body and put on my robe. I went to the computer and opened chapter ten of *Jerissa's Journey*. Maybe, I needed to take a walk in the woods to hear my characters speaking. Inside that tiny bedroom/office, Jerissa was quiet. I decided to sign online and download the rest of JoyJoy's wavs.I opened my mail box. Three emails from MastrThief topped the list. Nervously I opened the first one.

Subj: **Where are you, Sweetie?**
Date: 3/10/99 10:49:088 pm Central Daylight time
From: MastrThief
To: SilkyDreamGirl
Power outages here, could not sign on until late. Hope to see you
   tomorrow night around ten.

I missed him by two minutes. He would be here tonight. I mean that was like making a date, right. At least that's the way I took it. I was jittery, nervous. I opened the second one. It was a wav. The man sent me music! I downloaded the wav and Barry White's deep voice filled me with emotions. I shivered with pleasure. I played the wav three times before I moved to the next email. The man was sexy. He stood before a turquoise blue ocean in a pair of red Speedo. The masculine lines of his cheek and his legs satisfied my fantasies. I pressed my lips against the monitor. The screen crackled with static. Then reality hit me. I was not alone with these feelings, this giddiness. He thought enough about me to send not one but three e-mails. Yeah! I hugged myself and signed off without visiting my old haunt.

By the time the boys arrived home, I realized Jerissa had not found a love. The plot was not working. I surprised the boys with a chicken pot pie and a whole lemon meringue cake (that's one moist cake). Over dinner we laughed about the time Darius tried to surprise everyone by cooking breakfast.

"He had grits everywhere," CJ laughed. "He cooked a whole box."

"Dad was mad!" Darius exclaimed. "I had to clean those sticky grits up by myself. They were stuck on everything, and when they turned cold, they were hard little boogers."

We talked about Bill Nye, the science guy. He understood the workings of an idiot's mind and broke down scientific principles in idiotnese. Precious angels that they were, the boys went to bed as scheduled. I took a bubble bath, scented down, lipsticked up, and was sitting at the computer when the phone rang.

"Hello," I answered in a sultry voice. I heard my voice from a long way. It was the kind of voice used by women in movies to seduce unsuspecting men.

"Kay-Jay?"

"Clarence, " I said in my normal bland voice.

"Who were you expecting?"

"What do you want, Clarence?"

"May I speak to the boys?" he asked.

"You know the boys are asleep," I snapped. "It's nine thirty."

"They are asleep, already?"

I didn't answer. I thought of Matt waiting for me and JoyJoy and MaryMacaroni. I thought about my protector, DogAround, and how nice he was to me. I was silent.

"So you're not talking to me?" Clarence broke the silence.

"What can I do for you?" I asked politely.

"I've tried calling at different times but the line stays busy," he said. "You never talked on the phone before."

"Things change."

"Who is he?" he asked laughingly but I could hear the seriousness in his voice.

Clarence? Jealous? Ha! He simply couldn't believe someone else found a use for his old shoe.

"Who is who?" I asked.

"Don't play innocent," he said. "I know you. I can't believe you would have men over with my boys."

Click. I hung up and hurriedly signed on line. The modem connected with the familiar beeps and screeches. Finally a voice from the computer boomed, *You got mail.* I quickly scanned my buddy list and there he was. What now? I opened the mailbox and saw nothing from him. Do I send an instant message to him or wait for him to send one to me? What was the correct procedure? I was thinking so hard about protocol that the soft beep of his instant message startled me.

MastrThief:	Hello Sweetie.
SilkyDreamGirl:	Hi

I said it shyly. At least, that's how I heard it in my voice, shy, coy, and timid. I wondered what he heard. Any thoughts of Clarence disappeared.

MastrThief:	Did you do anything special for yourself today?
SilkyDreamGirl:	Yes. I took a bubble bath.
MastrThief:	Sweetie, what a wonderful image that creates in my head.

All I could think was, *I am not alone with these feelings.*

CHAPTER 11

OBSESSION. What a magnificent word! The hissing of air behind my teeth caused a slight vibration on the tongue, like the first tickling of sexual stimulation. I was obsessed with MastrThief. I knew more about that man than I did Clarence. I knew his phobias and his joys. I knew that a crisp Cabernet Sauvignon across his tongue excited him like a hot kiss on the lips. I knew he loved his children deeply. I knew he didn't tolerate fools, and I knew I wanted him. Every night I sought his screen name in my ever growing list of buddies. When he signed on, I ignored my roomies and the continuous stream of IM from other men begging for my attention. MastrThief captivated me. His words haunted me as I checked the boys' homework. *Sweetie, I want to feast on your lips.* His image promenaded in my head between creaming butter and whipping eggs. His tanned, muscular legs invited my starving lips to nibble, nibble, nibble. Now, I had a joyous reason to rise in the mornings, to rush through housework, and to let my fingers fly through silky cake flour. I wanted nothing to interrupt my time with Matt. We talked long into the night. Our fingers tapped out questions, answers, comments, and sweet talk until sleep dragged him away from me. How could I sleep? His image tortured me.

You got mail became my catch phrase. I clicked online two and three times a day looking for mail from him. We were into the third week of our relationship and he was begging for pictures. He had sent me several of him and each was better looking than the last. His deep tan gave him a swarthy look. In one picture, he stood next to a black stallion. He and the horse merged into a collage of strength and beauty. I imagined myself astride that horse with him behind me. He held me tightly against his hard sinuous chest and buried his face in my hair. I had only to close my eyes to feel the wind on my flushed face and to smell the crispness of the ocean. Yes, we were always riding high above the ocean, along a rugged cliff. He guided the horse, loosely holding the reins in his strong hands. The sunlight glinted off the fine blond hairs on his arm. We moved with the rhythm of the horse. In my dreams, I felt him pressing against me. Oh, yes, between errands and sleep, I drooled over his pictures. Matt had no pictures of me. I refused to send him a picture.

MastrThief: Sweetie, there were no pictures in my mail
                     box. I want to see what you look like. I'm
                     going to like you regardless.

Right. I believed that one. We all have criteria, things we seek in a mate. My first criterion will always be a well-built man. Flex biceps and I fall in love. Clarence was a dusky brown man built like Arnold Schwarzenegger in his Mr. Universe days. My first husband, James, had a dark chocolate body so well sculptured that I spent hours following the def-initions of it with my hands, my lips, and my tongue. Joe, my third husband, sleazer that he was, had a body that could double for Wesley Snipes. Matt met my criteria with his washboard chest and well-defined legs, but did I meet his at a hundred seventy-four pounds? Was his ideal woman simi-lar to a blond, blue eyed, skinny Paltrow-type or would it be a voluptuous, sensuous Katie-type? Oh, yes, I was losing weight but not enough to run to *Glamour* shots and take pictures.

SilkyDreamGirl:	What's your ideal woman?
MastrThief:	Sweetie, I don't have an ideal woman.
SilkyDreamGirl:	Oh?
MastrThief:	No. One woman may have a great wit, like you.
SilkyDreamGirl:	Thank you. LOL.
MastrThief:	One woman may have charisma, like you.
SilkyDreamGirl:	Oh, my
MastrThief:	One woman may be devastatingly beautiful.
SilkyDreamGirl:	LOL. Like me.
MastrThief:	Sorry, I don't have pictures of that devastating beauty.
SilkyDreamGirl:	Ok. Ok. I get the point.

I decided to find an old picture from my thin and almost cute era. I found a picture taken by Regina on the beach at Monterey. My hair was full and flowing. Large sunglasses hid my eyes. Regina had taken that picture with love and laugh-ter. I had a bamming body. Curvy. I also scanned in the en-tire leg picture. Clarence had taken that one on our family honeymoon in the Black Hills of South Dakota. I scanned the two pictures and sent them to Matt. I signed off and crawled into bed. Miserable again. I had lied to Matt. Lied again—period. For the first time, I felt rotten about lying. Really, rotten.

***

I spent the morning baking cinnamon raisin cookies and cleaning the apartment. At nine-thirty the house shone from lemon furniture polish and elbow grease. A pleasant aroma of cinnamon filled the air and an Ottmar Liebert CD played softly in the background. I ran bath water and poured the last of my vanilla scented bubble bath into the tub. I lay in a steamy tub, with all too vivid images of MastrThief playing in my head. I forgot no money, no man, no job, and no prospects. If my hands happened to linger too long on my hardened nipples, it was okay. When the first spark of heat ignited my primal urges, that was okay too. He was there in my mind, tall, brown hair, with a flat stomach that rippled and eyes such a murky green I was not sure whether the green was true or some computer glitch. It didn't matter as my finger traced the cavity of my navel. I caught my breath and wondered how his hand, his tongue would feel in place of my own hand. I trembled beneath that mound of bubbles and . . . the phone rang.

A short stout woman cannot climb out of the tub as quickly as other people. By the time I got to the bathroom door, the ringing stop. I padded to the phone and picked it up. The caller ID flashed Chicago Board of Education and the number for CJ and Darius's school. I pressed *69 and waited for the answer.

"Truant office," a masculine voice answered.

"Hello, this is Katie Coomers," I said. "Someone there called me. I have two sons . . ."

"Yes, Mrs. Coomers," the man interrupted. "Darius is in my office. He had a slight altercation in his PE class."

"A what?"

"A fight in his gym class," he said like I was an idiot.

"Uh huh," I answered like an idiot.

"We need you to pick him up," he informed me. "He's been suspended for two days."

"Why was he suspended?" I asked. "Was the other kid suspended too?"

After all it takes two to tangle, I thought. Darius was smaller than most boys his age. I could not see him initiating a fight. I looked out the window at the thick sheet of falling snow. My pores were open.

"The other child's mom had to take him to the dentist," the man said. "Darius knocked out his tooth."

"Oh," I whispered. "I'm on my way."

My body was half-dry by the time I left the apartment. I prayed that I wouldn't catch my death of cold. I could not take any more nursing from Mama Jeffries.

***

Darius sat in the truant office looking as forlorn as I imagined Oliver Twist looked in the debtors' prison. His head was down, his hands dangled between his legs. His hair was rolled in tight balls and his gym shoes were scruffy. Oh, my goodness! It had been months since he had new shoes. The truant officer, on the other hand, rose from behind a wide dark mahogany desk. He was five feet wide by five feet tall and had the self-righteous demeanor of many short men in authority; his chest was puffed out, his lips were down turned, his eyes were narrowed, and his arms were crossed. My heart went out to Darius for having to endure his presence.

"Darius?" I called. "Are you all right?"

The child looked at me with such sad eyes I had to think of my flourless cake to keep from crying. It's a wonderful cake to think about in moments of distress. Chocolate is an antidepressive, at least that's my theory.

"Mrs. Coomers," the man said and rose. "I'm Mr. Buckingham."

I arched my eyebrow at him and thought, *How dare you make my son feel small.* I limply shook the truant officer's hand.

"What happened?" I asked.

"Darius . . ." he started.

"Excuse me Mr. Buckingham," I said and held up my hand. "I'd like to hear Darius first."

The man blanched and turned beet red. I'm not one of those mamas that think Little Johnny can do no wrong. When I was a child, contradicting an adult was unacceptable. I could not say *Uh uh, it didn't happen that way* without inevitably calling Mrs. Jordan, Mrs. Anderson, or whoever a liar. *Why Pat gonna lie on you,* Mama would ask. I always listened to my sons first. I knew none of the boys lied. Clarence insisted that the boys tell the truth at all times. Clarence. *Son,* he said often enough, *tell the truth, it goes easier. Don't lie to me. I need to believe in you. Don't let me lose confidence in you.*

They were the only boys I knew who admitted to wrongdoings like confession was a badge of honor. *I did it,* they proclaimed with fortitude. I never believed the myth about George Washington and the cherry tree until I witnessed Clarence's influence on my three sons.

"I hit him," Darius admitted his crime simply and directly.

Buckingham sucked in air. He had not expected such a direct statement.

"Why?" I asked.

"He said I was a punk. So I showed him who was a punk."

"Is that your version, Mr. Buckingham?"

"The gym teacher said Darius just hit the other student."

"Well, nobody just hits another person without provocation, Mr. Buckingham."

"Darius has to learn not to go around hitting people for the things they say."

I smiled my simple smile. That man didn't know how many people I wanted to hit. Maybe Darius was acting out my suppressed anger.

"You are right, Mr. Buckingham," I agreed, nodding my head. "He will be punished accordingly."

He arched his eyebrow as if to say, *Yeah, Lady, right.*

"He can return to school Monday," Mr. Buckingham said.

"You are sending schoolwork home with him," I said.

"Yes. He has assignments from Mrs. Perkins in his book bag."

"Thank you, Mr. Buckingham," I said. "Darius will not fight in school again."

When we left the building, the snow had stopped. A blast of winter air filled that March day. Darius zipped his coat up to his neck and pulled the strings of his hood tight.

"Darius," I said as I took the strings from him and made a quick slip knot. He looked at me with scared eyes. I smoothed his wild eyebrows and tugged him to me. "Next time, don't fight on school property. Wait until you are almost home. That way, the school can't suspend you."

Oh, did you really think I would tell him not to fight? We lived in Chicago. We lived in the real world. Words hurt.

***

Darius and I packed the last box of books to ship. We drove down Clark Street to the post office on Devon Avenue. Clark Street was always busy, no matter what time of day or night. It was one of those arteries that ran through the city like State Street, Western Avenue, and Madison Street. The traffic crept like a snake that had just eaten, lazy and slow.

Between Ridge Avenue and Devon, the sidewalk people scrambled around like a colony of ants. In and out stars, hawking wares on the streets, packing into taco joints, and resale shops. The area was dominated by Mexicans and Hispanics. The area seethed with the spicy aroma of authentic Mexican cuisine. Many windows were filled with unexpected black velvet art, piñatas, paper flowers, and posters of a serene beach in the Gulf of Mexico.

The drive to Devon usually took ten minutes. That day, the trip stretched into thirty minutes. I twisted in my seat, desperate to use the bathroom. I rolled my window down and stuck my head out. An eighteen-wheeler blocked the street. The driver had problems maneuvering the truck into the construction site of the new public library. I rolled the window up. Suddenly, I heard Darius muttering to himself. He didn't say the senseless things most kids say in play, you know, *Here comes Batman in his batmobile. He's gonna crush the Joker.* No, Darius was having a full fledge conversation about Clarence and me.

"She could go to California if she wanted to," he said in his normal voice.

"She's got to stay here and bake cakes," he said in a different, lower voice.

"She can bake cakes in California," he said in his normal voice.

His murmurings were so low, and in such distinct voices, that my hand gripped the steering wheel. Sweat ran down my face.

"Darius ?" I asked. "What did you say?"

"I didn't say nothing," he answered in his regular voice.

"You were talking."

I looked at him. He turned his head slightly and looked at me. His eyes moved from my face to the dash board. *Oh, my goodness,* I thought, *What are we doing?* I did not want to go to California but I did not want the boys to develop deep psychological problems because their dad and stepmom were nuts.

"Darius, you know I love you," I said.

"Yes, ma'am."

"You know there's nothing in the world I wouldn't do for you."

"Yes, ma'am."

"Sometimes, Darius, adults do not have all the answers."

He was quiet. He pressed the latch on the glove compartment. It dropped down and revealed a stash of peppermints. Darius took one, opened it, and popped it in his mouth. What do you say to a child having difficulty with his parents' separation?

"Do you want to go to California?" I asked.

"Don't we have to go?" He countered.

"Your dad is there."

"Do you love Dad?"

Now didn't I say Darius had a way of cutting to the chase of the matter? I thought about loving Clarence. Did I love him? Of course, I did. I love many things about him. The man catered to my whims. I would say, *I really want some ice cream*, and Clarence would get me ice cream. He ironed my clothes, ran my bath water, massaged my back, did the laundry, cleaned the house, massaged my toes, cooked the best chili in the world, and on top of all that was helpful to everyone around us. People loved him. Once I had loved him, but the man would not work. Love never fed a starving dog.

"I love your dad, Darius."

"Then why aren't you going to California with us? Does he love you?"

How do you explain love to children? How do you explain the many levels of love? I was close to ancient and I didn't understand love any more that day than the day I told Alex's father I was pregnant. Was Clarence in love with me? I didn't think so. Clarence saw me as a permanent babysitter for his boys. No more. No less.

At nineteen, Clarence sloughed off the West Side of Chicago. He sloughed off his civilian clothes and packed his closet with U. S. Navy–issued beige, white, and blue. Finally, freed from Roberta's choke hold, he met Valerie. For years, the two of them sailed to every Navy port-o-call presented to them. On his leaves, they explored exotic places in the South Seas, the Caribbean, Europe, Africa, and Asia. The adventures, the wondrous sights, did nothing to quell the growing maternal desires wrapped around Valerie's heart. The woman, who had agreed that children were not an option, wanted a baby. After years of marriage, the joy of exploration died within her heart. He surprised her with a trip to the Holy Land and another junket to Kenya. Still, discontentment rankled her mind.

"I thought," Clarence told me, "if we returned home, her maternal bug would die. I thought if she visited old friends and saw the rusty rut of their lives she would give up the notion of a baby."

The plan backfired. After years of jetting around the world, they returned to Great Lakes. Valerie spent weekends in Milwaukee with her family and old friends. While Clarence thought Valerie was over her maternal desires, jealousy picked and nicked at her until her breasts swelled with imaginary milk. With no discussion, no hint of her plans, she set about making a baby.

"Valerie was not a romantic woman, " Clarence whined. "So I should have connected the dots, but I never thought she could be deceitful."

When he learned that she was three-months pregnant, he was stunned and dismayed. The news slammed into him like a vicious blast of cold air. Without thinking, he asked if it was possible to have an abortion at three months. Yeah, when Clarence told me that, I cringed. Of course Valerie had been devastated. What woman, wife, would not have been. Her rage and her language shocked him. Valerie called him all kinds of selfish parasitic bastards. He crawled into a safe dark cave and didn't slither out again until Clarence Coomers Junior was born. Four months after CJ's birth, Valerie informed Clarence that she was pregnant again. Instead of submitting to the rage boiling inside his soul, Clarence silently had a vasectomy.

Then came another problem, Valerie wanted to settle. Clarence thought if he had to settle they should choose a beautiful exotic place where they could live cheaply on his retirement and the small savings they had accumulated. Valerie wanted a house in Milwaukee. She wanted her family and friends to share in her children's lives. House shopping shoved all other obligations off Valerie's daily calendar. She swaddled her children in winter gear and hunted high and low for that perfect home.

"All I could see," Clarence said, "was years of sameness."

One evening, Clarence refused to look at another house with a white picket fence. Valerie stormed out of their base quarters without Clarence or the boys. She never returned. She died in that big accident on I-94. Guilt and shame pithed the core of life from within him. Only Roberta could drag him back to breathable ground. When he met me, he thought I was a woman of dreams and visions. How sadly my dreams disappointed him. Love me. No. He saw me as a plush lap for his sons.

"Darius, your dad and I will always care about each other," I said. "Our feelings for each other have nothing to do with what we feel for you. I love you. Your dad loves you. We know what an exceptionally bright boy you are. We know you will do some things wrong like get CJ in trouble, but we still love you. That's never gonna change. Ok?"

The tip of the truck pulled out of the street. The traffic eased forward. I concentrated on the icy road and followed the traffic around the truck. I thought about the million little idiosyncrasies that were quickly adding to the complexities of my life. Darius was silent as I drove passed Mickey D's, the police station, and the hardware store.

"I don't want the family to break up," Darius repeated Clarence words.

My hands gripped the steering wheel as I made a slow turn on Devon. I could not believe Clarence was using the boys.

"Just think, you guys will be out in sunny California with your dad, away from the freezing wind and all this nasty, gray snow. You'll be right up the road from Disneyland, and so close to the ocean that you can probably taste the salt."

"How far is the ocean from Dad's apartment?" he asked.

"Closer than Disneyland, I think."

"We can go to Disneyland!" Darius exclaimed.

"I'm sure your father will take you."

"Wow! Disneyland!" Darius sighed.

How quickly children will toss away one parent's program for the other's.

***

Friday, I drained and closed a rainy day account and treated the boys to a shopping spree. They wanted the new Jordans. I wanted Pay Less. We compromised and bought low-cost Nike's. We moved over to J.C. Penney's and caught a sale. On the way home we laughed and cracked "your mama" jokes.

"Your mama is so fat," I told Darius, "she uses the lake for a bathtub."

"Ah, mom, that's a dub," Darius said. "I got one, CJ, your mama is so fat the butcher thought she was a cow."

"Man. You're talking about mom!"

"She doesn't care," Darius said. "She knows she's fat."

I laughed. Yes. I was fat and for the moment, happy.

Sunday I made a beef burgundy stew, crusty Italian Bread, and a cool lemon ice box pie. We ate like starving dogs, snatching the homemade bread away from each other. When the meal was over, we left the dishes on the table and fell before the television. Darius put in *Dr. Doolittle* with Eddie Murphy for the thousandth time. We followed that movie with *The Empire Strike Back* and finally, as the boys prepared for bed, I slipped in *The Housesitter.* I must have fallen asleep because when I woke, Goldie Hawn was falling off the bus into Steve Martin's arms. The End.

I sat up and scratched my back. I flicked off the TV, ignored the messy kitchen, and headed for the bedroom. I logged online. MastrThief did not appear in my buddy list. I immediately checked my email, and found nothing from Matt. After Darius's suspension, I had spent every moment, Wednesday to Sunday night with the boys. Wrapping myself around the boys had distracted me from the fact that I had received no email from Matt. I could no longer avoid the truth. My pictures had scared him off.

***

My regular room was usually packed from eight o'clock to midnight Friday nights, Central Time. That night, I entered the room to find JoyJoy typing:

Baby, take off your coat . . .
Real slow
Take off your shoes
I'll take off your shoes
Baby, take off your dress

yes, yes, yes
you can leave your hat on
you can leave your hat on
you can leave your hat on

SilkyDreamGirl:	What's that, Joy?
JoyJoy4U:	Silky, you don't have the strip4u wav?
SilkyDreamGirl:	No.

She sent the wav and played it after I downloaded it. Gypsy Rose Lee couldn't ask for better stripping music.

SilkyDreamGirl:	Let's party!
SilkyDreamGirl:	*Climbing on table.
SirGuyOne:	Ah, Silky? Whacha doing?
SilkyDreamGirl:	*Twirling hips
MaryMacaroni:	Well, Silky's not new anymore
SilkyDreamGirl:	(((!)))
DogAround:	Man! Look at that a@@
KissDaLady:	Woo Hoo! Joining Silky on table.
KissDaLady:	taking off blouse
SilkyDreamGirl:	(.) (.)
DaJudge:	— prefers cantaloupes.
TereseSpins:	ROFL
DaJudge:	Silky, do it gurl
SilkyDreamGirl:	*Twirling dress over head
DaJudge:	Woo hoo, Baby! Take it all off.

I ran into the kitchen and grabbed my bottle of tequila. I took one quick swig and carried the bottle back to the bedroom. I might as well enjoy myself. I was not going to cry over a man I had never met. I took a second swig from the bottle, plopped into my chair and resumed my role as exotic dancer.

That was the first night I did my table dance. I typed vigorously-chatting with everyone, laughing at silly inane jokes, and trying to forget that I had not heard from MastrThief. He had disappeared, opened the email with my pictures and disappeared. As I chatted and kept my activity in the room going, I called myself many names: Foolish, silly, dreamer, dreamer, dreamer.

I woke up with my throbbing head on my keyboard. The tequila bottle was empty. The booze had grabbed my feeble brain and squeezed it until I could barely hold it up. I clicked on and checked my email. SilkyDreamGirl had a mailbox full of wavs and messages. I downloaded the wavs and read the jokes. Half way through my email, I saw his name. I saw and I dreamed it all at once. His message read:

> Katie,
>
> I'm sorry I could not send mail before now. I've been out of the country on a security job. I hope we can talk tonight. TALK not chat. If you want to call me my number is 1-404-555-3475, or if you are more comfortable with me calling you, please email your number.
>
> Matt.

Uh-huh! No way. He left his number. My pictures didn't scare him off. He did like me. He did. There was another email another from MastrThief. He remembered how much I liked Curtis Mayfield and sent me *Gypsy Woman*. I downloaded the wav and clicked off line.

It was Monday and Darius had returned to school. My poor head. I made a large pot of black coffee and drank four cups to flush down four aspirin. I showered, then did my few chores. The tequila released my brain at about eleven. I went back to the computer and played the wav from Matt. I twirled around my bedroom.

From nowhere through a caravan
around the camp fire light
a lovely woman in motion
with hair as dark as night

Now, why would a man send such a song? *Unless . . .*
Don't you dare think it, Katie, I told myself. Like the woman
in the song, I danced around the room, imagining that I was
dancing for Matt, and yes, it was a seductive dance. I undulated my hips, grabbed a scarf from a hanger and moved
slowly and sensuously, letting the scarf flutter across my
body. That song had a hidden message. One verse shouted
love:

Ooooo how I like to hold her to me
and kiss and forever whisper in her ear
I love you gypsy woman, I love you gypsy woman

By nightfall I was anxious for the boys to sleep. For once,
the little rascals took their time preparing for bed. They
were cantankerous and sensed my urgency. Finally at 9:15 I
heard their heavy breathing. I entered my room and closed
the door. I nervously dialed the number and listened to the
long intermittent ringing. On the fourth ring he picked up.

"Hello," his voice was as musical as I imagined.

"Hello, may I speak to Matt?" I asked, just in case.

"This is Matt."

"Hi, it's Katie, Silky,"

"Hey you."

"Hello," I said.

"Your voice is different than I expected," he said.

"Oh, what did you expect?" I laughed. "A sensuous hot
voice?"

He laughed, a hearty laughed. I pressed the phone to my
ear and melted into my chair. I spun around in my tiny bedroom, made even smaller by the computer desk and file cabinet. The smallness didn't matter. The sky was falling. I was

spinning. My heart was pounding. That man's rich laughter rang in my ears, and I forgot everything.

"I didn't expect you to call, Sweetie," he said.

"Why."

"No, email confirming," he said.

"Busy. Baking. Packing," I said.

"It's almost time for the boys to leave," he said.

"Two months and twenty days," I said.

"What are you going to do with all that Freedom?" he asked.

"You go straight for my jugular," I laughed.

"How, sweetie?" he asked.

"I was avoiding that issue."

"Well, time is moving forward," he said.

"I know," I whispered. "I guess I do need to examine my future."

I twirled around in my chair again. I curled my feet in the chair and I chatted. I openly and HONESTLY shared things with the man that I could not share with Mama, Georgie, LaDell, Clarence, or Donna.

"You are so thoughtful," I said after an hour of conversation. "I can't believe you're not taken."

"Taken?" he asked.

"Married, dating."

"I am dating, sweetie."

You wanna talk about a heart dropping to the bottom of a shoe! My heart crashed. Mist formed behind my eyes. Did I really think a fine man from Atlanta would be single and available?

"You are?" I asked. "I thought you said you were not taken?"

"Dating is not taken, sweetie. Dating is just that."

"Oh."

"I've been dating this woman off and on for a couple of years," he said.

"Oh."

"I don't know where the relationship is going."

"It will go wherever you want it to go," I said.

Please, I thought, *don't want it to go anywhere.* He did not respond. I waited and waited. He said nothing.

"When you make a decision, the relationship will either go forward or die," I said.

He laughed, that rich sexy laugh, "That's true, sweetie."

Okay, Katie, I said, *he obviously has someone in his life. You need to end this thing now. What thing?* A voice in my head asked. I continued to talk with him. He told me about his vacation on the beaches of St. Croix. I told him about my table dance. It was two a.m. when we finally said good night. I didn't think about the phone bill that would come later.

Matt and I began a rigorous online and phone relationship. When he was home, he called. When he traveled, we were online. When the phone rang, I didn't know whether it was a bill collector or Matt. I didn't care. I listened to creditors ask me for money I didn't have and cheerfully told them, *I'm broke. I have no money. I have no job. Could you just not call me? I'm waiting for my gentleman caller.*

Did we cyber? Did we phone sex? Oh, the man was as smooth as a good bottle of tequila. I can vaguely pinpoint the first night we cybered. I remember it began innocently enough with a string of questions from him. I simply answered his questions.

"Are you dressed for bed?" he asked one night.

Uh-huh.

"What do you have on, sweetie?"

"Why?"

"I have this image and I want to know if it's true."

"Oh? What is it?"

"Sensuous."

I let loose a gut ripping laugh. "Okay, tell me," I said. "How did you come up with sensuous?"

"Sweetie, you are a sensuous woman. I think intelligence is the sexiest attribute a woman can have."

"So, if we were rutting, would it be my intelligence causing your pleasure?"

He laughed. "Touché, sweetie."

"What are you wearing?" I asked.

"A pair of boxer shorts. Silk boxers."

Oh, my! I saw him as clearly as I saw my pudgy fingers playing with the telephone coil. He was tall, bronze, and almost naked.

"Deeeelickable," I smirked.

"You are naughty. Tell me what you're wearing."

I made up a sexy fuchsia thing—the kind of outfit Victoria has in her stores. I exaggerated the pleasure I received from a foot massage. I told him about the hot coil in my belly. By the time Matt finished with me, I writhed on my bed like a sex-starved lap dancer.

In the back of my mind was the nagging knowledge of *HER*, the woman he was dating. He didn't mention her and I didn't ask. *Give it up, Katie.* I told myself. *Give it up.*

CHAPTER 12

Mama, Georgie, and their church group celebrated Easter with a feast that rivaled the spread found in one of those all-you-can-eat places. Those women chopped, diced, whipped, stirred, kneaded, and mashed until Georgie's banquet tables groaned under the weight of bowls and platters piled high with Turkey and dressing, leg of lambs stuffed with mint butter, seven-layer salad, ambrosia, broccoli and cheese casserole, mustard-turnip greens, candied yams, potato salad, and of course, my desserts—a four-layer coconut cake with pineapple filling, an angel food cake drenched with strawberry topping, and lemon mousse.

I avoided religious holidays. I learned, through my studies of history, literature, and philosophy that most things practiced in organized religions had pagan roots. Mama claimed that higher education eradicated my belief system.

"I didn't raise an atheist!" she once shouted at me.

"No, Mama, you didn't," I reply. "I'm not an atheist. I have a very deep belief in God."

"Then your butt needs to be in church."

I smiled at her. I didn't remind her of my short stint as a Sunday school teacher. I didn't remind her how the pastor chastised me when I questioned the validity of the church holding an Easter egg hunt.

I'm off track. What were we discussing? Oh yeah. Sunday I packed a Carson Pirie Scott bag with plastic containers and headed for Georgie and LaDell's. I had very little food in the house and my unemployment check was three days away. Seriously crippled, my bank account begged for some type of relief, government or otherwise.

Cars lined both sides of the street on LaDell's block. Unlike the city with its congested skyline and neighborhoods, the far south suburbs were flat and airy. The sky street endless overhead with nothing to block the view of the horizon. I parked a block away and cut through his backyard. Mama, Mrs. Anderson, and Mrs. Jordan's voices ripped with laughter as I entered the kitchen. They were Bertha-butt women who enjoyed turnip greens and cornbread and appreciated a rich cobbler. They were busybodies with their noses in everybody's garbage. They had lost their husbands either to death or to other women. When the women set eyes on me, the laughter stopped and disparaging sneers marred their faces. I stomped my feet on the grass mat and greedily sniffed the aroma of roasted lamb.

"Hello, Katie," Mrs. Anderson spoke.

A tall honey brown woman, she wore a peach skirt with a paler peach blouse. Her eyes shifted back and forth, constantly seeking other folk's business. Mama and Mrs. Jordan also wore pastel skirts and pale blouses. The women wore Aprons with tough bibs to protect their Easter outfits.

Somewhere in the house, matching hats and suit jackets laid at Easter parade rest.

"Katie," Mrs. Jordan spoke.

She stirred a pitcher of lemonade on the counter next to the back door. She always wore beautiful wigs, not cheesy synthetic wigs but soft brown human hair wigs that framed her face with feathery wisps. Mrs. Jordan's complexion was the color of weak tea with golden highlights. She never criticized me. However, her soft, high-pitched voice evoked guilt in me. I gave a weak hello to everyone with a wide smile on my face. I hoped that would appease them. It did not.

"You should have been in church," Mrs. Anderson threw her comment over her shoulder without turning from the stove.

"Yes, ma'am," I said.

"We would enjoy seeing you in church again, Katie," Mrs. Jordan said as I walked passed her to the center island where Mama folded linen napkins.

"Clarence did a good job raising those boys in church," Mrs. Anderson said.

My lips quivered, but I continued to smile. I placed the bag on a kitchen stool, shrugged out of my jacket, and hung it on the coat rack. Those women knew how to push buttons. They had years of practice at pushing buttons, meddling, and sharpening their wits on weaker women and men who were afraid of the word *no*. In Georgie's huge designer kitchen with the center island, those women tried to designate me to a child's place. Unfortunately for them, I was born into their fold. I knew how to stand toe to toe with them. I was, after all, Mama Jeffries' only daughter.

I washed my hands at the kitchen sink and fixed myself a plate from the various pots and pans on the stove and counter tops. I positioned a perfect hot pepper on the side of the plate and took three wings from a mound of fried chicken. I piled greens and cornbread on the plate, along with potato salad. I bit into the pepper and the seeds exploded in my mouth. The heat rushed to my head. I heard a distinct tsking from Mrs. Anderson but never looked at her. Georgie's yellow and white kitchen invoked memories of country bakeries. Stenciled daisies danced around the border. Copper molds bordered the cabinets. Cactus plants and potted herbs sat in a box window over the sink. Like Georgie, the kitchen welcomed me with warmth and coziness. I ignored the women and enjoyed my food. Finally, Mrs. Anderson and Mrs. Jordan carried dishes through the swinging kitchen doors into the dining room, and Mama lit into me.

"Why did you come here like that?" she asked and wiped imaginary crumbs from the ceramic counter. "You knew LaDell and Georgie were having company over. Do you have to embarrass them? You could have worn a dress."

"I'm not trying to embarrass anybody," I said. "All my clothes are too big, Mama. I'm losing weight." My hair was in a ponytail and I had on sweats.

"Hmph! I see you brought enough containers to take away half the dinner!" she barked.

Mama didn't acknowledge that I had lost over thirty pounds, dropping from one hundred and ninety-five big pounds to a healthier one hundred and sixty pounds. I knew she could see a difference. The sweats were sagging on me. Mama and Donna never acknowledged any of my accomplishments. That Easter, Mama was itching for a fight. I said nothing but scraped the last bit of potato salad onto my fork. When it came to greens, smothered chicken with gravy, cornbread, and candied yam, those South Side church ladies outdid any world renowned chef. Crushed red peppers dotted tender turnips and mustard greens, flavored with smoked turkey. The crunchy potato salad (yes, I tasted the granny smith apples) cooled my mouth after the peppers.

"It's embarrassing," Mama continued, "for you to come over here with your hair half combed."

"It's a ponytail, Mama."

"You're too damn old for a pony tail," she said and moved to the counter. "Oh! Pat forgot the Lemonade."

Pat was Mrs. Anderson. She was also Donna's mom. Mrs. Jordan's first name was Dorothea. Mama grabbed the pitcher and left the kitchen. While everyone was out of the kitchen, I took the opportunity to pack my containers with food and to refill my plate. I had the plastic ware neatly stacked on the island by the time Mama reentered the kitchen.

"The boys say they have their tickets for California," she continued. "CJ said his dad wanted to send you a ticket."

Ah, so we were at the gist of this discussion-my failed marriage. She wanted my marriage to Clarence fixed. I chose to ignore her and shoved candied yams into my mouth. Somebody had added nutmeg. I pushed the yams aside. Mama carried empty pots to the sink. She spoke over her shoulder as she washed them. She would not let me eat in peace. Mama walked to the opposite side of the island and wiped imaginary crumbs again.

"Why don't you join your husband?" she asked.

Falling back on the old faithful charm, I smiled, hoping to disarm her. Again, my charm did not work.

"Wipe that silly grin off your face," she said. "Why won't you join your husband? You got those two boys in there who need you and Clarence."

"What about Alex?" I asked. "Am I supposed to move half way around the world and forget him?"

"Don't use Alex!" Mama snapped. "You talked me into letting him go to some Godforsaken place with his father in June. Remember?"

Ever wanted to tell somebody off but was too afraid of hell to do it? That's the way I felt that day. I wanted to say, *Old woman, get your nose out of my business.* Instead, I listened as she fussed. Mama threw the dish cloth on the counter next to my plate. A dingy dishtowel does not help the appetite. Obviously, the woman was not going to let me enjoy my last bite of greens and cornbread.

"Why do you want so much?" she asked.

Mrs. Anderson pushed through the swinging door with an empty platter and walked to the stove. "Can you believe they went through that chicken like a buzz saw through sawdust?" she said. The tension stirred around Mama and me, stirred until it scooped Mrs. Anderson into its midst. She turned and looked from Mama's angry face to my benign smirk.

"Helen, are you okay?" she asked.

"You're never satisfied," Mama hissed.

"A working husband would satisfy me," I flipped and dropped my fork.

"Oh, really?" Mama mocked. "Clarence brought home more in retirement benefits then most working men, but that wasn't enough for you. You've always been a greedy, grabby thing."

I wanted to say "F" Clarence. Mama knew everything good about him. He told her about his retirement benefits, his disability benefits, all the medals he earned during this twenty-year stint in the military, and his desire to find the perfect job. He painted this wonderful picture of himself as a man, husband, and father. Mama bought into it. Hell, I bought into it.

"You're living in a dream world Katie Coomers," Mama said.

"Well, sugar, no sense worrying about Katie," Mrs. Anderson said, like I wasn't in the room. She used a pair of tongs to lift chicken from the roasting pan to the platter. "The gal got Mr. Pete's house and Verna's good jewelry." I stared down at my plate, too embarrassed to hold my head up as that biddy raked me over hot coals.

"Now she got Donna and Mike begging her to take their money for her cake baking business," Mrs. Anderson said.

I've been very honest about Donna and that damn catering business. Fact one: The business was Donna and Mama's idea. Fact two: Donna kept offering money and ideas for the business. Fact three: I kept saying no.

"I've never asked anybody for a dime!" I snapped.

"Well, you were quick to take three thousand dollars from me back in January," Mama said.

"Quick to marry crazy Pete for his money," Mrs. Anderson threw in.

"Why are you so mad at me, Mama?" I asked.

"You need to grow up!" Mama shouted. "You been floating from job-to-job and man-to-man, all your life!"

"Mama, do you really think I should waste my life with a man who doesn't work, or maybe you think I should kill myself cooking for a living."

Mama walked slowly to the island and leaned into my face. I smelled her perfume, a brand that I considered strictly for old women. When Mama was upset, her body temperature changed and that fragrance moved up a stinky notch.

"Why not?" she hissed. "I did for years."

"You didn't have to cook or clean for white people," I snapped. "You just did it to be ornery. Daddy left money to take care of us."

When those words slammed into Mama's face, she transformed before my eyes like Bill Bixby once transformed into the Incredible Hulk. Her face contorted and changed colors. She grew six, nine, fifty feet. Her dark eyes deepened into coal black beams of rage.

"How do you know what Alex left?" she asked in a low, ominous voice.

Her voice frightened me more than the electrifying third rail of the El track, more than a Stephen King horror novel, and more than a Chicago neighborhood at two in the morning.

"How do you know?" she enunciated, slowly like she was speaking to some foreign spy.

"He told me," I whispered.

"Told you what?" she asked, daring me to speak what I knew.

Then I saw it in her eyes, not rage, but a spark of something that I had never quite understood. I looked at my mama. My words caught on a latch in my throat. I could back away and say nothing. I could let Mama continue her self-righteous reign as Alex Jeffries's widow. I could continue my role as the wayward Katie Jeffries Cannon Smith Robinson Coomers.

"What?" she shouted and slammed the counter top.

That household shook on its foundation. The mountain of fear that I felt crumbled into the ocean. Georgie stood just within my peripheral vision. I don't know when she entered the kitchen. She twisted one strand of that chestnut mop she called hair.

"He told me about the insurance policies," I shouted. "He said that the house would be ours, free and clear"

"Katie, don't," Georgie walked up to me and grabbed my hand.

"He told me, Mama," I said. I emphasized *me* as I pulled my hand away from Georgie. "But you went around like we were death-poor, like we had nothing, were nothing. Scrubbing and cleaning and cooking and making out like he left us with nothing, like he wasn't a man to take care of his family. Why would I stay with a man that does less than my daddy? Why?"

"Keep y'all voices down," Mrs. Jordan said as pushed through the swinging door. "Folks can hear you."

"He had no business telling you those things," Mama said. "No business."

"My Daddy knew he could tell me anything," I said. "So you tell me, why did you pretend we were at poverty's door. Why didn't you spend one cent on my college education?"

"Well, if I had spent that money on you, it would have been wasted. You came home shaming me and since then you ain't done a thing with your life. Sitting around all day, talking to strangers on your computer!"

"How do you know I'm on the computer all day?" I asked.

But Mama was in a zone. She talked to the air, to the tiny audience that had gathered in Georgie's kitchen, and to a time past. "She was always there, always the first one to greet him each morning when he came through the door in the mornings . . ."

I interrupted with "You couldn't stand it that somebody loved me. You couldn't stand it. You were determined to punish me for that! Cause my daddy loved me . . ."

But Mama was lost in her thought: "Always the first on his lap in the afternoon, hugging on him, getting him to act improper with his own child, like he didn't have a wife . . ."

"My daddy never acted improper with me!" I screamed. "You were just jealous."

Honey, the word jealous snapped Mama out of her soliloquy. She leaned across the counter and whacked me so hard that I stumbled off my stool. If Georgie had not caught me, I would have landed, ass-first, on the floor.

"You get out of my sight!" Mama screamed. Her small

fudge eyes budged in her head. Her ashen lips quivered. "Get out of my sight before I give you the thrashing you need!"

Look, when your mama threatens to whop your ass and you're thirty-seven, you don't stand around waiting for her to do it. I was not so grown that I didn't know the penalty for striking my mama. I intended to live a long life. Tears swelled in my eyes but I didn't cry. My face throbbed from that whack but I ignored it. With all those wretched eyes on me, I held my head up and grabbed my jacket. I couldn't hit my mama or cuss her, but I could leave her with words to ponder. At the back door I turned and looked into her eyes.

"You got love for the world, Mama Jeffries, for your church members and every neighborhood kid with a snotty nose. You got love for nasty bums on the street but for your own flesh and blood, you have nothing. Where's the right-eousness in that? Even the prodigal son had a welcome."

"Katie!" Georgie shouted.

I opened the door and stepped out into that cold April day. Mama's voice droned in my head as I sped past people in their Easter finery trying to fight against the wind. I race up Interstate 57, to the Dan Ryan Expressway, where mon-ster eighteen wheelers and cars zoomed reckless low-riders competed for the road. My thoughts raced like the traffic. *So Needy. So Needy.* Why did I let Mama push me and push me with her ideas about my life?   Floating from man to man, indeed! James, my first husband cheated. Mr. Pete, dirty old man that he was died. Who knew where Joe Robinson, my third husband, had disappeared to? I zoomed past the empty spaces that once held the huge Robert Taylor's Hous-ing Projects, past the old State Way Gardens location, and the new Comiskey Park to Lake Shore Drive. The traffic thickened as I passed McCormick Place and my thoughts thickened with anger. Mama and her church pals did not know how difficult it was to manipulate money, or to lose weight, or to laden under the watchful eye of every nosey body on the South Side. I was moving on with my life but not one person could see beyond my past mistakes. I drove right into a bottle-necked traffic jam around Navy Pier and with the other drivers moseyed past a tumultuous lake. The waves crashed upon the sands and over the stone walls and I wished it could wash away the last hour, the last year, the last decade of my life. I wished my life was as stately and prestigious as mansions and buildings in Streetersville, an old Chicago neighborhood along Lake Shore Drive. I wished my life possessed Streetersville's quiet dignity instead of rough waves like Lake Michigan.

So needy. So needy. Those words bounced inside my head as the traffic loosen at Belmont Harbor. I sped the rest of the way home. Once inside my apartment, I tossed my jacket on my sofa and headed straight for my computer. I did not want to think about Mama and my life. I only wanted to sign online and lose myself in my chat room. My regular chat room was empty so I surfed the web until I ran across a chat room titled *IS ONLINE LOVE REAL?* Oh, how I wanted that to be true. I needed love. I laughed. *So Needy.* I entered the room. I watched the hellos and comments scroll by and then I typed:

SilkyDreamGirl:	Well, is it real?
FathomLovr:	Is what real?
SilkyDreamGirl:	Online Love.
Amasklwear:	Yes, Silky. It's Real.
SilkyDreamGirl:	How many people have found true love online?

Mostly everyone in the room claimed to be in love or to have found the perfect love. Some roomies spoke of storybook romances with happily ever after ending. Some roomies spoke of bitterness, love hindered by distance, spouses, or ill-nesses.

| AmaskIwear: | Are you in love, Silky? |
| SilkyDreamGirl: | Yes. |

There I had admitted what I did not whisper to Matt or to myself. I love the way he made me think, feel. I love the way I told him everything and anything. I love the way I was honest with him. No lies. Well, okay, he still didn't know about my weight, but I didn't lie about it. Although my mother thought I was nothing more than navel fuzz, some-body, somewhere saw value in me,

VanityFair28:	Have you talked to him by phone?
SilkyDreamGirl:	Yes. He calls me about three times a week.
VanityFair28:	LOL. Silky, I think he cares for you too.
SilkyDreamGirl:	He has the hots for me. That's not love.
AmaskIwear:	True dat.

We talked about the advantages and disadvantages of online love. Five of the women and I bonded: AmaskIwear a.k.a. Dee, TTSGURL a.k.a. Josey, MushMouth a.k.a. Carol, VanityFair28 a.k.a. Nancy, Porky2love a.k.a. Lori. We ex-changed pictures. Dee and Lori were heavy women. Both had dark hair and dark eyes. Lori, however, was white with a serious case of acne that poked out of her thick layer of make-up. Dee was gorgeous, a big woman with sensuous features and smooth skin. She was deeply dark with sparkling eyes. Small and delicate, Nancy provoked all my natural jealousies. She was beautiful with large brown eyes and thick curly eyelashes. I imagined that she was the type of woman Matt wanted. Josey had thick curly red hair.

Carol, MushMouth, was a washed-out blonde. Her plight was evident in the dark circles and bags around her eyes.

MushMouth:	My husband is abusive. If he knew I was chatting with Steve online, he would kill me.
SilkyDreamGirl:	If he's abusive why are you still with him?
MushMouth:	I have three kids and no money.
VanityFair28:	Isn't there a woman's shelter in your town?
MushMouth:	No. I live in a small town in Indiana, near Lafayette.
VanityFair28:	OIC.
MushMouth:	Steve is working on a plan to help me get away.
SilkyDreamGirl:	You love Steve, right?
MushMouth:	Very much, Silky. Truly I do.

***

LaDell brought the boys home around ten o'clock that night. CJ and Darius dragged into the apartment, sleepy, cranky, and sticky dirty from candy and desserts. LaDell walked past us with my Carson's bag, the one I had left in my haste to escape Mama Jeffries.

"Do we have to take a shower?" CJ asked.

"Boy, get your nasty butt in that shower?" I snapped.

I closed the door and locked it, knowing LaDell would not budge from my kitchen until I heard him out. You don't mess with LaDell's mama and not reap the punishment.

"Me too?" Darius asked.

I lifted my left eyebrow and he threw up his hands. Darius turned and walked out the room. I entered the kitchen to face my executioner. LaDell stood in my open refrigerator, unpacking the Carson's bag. A gray scarf dangled from his soft black leather jacket.

"You need money?" he asked and pointed to the lonely plastic containers inside the empty refrigerator.

"No!" I snapped.

"Hey!" he said, throwing up his hand. "I'm just asking cause your cupboard is bare." He closed the door slowly, like he was closing the lid of a coffin.

I sighed and slipped into a chair. "LaDell, I haven't asked anybody for anything."

He pulled out a chair, flipped it around, and straddled it. He searched his jacket pockets. I knew he was looking for cigarettes. It was an old habit. He had not smoked in months. He finally found a tooth pick and placed it in his mouth. We stared at each other. His eyes, so much like Daddy's while the rest of his face had the same curves and coloring as Mama's.

"You gonna tell me what happened?" LaDell finally asked.

"If I knew, I would," I answered.

He moved the tooth pick to the other side of his mouth with his tongue. He waited. A vicious quarrel came from the boys' bedroom.

"Okay, you guys!" I yelled. They stopped arguing.

"If it were only that easy between you and Mama," LaDell said.

"What do you want me to say?" I asked.

"Just tell me your side of the story."

I sighed again and leaned back. I looked at my brother. LaDell had been the official mediator between Mama and me ever since Daddy died. Delicate wrinkles lined his face like fine webbing. I reached across the table and took his hand. His callouses felt like tiny pebbles.

"My Dear Brother," I began as if I were reading a letter, "How can I tell you my side of the story? I don't know the truth of the matter. This story began long before we were born. This entire thing is all in Mama Jeffries head, not mine."

"Katie . . ."

"Sh, dear Brother," I said. "The feud between Mama Jeffries and me has nothing to do with you, nothing to do with her loving you or me loving you. You can't make peace between us. You can't talk me around. It's time you move on."

He was quiet for a moment. We listened to the shower, the clock ticking, and the crackling of a breaking family. LaDell squeezed my hand.

"She's your mother, Katie," he said. "You need to apologize."

"Not this time, LaDell," I affirmed. "I won't."

CHAPTER 13

Donna and I delivered a wedding cake, six layers with purple and pink roses, to a banquet hall on the South Side. I did the best I could with purple and pink. Donna claimed it was a work of art. Truthfully, after that atrocity, I made a mental note never to put another purple rose on a cake. As we left the banquet hall, the wedding party arrived. Seven grotesque bridesmaids with tear-streaked mascara stormed behind a gorgeous bride. Cinderella's stepsisters would have rejected those dresses with their puff-puff sleeves and tiny purple and pink roses around the neckline and hem.

After delivering that monstrosity, we stopped at a specialty shop to check out pans for children's birthday cakes. Saturday afternoon shoppers meandered up and down the aisle of the tiny shop. Silver-haired ladies searched for that perfect shade of rose food dye. Excited children searched for Hercules or Pocahontas, the best Disney pan for their super-duper birthday cake. Donna and I stood before the display of cake pans shaped like *Sesame Street* characters. I personally preferred simple cakes with flowers and balloons, but children wanted more flash than flavor. Nonchalantly, Donna twirled an Elmo pan in her hand.

"Geez, this is an ugly thing," she sneered.

I took the pan from her. Elmo was one of my favorite *Sesame Street* characters. Before Marjorie fired me, I had bought my niece, Shanna, a Tickle-Me Elmo doll, a pair of Elmo pajamas, and an Elmo backpack. He was a goof-ball. I like that about him. Donna could not understand the value of just being goofy.

"Mike was wondering what happened to your stepmom screen name," she said. "Why doesn't he see you online anymore?"

"Oh, who has time for that," I said.

Irritated by Donna, I examined the pan. It was costly and had many cracks and crevices. The decorating would be time consuming, a challenge.

"He doesn't see your other name, Katie's something, either."

"Oh, is Mike my online angel?" I snapped. I wanted the pan. If a kid wanted flash, who was I to deny her Elmo.

"Damn, Katie, why are you so edgy?" she asked. "We're just curious that all."

"Well, be curious about somebody else's business!"

Donna peered at me over her sunglasses. Donna always wore those large gold sunglasses that look elegant on her face. Sometimes I wanted to scream, *It ain't fair!* Whatever the woman put on she looked as elegant and classy as Leontyne Price, Jessye Norman, or any other great lady. Large gold sunglasses would swallow my face and make me look like a child playing movie star. I held onto the pan but examined others in the *Sesame Street* display rack. Donna cocked her head and leaned closer as if she were peering into my soul, trying to find the real me.

"You're cybering!" She exclaimed.

The Tickle-Me-Elmo pan slipped from my hands. A lady with fluffy silver hair stared at us. I turned and walked away. Fire ran up my back. My face was hot. I felt the frosty, judging eyes of the women boring holes in my back as if I were a two-bit whore.

"Katie!" Donna called.

I pushed open the door and hurried across the parking lot. Don't embarrass me and expect me to stick around. I searched my pockets for keys then realized we were in Donna's car. We were out in the boondocks, the southwest suburbs, so all I could do was wait. Donna finally came out the store, without bags, and unlocked the door.

"Girl, I can't believe you are cybering," she said as she climbed in the car.

"I am not cybering," I said.

"Uh, huh," she contradicted me.

That was the thing about a lifelong friend who had crawled across the same dirty floor, who knew all my Mississippi kinfolks, and who had been a bridesmaid at three of my four weddings. She knew when I was lying. We were silent as she maneuvered the car out the lot. I stared at the countryside as we drove along Highway 53. I detested the desolate look of open space: Fields, trees, and sky for miles and miles. I wanted the congestion of the city. I wanted the safety of my box of an apartment. I wanted to be free of Miss Prissy. Ever so often she turned her head toward me. I kept my eyes glued to the emptiness of the suburban sky. I fell asleep at some point and had a weird dream.

In that dream, hundreds and hundreds of faceless people, men and women, twirled around me. That was okay. I expected them to be faceless. However, above them, in a black sky was a large yellow smiley face that rocked back and forth. Smiley floated toward me and the people twirled faster and faster. Smiley loomed closer and closer, growing bigger and bigger.

Donna braked suddenly, and I jerked out of the dream. Bumper to bumper traffic snail crawled out of O'Hare, north on the 294 tollway. When I looked at Donna, her face was tight and mean. She swerved, barely missing the car in the next lane. I said a quick prayer. She swerved again and maneuvered the car into the far right lane. She zoomed off the expressway at Touhy and Dempster.

"Why did you come this way?" I asked.

"You slept through an accident," she said.

I eyed the Wendy's restaurant. I was hungry but knew Donna would refuse to stop at any fast food restaurant. Donna and I had so little in common. Donna's idea of music was soft jazz. My idea of music was D'Angelo, Joe, or any other male that made me salivate. Donna wanted potato chips. I wanted popcorn. Donna's idea of a good book was a super romance novel. My idea of a good book was one made up of truth, fallacy, myth, or legend like *Middle Passage*, *Great Expectations*, and anything else with more meat than cheap sex scenes. What the hell were we doing with each other? Our last good moment together happened before my marriage to Clarence and before Regina's death.

Donna, Regina, and I were speeding on Lake Shore Drive, singing Whitney Houston's *The Greatest Love* along with the radio. Donna had a big fat engagement ring on her finger. Regina had inked the deal with a play in New York. I had a wonderful boyfriend, Jackson, who was a city cop. We, the three of us, were all happy at the same time-a rarity. That was the last time I remember everything being in place, in order. After that I made one bad decision after another, and so did Regina. She left Chicago as a gorgeous black woman with enough confidence to take on Broadway. Two years later, Regina returned to Chicago a mess, really a mess—skinny, balding, and jittery. When she walked off that plane, her appearance appalled us. The pressures of New York, the play, and a lover, who was married to a wonderful, adored actress (one of my personal favorites), left Regina ready for a basket. On top of that, she was pregnant.

Regina wanted an abortion, and Donna agreed it was the best thing. I tried to talk her out of it. We discussed adoption or raising the baby as a team. We even considered letting our mothers raise it. Mrs. Jordan would have welcomed another Jordan. Even Mama would have helped. She had an easy relationship with Donna and Regina. They shared things with her that they didn't share with their own mamas. I was the only kid in the neighborhood who thought Mama Jeffries a little too rigid. In the end, Donna and I sat in the waiting room laughing about some silly hat we had bought Mama for her birthday. When Regina came out, she was ashen and shaky.

"You okay?" Donna asked.

"Yeah," Regina whispered

We took her at her word. The last weeks of her life had been traumatic, so we just shrugged her appearance off as another bad thing. The next day she was dead from an overdose of propoxyphene, and yes, in my heart of hearts, I did blame Donna. She persuaded Regina that an abortion was the best thing, the safest thing. Maybe it should have been, but my friend, my sister, my heart died. For the first time in my life, I felt completely alone. In the letter Regina left behind, one line for Donna and me, cemented us together.

Katie and Donna, I love you both. Please, take care of each other.

After Regina's death, nothing went right for me. I married Clarence. He left. I floated. I didn't know how to be happy, and my friendship with Donna did not provide any joy. But Regina had been dead for nine years and I no longer wanted to take care of Donna at the expense of myself.

"How could you?" Donna broke into my thoughts. We were driving under the Milwaukee Road overpass.

"How could I what?"

"Cyber?"

"See that's your problem," I said. "You're such a prude!"

"That's why you have four ex-husbands," Donna retorted. "You are sex-crazed."

"You are married and sexless!" I exclaimed.

"You're a pervert, Katie," she said.

"Why, because I chat?"

She tsked me like her mama tsked me. She sat behind the wheel of her cream color Volvo, in a pale pant suit, tsking me.

"Don't tsk me!" I snapped. "Your husband is online chatting all the time."

"He only chats at lunch, and he doesn't cyber."

"Yeah, that's what everybody says."

"You're having sex with strange men!" she snapped.

I laughed, "I don't remember any man taking off my clothes and inserting his penis in my vagina."

"You are nasty, Katie! Downright trifling!" she exclaimed.

Yes, the girlfriend called me nasty and trifling. I heard the rest of her castigation in snatches, *wallowing in self-pity, fool, man-jumping heifer, disgraceful sinner.* How long had enmity curdled in her toffee body? Heat bristled at the root of my hair. My eyes watered. The world shimmered before me. Red strobe lights, sparks of anger flashed before my eyes. A tightness centered in my chest. I trembled and dug my nails into the palm of my hands.

"You bitch!" I hissed.

"What?"

"You heard me," I snapped. "Why would you call me nasty? You don't know whether I cyber or not. You're just a narrow-minded, tight-ass prude. You look down on me like I'm a scab on your rusty knee. I'm tired of you trying to change me, trying to get me to do things your way. Why do you come around me? Obviously, you don't like me. You criticize everything I do and everything I am. I think you hang with me because of some sick obligation to Regina. Regina is dead, and I can't soothe your guilty conscience over the abortion. It's over. You owe me nothing. I owe you nothing!"

"Get out!" Donna screamed. She swung over to the curb and stopped the car. "Just get out!"

I got out at Dempster and Waukegan Road which was more than twenty-five minutes from my apartment by car. Donna skittered away from the curb and my cake baking business skittered away with her. I waited on the corner for the north suburban bus to carry me into the city. It was a long time coming. By the time I got home my mind was set. Did Donna really believe that life ugliness dared not enter her perfect world? She wore her furs and gems like badges of honor, as if her narrow-minded, prudish attitude entitled her to things. *Bitch!* That one word played in my head all weekend.

Monday, I went looking for old WhiskyLips. I placed him in my buddy list, sat, and waited. I chatted with my buddies. The number of people online during the day amazed me. JoyJoy4U was always online. RedDoll popped off and on. DogAround and I chatted and exchanged pictures. The man had a gigolo body. His upper body had the definition of Sly Stallone. He had eyes like Will Smith, a mouth like Taye Diggs, and the rich brown color of a lickety Fudgesicle. Uh-huh! In other words the man was fiiiinnnnnee. Unfortunately I was not his type.

DogAround:	Beautiful eyes.
SilkyDreamGirl:	Thanks.
DogAround:	Too bad.
SilkyDreamGirl:	What?
DogAround:	You're not in church.

So I laughed as he crossed me off his list of potential mates. At 11:30, WhiskyLips signed on. I gave him a few minutes to check his email then I switched screen names to Jaded-Womn49. I used the search engine and found him in a room titled *Men Over 40 Seeking*. If Mike didn't cyber, what was he seeking? I entered that room. I chatted for about ten minutes with everyone in the room then I focused on him. I flirted outrageously with him. It took exactly fifteen minutes for him to IM me. We chatted in general about our lives—who we were, what we did. He was straightforward. He did not lie about his marriage nor his job. I lied about everything. I did that for three days. On the fourth day, I went straight to my purpose.

JadedWomn49:	How bored are you, sugah?
WhiskyLips:	Very.
JadedWomn49:	You have a picture to trade?
WhiskyLips:	Yes.

Mike sent me his picture, a good one of him taken two years before at his kid sister's graduation party. I recognized it because I could see Clarence in the background. When you are married to a guy for seven years, you can recognize his balding head anywhere.

I sent Mike a picture that some jerk had shared with me.

The picture was of a beautiful naked brunette with a body straight from a surgeon's knife; firm breasts and not an inch of fat. The woman squatted with her legs opened.

WhiskyLips:	You have a dynamic body.
JadedWomn49:	Thank you.
WhiskyLips:	I wasn't expecting that!
JadedWomn49:	Does it disappoint you?
WhiskyLips:	Not at all.
JadedWomn49:	do you ah . . . have many girlfriends?
WhiskyLips:	I told you I'm married.
JadedWomn49:	Happily?
WhiskyLips:	After 9 years?
JadedWomn49:	So you're bored with your marriage?
WhiskyLips:	LOL. You are an insightful miss.
JadedWomn49:	Well, I didn't expect you to be the my-wife-doesn't-understand-me type of guy.
WhiskyLips:	She understands me.
JadedWomn49:	How many children do you have?
WhiskyLips:	None.
JadedWomn49:	OH?
WhiskyLips:	She has a friend who almost died giving birth to her son.

That's not true. The woman lied. Well, okay. It was not an easy birth. It was a dry birth. My water broke long before I went into hard labor. My screams drowned out the other ten women delivering babies that night. Regina was in the room with me as my birthing coach while Donna and Mama paced the waiting room floor. It was difficult, but I never came close to death.

WhiskyLips:	My wife thinks that having a baby will make her a pig.

JadedWomn49:   Your wife thinks <u>her</u> best friend is a <u>pig</u>?

WhiskyLips: Yes. Her best friend is huge. My wife says
                      motherhood makes losers out of women.

Loser. I was about to release her adorable hubby and protect
the sanctity of her marriage, but the cow called me a loser.
My anger renewed itself. Trifling? How trifling was her husband?

JadedWomn49:   Sugah, I'm sorry about your difficulties. What
                      can I do to help you laugh this afternoon?

WhiskyLips: LOL

JadedWomn49:   That was easy. My job is done.

WhiskyLips: No. LOL. Don't go.

JadedWomn49:   Oh. So, the man is interested in little ole me.

WhiskyLips: Very interested.

JadedWomn49:   Can you unzip, sugah and set your manhood
                      free?

WhiskyLips: One moment let me lock the door.

JadedWomn49:   Be right here, sugah.

Now, as far as I'm concerned there are people who cybered
and people who don't. As SilkyDreamGirl, I refused to
cyber. (My relationship with Matt didn't count.)   I was
NOT a cyber girl. I enticed and titillated but delivered nothing. Yet I would give Miss Prissy's husband the pleasure of
his life.

WhiskyLips: Baby, I'm back and rock hard. What about
                      you?

JadedWomn49:   I'm touching myself now.

Of course I was lying. I was not touching myself. I had no
intentions of deriving pleasure from that session. Cybering

with Mike was about revenge. I had an add-on program that managed my IM's. The program also tracked my chat room conversations and instant messages. Miss Donna would get an anonymous email with that cyber session. So what if she knew who it was. It would definitely serve her right.

WhiskyLips:	ready to get all wet with your juices. Ever play the rusty trombone
JadedWomn49:	what's that?
WhiskyLips:	that's when blow my a@@ and reach around and stroke me.

Whoa! That shocked me and I always considered myself un-shockable. Now I understood why Donna didn't want to nibble on him. I wouldn't even let him kiss my cheek. It gave me more insight into Donna's bedroom than I wanted. I immediately switched from JadedWomn49 to Silky-DreamGirl. I deleted JadedWomn49 and signed off without sending the instant message to Donna. You never know how tight another woman's panties are until you put them on.

***

Donna and I were kaput. Mama and I were kaput. Talking to Alex was like talking to a travelogue. He was excited about his upcoming trek through the Middle East with his father. The only grown up talking to me offline was Georgie. Georgie usually wrapped her life around her husband, her children, and her patients. Our relationship was friendly but I knew I was not high on her list of priorities. Don't get me wrong. I appreciated and admired Georgie. If I made her life sound as sweet as a basket of cakes, shame on me. Although Georgie's personality sparkled like those glittery outfits she wore, she was a care giver. The woman worked hard to make her life and the lives of those around her pleasant. After my arguments with Mama and Donna, Georgie decided to nurse me back to a healthy reality. She implored me to call Donna, Mama, or Clarence. I refused. It amazed me that everyone thought something was wrong with me simply because I was stepping out of familiar. Finally fed up with me, Georgie came to my house with a care package and some words of wisdom.

"Katie," she said and placed the package on the table.

"Georgie," I answered, slipping into a chair between the sink and the table.

Georgie had on a black pantsuit with more colored sequins than an after-five dress. She had an armful of silver bracelets that clanged as she unpacked the bag. She didn't say anything about the bags under my eyes or the fact that my hair stood all over my head. It was one o'clock in the afternoon, and she never reminded me that I had slept my day away.

"I brought you some asparagus. I know how much you love them and I got your Eight O'clock Coffee at a good price."

"Georgie," I whispered. "I do appreciate this honey, but you don't have to take care of me."

"Did I tell you, Mike and Donna have split?" she asked. She looked at me, expecting me to utter some type of regret. I was quiet.

"Maybe you should give her a call," Georgie said. "She's got to be hurting."

I picked up the carton of cottage cheese Georgie had set on the table and opened the container. I leaned back and pulled a spoon from the drawer.

"Katie," Georgie laughed. "You are a hard woman."

"You think?" I said and began eating the lumpy curds.

Georgie patted me on the head like I was a difficult child. "You'll figure it all out one day, Katie."

"Figure what out?" I asked with a mouthful of cottage cheese.

"Whatever's got you confused," she said. "Stop fighting life."

"Is that what I'm doing?" I asked.

"You deserve to be happy too."

"You think?"

She shook her head. "Katie, everybody gets it but you."

"Gets what, Georgie?" I asked.

Georgie pulled a chair from the table and sat. She leaned back and ran her hand across her face. Her fingers were puffy, smooth-absolutely wrinkle-free. I smiled as a nudge of suspicion entered my mind. Georgie was pregnant. With both of her pregnancies, Georgie's wrinkled, hard-working hands transformed into soft dewy beauties. I always pondered the amazing effects pregnancy had on some women. Some women assumed that wonderful glow of motherhood. Georgie was such a woman. I had assumed the grotesque features of a bloated walrus. My nose spread across my face. My skin became dry and patchy with forty different shades of browns and black. That wonderful glow of motherhood never washed over me.

"Do you remember my mama?" Georgie asked.

Who on the South Side of Chicago didn't remember Georgie's mama? Mrs. Packard went all over the South Side helping people out. Her help came with a dour expression and a sermon. Mrs. Packard always preached on the pitiful state of people and how some people were in such a pitiful state because of their own wickedness. *Sin*, Mrs. Packard preached, *sin will keep you down. Sin, oh yes, it will, rob you. It will empty your cabinets and rob your storehouse. Get right with God. Get your life on the right track. Repent.* That woman kept a Bible in her purse. If she felt led, she removed that Bible from her purse and thumped the stunned sinner on the head with it.

"Yeah, I remember your mama, Georgie," I said, looking at her quizzically, wondering where she was going with that thought.

"Do you think my mama was a happy woman?"

Actually, I never thought about her being happy or unhappy. She was crazy, Bible-toting Mrs. Packard. The woman had eight girls and not a torn dress or hair out of place among them. Her husband had been a quiet man that moved in and out the house like a mouse. She died long before Alex was born, long before any of us graduated from high school. Had she been happy?

"I don't know," I said.

"My mama cried every day of her life," Georgie said.

"Why?" I asked.

"She didn't know how to seize her happiness, Katie," Georgie said. "She was always looking for the next great problem to solve so others could appreciate her. She lived to hear somebody say that she was a saint."

I laughed. "I don't remember anyone calling her a saint."

"No one ever did," Georgie said.

"I don't get it."

"How could anyone call her a saint, when she didn't see herself as a saint?"

"Huh?"

"Think about it, Katie."

"You are confusing me, Georgie," I said.

"It's so simple, Katie."

Okay, I'm not the brightest light, but I've always thought I was smarter than Georgie. I thought of Georgie as a dipsy woman concerned about things and status, not about what keeps the world on its axle. The seriousness on Georgie's face, a face that usually sparkled with joy and lightness, made me pause and give thought.

"My mama died because no matter how many problems she solved, no matter how much she helped other people, she never felt appreciated," Georgie said. "You know how my mama referred to herself in our house?"

I shook my head.

Georgie sighed and continued, "as a fighting heifer. That's how we all saw her. She was nobody's saint."

I thought about Mrs. Packard dying of a broken heart because nobody thought she was a saint. Life was strange. Twenty-five years after Mrs. Packard's death, her daughter had become my saint.

CHAPTER 14

On television Alex's dad appeared regular height, chunky, and nondescript. The man forging through the crowded lobby of the University of Illinois Chicago auditorium was a tall, slender man with a weary smile. He scanned the mob for Mama or Alex. I raised my hand and called to him. The din of voices surrounded us and the blare of traffic on the street smothered my voice. I plowed through the crowd with *pardon me, excuse me* until I was close enough for him to hear me. I called again. He turned and raised his eyebrows in puzzlement, then recognition brought a smile to his face.

"Miss Katie," he said with a professional smile on his face. The crow's feet around his eyes, his silver gray hair, and the wire rim glasses created a seasoned but extremely hand-some looking man. He reached out, took my hand, and placed it on his heart, a gesture that once caused my own heart to flutter. After eighteen years, the man had not

changed his modus operandi. Did he think I had forgotten
his techniques and habits?

"So, you made it," I said and searched his face for the
young man I once knew.

"I wouldn't miss my son's graduation for anything, even
for the scoop of a lifetime."

I laughed and punched him on the arm, an old habit
from our college days. "I meant your career. You made it."

"I did but it was a lonely trip," he said and turned and
looked toward the auditorium where Alex would end his
childhood and begin manhood. He looked at me again and
a swell of emotion filled his eyes. "Thank you for him," he
said. "Without him, my future would be hollow."

Christenings, graduations, and weddings were times of
intense joy when families settled their feuds. Alex's graduation should have been such a moment. Mama Jeffries and
I should have fallen into each other arms, begged forgive-
ness, and cried eternal love. Instead, we sat at the opposite
end of the family row. The arrangement was Mama Jeffries,
CJ, Darius, my niece Shanna, my nephew Terrence, Georgie,
LaDell, Tameka, Alex's dad, and finally, me. Yes, I came after
the infamous dad like a token member of the family.

Alex chose Scoozie's for his graduation dinner party. It
was the perfect place for children to suck up spaghetti while
the adults pretend sophistication over Italian cuisine. That
decadent restaurant with its gold facade and rich tapestry
trimmings was bold and big enough to hold a wedding re-
ception for three hundred people. That night it was loud and
busy. Mama and I never glanced at each other, never acknowledged each other. Even with the family laughter ringing like church bells, even with the bantering and the
hilarious discussion of Alex's mishaps through childhood,
we ignored each other. That night I learned how difficult ignoring a person deliberately was. That task required more

concentration, more effort, and more pain than birthing a baby.

***

Clarence's telephone calls were clock ticks. Every Sunday evening, after he had heard some preacher's sermon on the sanctity of marriage, he called me with a plea for reconciliation. Every Sunday evening, I gave him the same answer, *no*. His final call came six days before the boys' flight date, six days before the life I knew dissipated. The boys were spending their last weekend with my brother and his family. I was trying to get used to a silent and lonely apartment. Oh, yeah, my maternal instinct was screaming. I wanted to hold on to my boys. Especially since Alex had left for Europe the day after his graduation. He and his famous dad would spend the summer in Europe—Spain, France, and Italy—before heading for those heathen (Mama's word) Middle East countries.

"I want you back, Kay-Jay," Clarence said.

"Oh?"

"The boys need their mom," he stated with all the romance of a troll.

I translated that to mean, *I need a babysitter, Kay-Jay, and the boys love you.* In my small kitchen, with that phone pressed to my ear and the aroma of smoked meat wafting up from my neighbor's grill, I toyed with the idea. Our reconciliation would choke Donna and please Mama. The boys would dance on moonbeams, and Bertie would hang herself with a golden thread. Yes, the rewards were boundless. If Clarence had spoken one word of devotion, I might have considered it. The man did not bother boosting my ego. He did not tell me I was beautiful, desirable, or the love of his life. Instead, he snapped his fingers, hit his thigh, and called to me like I was a puppy. He bent forward and held out a bone, *Here, girl, the boys will miss you.* He expected the old

Kay-Jay to wag her tail, pant with tongue hanging out, and run happily to those snapping fingers. I was tired of being Clarence's pet. I was tired of his *good girls* and belly rubs. I was tired of rolling over, fetching bones, begging with my soft fudge eyes.

"Are you still working, Clarence?" I asked.

Clarence shattered any hopes of reconciliation with his next words.

"I tried, Katie," he said. "That job wasn't for me."

"So, what are you doing?" I asked. "How do you intend to take care of the boys and me, if I decide to join you?"

"I'm working on some things I can't tell you about now."

I rolled my eyes toward the ceiling and walked to the backdoor. A dusky sky covered Chicago. It was the second week of June and the sun had not decided whether it would grace us with long hours of daylight. Summers in Chicago can consist of chilly rainy days. Still, observing the sky was better than listening to another one of Clarence's get-rich-quick schemes. Clarence lived on those highs. I didn't want to know what direct marketing miracle was sucking money out of Clarence's pocket.

"Clarence, when your preacher was telling you about the sanctity of marriage, did he tell you about that little known Bible verse that goes if a man doesn't work, he doesn't eat."

"You need to trust me. Come out here with the boys, and let's be a family."

"You need to get a grip on reality, Clarence."

I hung up. I was one of those people who believed that California would go the way of Atlantis. Every inch of land, from Smith River to Chula Vista, would slip right into the Pacific Ocean. California would become a legend, a fable, a golden vision for future explorers. I also believed that the day I stepped into LA, the ground would tremble, shake, and crumble. I would disappear under a mound of debris. Those belief and fears were surmountable, but my aversion to Bertie was not. LA was the enemy's camp and Bertie was the enemy. I piddled around the apartment until I heard Darius and CJ's loud voices in the stairway. I opened the door, anxious to have them home.

"Mom! Mom!" Darius bellowed as he ran up the last flight of steps. "You should see all the stuff Aunt Georgie and Uncle LaDell bought us."

He carried a huge Toy's "Я" Us shopping bag. CJ followed him with an equally large bag, and finally, LaDell huffed and puffed his way up with an armload of packages. LaDell was freshly shaven for the summer months. He had replaced his small hoop earrings for a dangling cross. I knew Mama Jeffries was somewhere frowning over that latest piece of jewelry. I pressed against the wall to let the boys and LaDell pass. The boys flew past me into the living room and dumped their bags on the cocktail table.

"Wassup," he said. "These boys have worn me out."

"What's all this?" I asked.

"We took the kids shopping for summer," he said. "Tonight I feel like an old man."

I laughed. "You want something cool to drink."

"Naw," he shook his head. "I got the family in the mini-van and you know Georgie, she'll be honking in a moment."

He turned to the boys, "Okay, guys," he said, "give me some dap."

The boys ran to him and hugged him. That threw him. His eyes watered. "Hey, little men, I said dap."

The boys laughed and each hit his fist lightly with theirs.

"Yeah, that's it," he said. "And tell your mom to call her mom." He looked into my eyes.

"Yeah," I said. "When Chris Rock is president."

He laughed, "Well, there's hope, yet."

By the time the boys and I packed one final box and squeezed their gifts, except the Game Boys, into their suitcases it was after nine o'clock. They were exhausted and, as usual, fell asleep instantly. I stood in their doorway listening to their breathing. The back porch light illuminated their faces. My heart caught in my throat as I looked at the long lashes concealing eyes that would not look upon my face for months. I gently closed the door and went to my bedroom.

I signed online and chatted with Louis a.k.a DogAround for a spell. We didn't want to enter our regular room with its craziness. I created a private room and invited Louis and MaryMacaroni to join me. We had a gossip session until midnight. Louis and Mary got into some love talk so I said good night to them. Matt had not signed on.

***

We were in the final week of the school year, five days from the boys' flight date. After they left for school that Monday morning, I took the last box to the post office. Up and down Clark Street, there were parents with their children: mothers, fathers, sisters, and brothers. In the post office some bratty kid whined for the Bugs Bunny stamp series and his dad happily obliged him. At the fruit stand, a young girl explained to her mother how a Kiwi had a higher concentration of Vitamin C than an orange. Her mother didn't believe her. I completed my errands as quickly as possible, hurried back to my apartment, and locked myself away from all that family activity.

After school, I let the boys play in Touhy Park until seven. I then took them to Parkside Grill for Vienna hot dogs and fries. Around us, other families were discussing their vacation plans—Disney World, Sandusky, Kings Island, over the woods to grandma's house, journeys to Mexico to visit grandparents. Of course, the boys went on and on about their trip to California. I tell you, by nine p.m. I was ready for some online excitement.

Matt signed on at ten o'clock. I had never been so happy to see a screen name. Yet within minutes of chatting with him, I wanted to shake my computer and scream, *It's never gonna work. How can you desire me and be with her?* Matt informed me of two things: His lady friend's name was Julia, and she was moving into his place the next day.

SilkyDreamGirl:	I guess next you'll tell me, you're getting married.
MastrThief:	No. I told you I'm never getting married again.
SilkyDreamGirl:	Yeah, I didn't expect this either.
MastrThief:	Nothing changed between us, Sweetie. We're still friends. We will always be friends.
SilkyDreamGirl:	I don't screw friends.
MastrThief:	Good because we've never screwed.
SilkyDreamGirl:	You think not.
MastrThief:	LOL. Okay we've come close.
SilkyDreamGirl:	So, despite what you say, our relationship will change.
MastrThief:	It must.
SilkyDreamGirl:	Well, I wish you the best.
MastrThief:	You too, Sweetie.

He signed off and devastation crawled around my head and choked the breath from my body. I had poured my heart out to Matt, and he had let me down. Dee had warned me that he would disappoint me. Didn't she call him a slutty shithead? Didn't I know our relationship could not last forever? We were online for Pete's sake! I was so numb I could feel the bottom of my feet tingling. Didn't I hear about others' tales of heartbreak? There were stories of people roping others into false relationships then borrowing thousands of dollars. The borrower's screen name and fake name always disappeared afterward. It happened to both men and women. Didn't I know men and women who traveled great distances for one-night-romps? Didn't I know a woman who sat nude before a digital cam all day long and cybered? Didn't I know a guy who paid women airfare to New York City so they could insult him in public? Didn't I know a woman who had met and slept with fifty-eight guys? Didn't I know at least ten people who were going through the heartbreak of a broken online relationship? Chat rooms could easily be considered brothels, gin joints, or sin palaces. Yes, my roomies had warned me. *Oh, Silky, it happens all the time. All the time. All the time.*

I sat and watched his screen name disappear, knowing that I would have no further contact with him. Knowing that whatever I felt was all for naught. Why break up with an online lover? I wasn't going to present him with a cyber baby. Truth is I had been dreaming—just dreaming, mind you—of meeting him. Like star crossed lovers we would meet in New York at the Ritz Carlton. We would look into each other's eyes and fall into each other's arms. In our suite, we would fall passionately on the floor and have the hottest, steamiest sex of our lives. Yes! I always imagined us meeting in some place neutral. When his screen name vanished, so did those dreams. Once again, my Internet experience had caused me shame! I cybered with him! I listened as he whispered obscenities to me over the phone. I was nothing more to him than a jolly. I stared at the computer screen, seeing but not seeing the IM flashing from Dee. Matt was gone and I was too humiliated to answered the IM. Maybe Mama and Donna were right. Maybe I was too much of a dreamer to face reality. Who else but a dreamer would spend time in a fantasy relationship with a man she had never set eyes on? Who else but a dreamer would along herself to be pull into a sleazy cyber/phone sex relationship? Disgusted, I signed off.

***

I want you back, Kay-Jay. Clarence's words swirled around inside my head the next day. I felt like a dog whose owners had dropped her off in the country—lost, bewildered, and looking for a way back home. We were four days away from the boys' take off. I was miserable. Then we were three days away from doomsday. I was desperate. It was two days before flight time. The only seat available on the boy's flight was a first class ticket that made my credit card scream, *ARE YOU INSANE!?!* Yes, I was.

One day before departure. The boys sat on the floor with a medium pepperoni pizza between them. I lay on the sofa with a little blanket thrown across my feet. I was still watching my weight so I had a small vegetarian delight salad on the coffee table. We were watching Dr. Doolittle with Eddie Murphy for the fiftieth time. Except for the pop cans, candy wrappers, and the pizza boxes on the floor, the house was immaculate. The boys traveling clothes were the only things hanging in their closet. All their books were in California. The apartment had a lonely hollow sound.

"Mom, we're really gonna miss you," Darius said with a mouth full of pizza.

"Yeah," CJ chirped, "we're gonna miss your cooking. Dad can't cook."

Kids reduced everything to the lowest common denominator. I was the cook, the babysitter, and the chauffeur—the disposable thing in their lives. Dad was the man.

"What if I decided to come with you?" I asked.

"Cool," CJ said. He said this with his mouth full of pizza so I discounted it. Give CJ food and he would agree to anything.

"We would be a family again," Darius said. "Me, you, loser CJ . . ."

"Don't call your brother a loser," I interrupted.

". . . okay, not a loser CJ, and Dad," Darius corrected. "Then we could go to Disneyland together."

"So, are you going with us?" CJ asked.

"Yeah," I said. "Maybe for the weekend, to see if I like LA."

"If you like it, then what?" Darius asked.

I smiled, "We'll see."

***

The flight Clarence chose made as many stops as a local train from Chicago to New Orleans. Once we landed in an airport so tiny, I swear the town's council was on the runway with banners that read *Welcome to Small Dale, USA*. We left Chicago at 6:05 A.M., central time, and arrived in Los Angeles at 3:30 P.M., Pacific Time. Do the math and let me know if the travel time was a bit excessive.

When we disembarked in Los Angeles, the boys spotted Clarence before I did and flew down the ramp. He had on white shorts with an open blue plaid short-sleeve shirt. Underneath that he wore a "wife beater" T-shirt, the kind Marlon Brandon wore in *A Streetcar Named Desire*. His biceps and triceps stimulated memories of pleasure. The man looked GOOD.

"We missed you, Dad!" CJ said.

The boys and Clarence were wrapped together. A tear touched my eye. This was right. This was family. How could I think about breaking up our home? Other families and couples greeted each other with hugs and kisses. Business travelers rushed past the groups. I waited for Clarence to acknowledge me.

"Mom, came with us," Darius said. "We're gonna be a family, again."

"Your mom?" Clarence said. He looked up and saw me for the first time. Disbelief and something else washed over his face. Had my weight loss shocked him? I was now down to one hundred and forty-two pounds. I had lost more than fifty pounds since he left.

"K-K-Katie," he stammered. "What are you doing here?"

"I told you," Darius said. "We're gonna be a family, again."

"Why didn't you let me know you were coming?" Clarence asked.

"We just decided last night," CJ said.

"Where's Aunt Bertie?" Darius asked. "I thought she was gonna be here too."

"She's at the house."

Clarence was uncomfortable. Realization dawned on me—Bertie didn't know that Clarence had been begging for a second chance.

"Are you okay, Clarence?" I asked. "Don't I get a kiss, a hug, a handshake?"

"Kiss her, Dad," Darius said.

Clarence gave me a dry peck on the check. True, I like my kisses dry but that kiss peeled the skin off my cheek. I cocked my head and looked at him. His small brown eyes shifted back and forth like a thief cornered by cops.

"Well, see, it's just that . . ." Clarence began.

"Dad, are we going to Disneyland?" Darius asked. "Do we have our own room?"

"Wait, son!" Clarence snapped.

I knew something was definitely wrong. We maneuvered our way through the bustling travelers, past gift shops, and snack bars. Clarence walked quickly and the boys kept up with him. I didn't want to power-walk through a busy airport, but I had no choice. Occasionally Clarence threw a fugitive glance at me, making sure that I was keeping up with them. I was peeved. He had not mentioned my weight loss. Fifty pounds is very noticeable. We retrieved our luggage.

"Are you all right, Clarence?" I asked.

"We need to talk."

"Well, we have the weekend to do it."

"Dad, mom's gonna make you chicken enchiladas tomorrow. She said so," CJ interrupted.

We exited the airport and merged into a permanent traffic jam. My intuition whispered, *Trouble ahead*. The stream of sweat that ran down Clarence's face was the first clue. True, the windows were up in his two-door clunker of a car but the air conditioning was at full force.

"Are you sick?" I asked Clarence as I touched his face and his ears, checking for fever.

He shook his head. He never took his eyes off the road, never looked in my direction. In the pit of my stomach, a grain of doubt fell. While the boys were excited about the possibilities opened to them in LA, Clarence was irritable.

"We can meet Will Smith," Darius laughed.

"Shaq!" CJ shouted.

"Y'all keep it down back there!" Clarence snapped.

The boys fell silent and my eyes narrowed. Something was definitely wrong. That grain of doubt became a pebble of fear. Soon, we were pulling into a subdivision of ranch houses. Palm trees rose high in the sky like lanky giants with mop tops. The streets were wide and baked white from the sun. Every so often we passed one or two children on bikes or a dog in a yard.

"I thought you lived in an apartment complex," I said as Clarence turned into a cul-de-sac.

"I moved a couple of months ago," he said. He aimed the

car for a green house in the center of the cul-de-sac. "Bertie owns this house along with two others."

"Nice," I said. "Why didn't you tell me?"

"Would it have made a difference?" he asked.

I said nothing.

"We live here?" Darius asked.

"Is there a swimming pool?" CJ asked.

When Clarence stopped the car I got out and held the seat up for the boys. Clarence got out like he was dragging a ball and chain. I stretched and turned around. It was a charming house. The house Clarence had promised me many times. The landscape was impeccable with low bushes and irises before a huge picture window. A lone palm tree stood in the front yard.

"Katie," Clarence said and moved around the car toward me. I pretended that I didn't hear him and followed the boys.

Bertie threw open the door with a happy face. Most women over forty were plump or curvaceous, but Roberta Coomers reminded me of a scrawny Christmas tree. She was all needles and tough bark.

"My babies," she cried.

Her skinny face beamed, gleamed, unnaturally. I examined her face and neck. Her skin stretched taut, plastic-like over her bones. She had wiped away all the wrinkles and sags accumulated through the years.

"You had your face lifted!" I cried.

Her smiled flip flopped into a hard frown. I heard Clarence's gasp behind me. The boys squinted their eyes and walked cautiously toward her. Darius peered at her face, looking for the telltale scar.

"What the hell is she doing here?" Bertie asked.

"I didn't know she was coming," Clarence said from behind me.

Okay, so Miss Bertie thought she had her little family

safely in her grip again. Big deal. I was not going to run from
Bertie. Clarence was too old to be afraid of his big sister. I
might fall in the ocean with the rest of the Californians but
I would be damned if I fell before Bertie. I strolled up the
short path, climbed the steps, and shoved past her. The old
girl fell against the door.

"She can't come in here!" she cried.

"I'm in," I stated and then exclaimed, "Oh, my goodness!"

The boys followed me into the house and crowded
against me. All our mouths dropped open. The living room
was stunning in rich toffee brown leather and southwestern
art. I walked slowly around the room taking in the details.
Brass studs trimmed the arms of the leather sofa and chairs.
An earth tone rug covered the gorgeous high-gloss hardwood floors. Lamps of sandstone stood upon wrought iron
tables. Bushy fauns sat around the room like comfortable
guests. A picture window overlooked the cul-de-sac. A
doorway led down a short hall with three doors opening
onto the sleeping quarters and the bathroom. The room also
flowed, to the right, through an oval arch way into a dining
room. Toffee leather chairs surrounded a marble table. Beyond the dining room, through sliding doors, were a patio
and I swear, a swimming pool.

"Man!" Darius exclaimed and walked around me.

"Geez, this is tight!" CJ said and walked to the picture
window.

Darius and I joined CJ at the window. I dropped my
purse on the nearest chair, removed my sunglasses, and put
my hands on my hips. I swirled slowly around. "Well," I said.
"Exactly what kinda job did you have?"

The boys also turned and looked at their dad. Bertie
closed the door behind Clarence who crawled into the room
like the lying snake he was. He had been living the life of

luxury while I struggled to provide a roof over his children's heads. Oh, I was going to enjoy my stay in that house. He dropped the luggage and held out his hand in supplication

"She can't stay!" Bertie shouted.

"Bertie," I smiled. I folded my arms and walked slowly toward her. The boys followed me. "You do remember the wedding ceremony?"

"I don't give a damn!" she screamed.

"Roberta, what's wrong?" A sweet melodious voice came through the dining room. "Is Claren" (not Clarence but Claren) "back with his sons?"

The boys and I turned back to the dining room. A beautiful Mexican creature with the lightest brown eyes, eyes the color of a fawn, walked through the dining room. She was no more than twenty-five years old. Even in my youth, I had not looked so sweet and angelic. A lump the size of a baseball rose in my throat. I looked quickly at Clarence. He stuffed his hands into his pockets. Bertie wore a smug, triumphant look. I turned to the stunning creature who stood in the arch way.

"Who are you?" I asked.

"His woman," Bertie said.

I looked quickly at the boys. Bewilderment washed over their faces. That spacious house shrunk to a hut. How could Clarence have a woman? I looked back at the girl. On closer examination, I wasn't sure whether she was of legal age or not.

"His woman?" I smirked but inside fear and humiliation gripped me. Could Clarence really be such a sleaze?

"That's what I said," Bertie snapped.

"Bertie," I said, turning on her. "Do you want me to kick your ass now or later? Cause you're all in my business."

"K-K-Katie," Clarence stammered. "Don't do anything rash!"

"Who are you?" the girl asked.

In unison, the boys and I answered.

"His wife, sweetie," I said.

"My mom," Darius said.

"My mother," CJ said.

The girl looked from me, to the boys, to Clarence who had inched between Bertie and me, and finally to Bertie for confirmation. The room was quiet for a full ten seconds. Trust me. Ten seconds stretched into infinity. I watched doubt, confusion, and finally outright disbelief cover her face.

"Didn't he tell you he had one?" I asked.

"Claren?" The young thing pleaded for an answer.

"How the hell you gonna come here with no notice?" Bertie asked.

"By invitation," I answered. "My husband has been begging me for another chance for months. In fact Sunday, he called and begged me to give our marriage another chance. Didn't you, Sweetie?"

Oh, yeah, Katie could be a bitch. I was two-thousand miles from home, with a pocket full of change and a purse full of false promises. Heat crept up my back, my neck, and my face. I felt stupid, hurt, and ashamed. AGAIN! Would these feelings be a permanent part of my makeup? Was I going to let Clarence or Bertie or Baby Girl see me crumple? Heat crept up my back, up my neck, and across my face. That simpleton smile spread until my face froze in a hard mask.

"You're lying, Miss Thang!" Bertie snapped.

"Claren?" the young thing whimpered.

Clarence looked from me to Bertie back to me. He never looked at baby girl. He dared not. I think he knew that one sympathetic glance in her direction would push me over the proverbial edge.

"How long have you been cheating on me?" I asked Clarence, hoping he would say Monday. Monday would be cool. It would mean that in anger he rushed out and found the first young thing that threw herself at him.

"He met Raquel a month after he got here," Bertie smirked.

"What!" I looked at Clarence. "You shitty ass bastard!"

"Katie, the boys . . ." Clarence reminded me of our agreement not to cuss in front of the boys.

"Claren?" The young thing was still begging for attention. No one responded.

"Whose house is this?" I asked. "You said this was Bertie's house."

"It is," Clarence said.

"And you're not welcome in it," Bertie said.

"Then we can't stay here either," Darius said.

"Darius!" Clarence said.

"I'm not staying if my mom's not staying!" CJ shouted. "I don't know who that Mexican lady is but she's not my mom!"

"I think you better take us to a hotel until we figure this out, Clarence," I smirked. I raised those boys like they were my own and now the dividends were overflowing.

"You are not going to a hotel," Clarence said. "Bertie, I think you and Raquel better leave until I sort this out."

"I'm not leaving, Claren," Raquel said. "You asked me to be a part of this day and I'm not leaving."

"So, you plan to sleep in the bed with us?" I asked.

It was a simple question, but horror crossed the girl's face. She looked from Clarence to me. Then she burst into tears. She ranted in Spanish, throwing her hands up. The only words I could make out were *gorda* which meant fat, *estúpida* which meant stupid, and *puta* which meant whore.

"I don't know if you're calling me a fat whore or yourself a stupid whore but I think you best be careful with that language," I warned.

"I'm not leaving," she cried.

"Cow, you're leaving if I have to sling your Mexican ass in the street," I said.

"You have to get through me," Bertie moved toward me.

I leaped and Clarence caught me. I struggled to get out of his arms because Bertie was coming toward me. Baby Girl had her hands on her cheeks, crying *no, no, no.*

"No, Aunt Bertie," CJ shouted and dived between Bertie and me. "You touch my mom, and Imma hurt you."

"Me too," Darius said and stepped to his brother's side.

Everyone froze. Clarence looked from his sons to me and then quietly said. "Bertie, take Raquel with you and leave."

"I know you're not kicking me out of my own house!" Bertie shouted.

"It's my house Bertie," Clarence said. "I pay the rent."

That may have been the first and only time Clarence asserted himself with Bertie. She huffed up like the big bad wolf and let loose a string of foul language. The boys' mouths dropped. I folded my arms. Raquel stopped her whimpering and stepped back. Clarence grabbed Bertie by the arm. I did mention that Clarence does not cuss, right? No? Okay, well Clarence had an aversion to bad language. Whereas I knew all the hells, damns, and some words too blue to mention in polite society, Clarence closed his ears, eyes, and mouth to such verbiage. Nevertheless, his big sister had no such distaste.

"This is my damn house!"

"Bertie, leave," he said. "You can't talk that way around my boys."

"If I leave, Clarence, I'm not coming back," Raquel said.

"I'm sorry, Raquel," Clarence said, "but my wife is here and she comes first."

Stop! My brain screamed. Rewind. *It is Labor Day and Hubby announces he is leaving me in front of my whole damn family!* Did I want a replay of that experience again? Did I really want this man who jerked women around like yo-yo strings? Did I want this man who could watch me struggle with bills and debts and not come up with one hustle to help? Everybody had a hustle, a way to get an extra dollar but not Clarence. How many more times must he walk out on me before I wise up. As sure as my name was Katie Jeffries Cannon Smith Robinson Coomers, when things got tight he would kick me to the curb, again. Yes, I had a moment of victory over Bertie and Baby Girl. Clarence had placed me first but for how long?

"No, Clarence," I said. "I'm not staying here. " I'm going home."

"We are going home," Darius said.

Stop! My heart screamed. What about the boys? I looked down at my two boys. Water sloshed in their large eyes. Fear ate away their carefree youthfulness. CJ's hands clenched and unclenched. Darius stared at Baby Girl like she was Godzilla's mama. I knew if he had Godzilla in his hand, he would have rammed it up her nose. I saw the hurt and devastation in the boys' eyes. We knew, we all knew, that whatever piece of marriage I had with Clarence was over. I turned on Clarence, rage boiled out of my mouth.

"You pus head jerk," I hissed. "You have no love for me or anybody else. When I look around and see how you've been living for months, I despise you. You know the shitpile you left in Chicago, the debts, mine and yours, and you never offered to pay a bill."

"I gave you five hundred dollars a month," he said.

"You didn't give me shit. You took six hundred a month out the household."

"It's about money," Clarence said.

"It's about respect," I said, "and love. How the hell can you say you love me and watch me drown in a financial cesspool, Clarence? Love doesn't pull a drowning woman to the bottom of the river. Love could not watch her die. Love saves, Clarence. When have you loved me?"

"You don't discuss leaving me. You just announced it in front of the world. My sister's sending me a ticket," I mimicked him. "You don't ask me if I will keep the boys, you just leave them on me with five hundred dollars a month and a bunch of debts. When I lost my job, you didn't step forward with more support. It's about money, indeed."

"We can discuss all this later," Clarence said.

"Why later, Clarence? Don't you want Miss Bertie and Baby Girl to know you're a worthless piece of bird dropping? If you had a million dollars stuck to your sorry ass, I wouldn't take you back."

I turned to Raquel who huddled next to Bertie. Confusion washed over her face. She looked from Clarence to me. Was I a mad woman? Was Clarence an ass? I knew those questions went back and forth in her head. I chose not to enlighten her. Bertie smirked and nodded her head slowly. Triumph, victory, all the glorious emotions of winning showed in her face. I shook my head.

"Somebody call me a cab," I said. What did I care about those two sorry women? Let them carry Clarence for the rest of their lives. I was finished. "I'll wait outside."

"We're going too," Darius said. He and CJ moved toward me. I dropped to my knees and stopped them.

"Look around," I said. "This is a wonderful house. I think your Daddy has a good job or a good business. Something is going on here."

"I have enough money to get back to Chicago. When I get there, I'll be flat broke. I don't have a job, and you know how tough times have been. If I take you back, I can't promise you food or clothes. I can't promise we'll have a place to stay in a month."

"We don't care." CJ flung himself in my arms. "I want to be with you. I love you, Mom."

Darius also threw himself in my arms. They bawled. A few tears slipped down my face. Oh yes, at that moment I despised Clarence. I never witnessed the effect of divorce upon children before. Yes, divorce. I had two boys clinging to me, wanting their mom. I could not make their wishes come true.

"Maybe your daddy will send you home for Thanksgiving," I said.

"You don't have to go, Katie," Clarence said.

"You are a jerk, Clarence," I hissed over the boys' heads. "Get me a cab here, quick."

Strength rolled from my short, stubby toes up to my big round head. I stood on the front porch with my luggage. The boys clung to me. I chattered on and on about the wonderful time we would have at Thanksgiving. I held back tears. I told a couple of elephant jokes. Finally, the taxi arrived and Clarence pulled the boys into the house so I could escape their tears. I held it together as the taxi crept to the airport. The plane departed from LAX, flew across country, and landed at O'Hare. Another taxi carried me to my apartment on Sherwin Avenue. I trudged up the three flights of stairs. I entered my dark, gloomy apartment, closed and locked the door, and crumpled into tears.

CHAPTER 15

The world was in the throbs of the new Millennium. Would I cry myself into it? Certainly. I was preparing for the end of my days. Every day, minute by minute, I felt myself slipping into a black hole. The longer I sat in that tiny, dark apartment, the more depressed I became. I cried about the boys, about Clarence, and about Matt. I cried about making that foolish trip to California.

When I was not crying, I moped around the apartment, from room to room. Like a phantom, I haunted myself. I thought about the Tylenol with Codeine sitting in my medicine cabinet. I could wash those pills down with the tequila gold. I could sleep out of life. There was no point. Tequila and pills. No point. Tequila and pills.

One morning, not able to stand my sour mouth, I stood over the sink, with my toothbrush loaded, and received the shock that probably saved my sorry life. The mirror reflected a woman who could have easily lived in the back of a garbage truck. My eyes were deep, hollow and circled. My hair, sprinkled with lint, stood around my head like tumbleweed. Sleep was piled in the corners of my eyes. A wide, white streak of dried saliva coated one cheek. I flushed with shame. A stranger stared at me from the mirror. With a wail, I crumpled to the cold ceramic floor. Weird guttural sobbing, like a basso seal, wrenched my body. My head fell into my hands. Mercy! I could not stop sobbing. Every problem I had surfaced and exploded into a catastrophe. I was alone and miserable. I was everybody's shame and nobody's pride. I was a marriage reject. I was a disowned child. I was a castaway. I was nobody's ideal woman. I was tired, tired, tired. I brought my knees up to my head, curled into a tight ball, and sobbed. I could not die. I could not, but I wanted to close my eyes and slip away.

I crawled over to the tub and stopped it up. I turned the hot water on full force. I pulled myself up and wiped my face. I gathered my beauty aids and hygiene products. How long had it been since I thoroughly cleansed my body? How long had I crawled around that dark apartment? I lowered my filthy body into the hot sudsy water. Dirt, grime, and sorrow puckered and popped off my body, floating away like scales. Dead skin curled into the tight naps of the loofah sponge. Tears rolled down my face as I tried to eradicate the sorrows of my life. I slipped down into the water, and submerged my head. I lathered my hair with shampoo. I scrubbed my body. The water cooled. I unstopped the tub, stood, and turned on the shower. I finished shampooing and conditioning my hair. Using a softer sponge, I rinsed the last hint of dirt and sorrow away. By the time I finished, the water running down the drain spoke my shame. It was gray and heavy, but I was light and clear. Why did I ever doubt myself, my decisions? Mama and Donna were wrong! There was nothing wrong with dreams.

A woman may cry for days, contemplate suicide, threaten murder, make a fool of herself, lose weight, gain weight, lose hair, grow bitter, scream, rage, but eventually she has to pull the strings of her corset tight and swallow the bitter truth. She has to take stock, and reinvest in herself. What else was there for me to do? I was nineteen again, on the campus of Washington State University, watching the father of my child walk away from me as if I were some small annoyance in the corner of his eye. I was twenty-five again, and standing before my green Gremlin with the missing hubcap, listening to my first husband James' deep baritone voice sooth the fear out of some other skank. I was twenty-nine again, standing before a judge, listening to Joe Robinson, my third husband, explain that he had grown accustomed to a life style that he was unable to maintain without alimony. I was married, but not married. I was dead, but not buried. Mama and Donna were definitely wrong; my mistakes were the results of poor judgment and trying to bend into others' image of who and what I was. *Oh, I get it, Georgie.* I thought. I see the mirror and the mirror sees me.

I slipped on a new pair of capris, bought for my trip to LA. They were too big in the waist. I weighed myself. I had lost the last twelve pounds. I was down to my original one hundred and thirty pounds, but there was no one to help me celebrate. I was famished and decided to make myself an omelet, but when I opened the refrigerator it was bare. I laughed hysterically and that frightened me. I had twenty dollars in my pocket, no food, and no unemployment compensation due. My utilities were past due. One Visa account was so far behind, I could not save it. Other creditors screamed for money. I had none to give. The only other funds available were in my 401K from Luft's Catalog Company, but I needed Clarence's consent to withdraw those funds. I refused to crawl to him for any assistance.

I slipped on my rundown sneakers and headed for Dominick's. Tuna, cucumbers, tomatoes, chicken breasts, and melons were on sale. I also picked up a pack of pita bread, a piece of feta cheese, and a few black calamata olives. Loading the items on the counter, I prayed that a sliver of credit was available on one of my credit cards. I wanted to save my twenty dollars for an emergency. My regular clerk looked at the name on the Visa and then at me. Her face wore a quizzical expression.

"What?" I asked.

She laughed, "I didn't recognize you until you spoke."

My mouth dropped. Had sorrow eroded all semblances of self from my face?

"You've lost lots of weight, huh?" she asked.

"Yeah," I answered.

"Whatever you did," she said, "you look good."

She swiped the card through the machine. *You look good.* Her voice followed me home. I walked the few blocks to my apartment and realized those were the first kind words spoken to me in weeks. After my family, friends, and supposed spouse had disappeared, I was relying on the kindness of strangers.

***

Men say women make them pay for the wrongs of other men. Yes, I was bent on revenge. I wanted MEN to suffer the consequences of my broken life. I would make them lust and long, pant and pine, and surrender all to me. I would make them pay for every sister, white, black, red, or yellow that ever cried her heart out in her lonely pillow. Those heartbreaking, wretched, dreadful, greedy, grabby creatures from another planet had worn my heart down to a thin artery, left me crying, *My man don't love me, treats me all so bad* blues. What else could a woman do but hone her seductive skills into a razor edge? What else could I do but go online and lose myself in fantasies and games? I changed my profile to read:

Name: Silky
Location: Capone City
Age: Never ask a woman
Marital Status: Are you strong Enuf to be my man?
Hobbies: I don't cyber. No Phone sex.
Occupation: The girl just wanna have fun.
Personal Quote: kiss-kiss, darling.

I was out for a good time. I wanted nothing more than for men to hanker after me. I flirted. I toyed. I was the dog on the prowl, the rover sniffing the meat. I was the bitee, the gnawler, an old school vamp, promising paradise but delivering nothing. I devised a filtering procedure. If a man were dim-witted, I clicked him off. If a man started with 35/s/m looking for fun, or any variation of that, I clicked him off. If a man asked me to cyber, I clicked him off. If a man were intelligent, witty, and charming, I flirted. Between table dancing to the Strip4U wav, my outrageous conversations, and that profile, I amassed a string of admirers from New York to California.

I scanned two new pictures, taken by my downstairs neighbor, into my computer. In one picture, I held my dress thigh high with one knee lifted. Even with my leg up, my curves were very visible. In that picture, huge oval sunglasses hide my eyes and most of my face. The second picture was a close up of my face. The sadness in my eyes offset my wide smile. I kept that one in reserve. I changed my personal quote to read: *A petite black woman with enough curves to keep any man on her track: forgive the face.* Men jumped out the screen at me. They typed: *Hi beautiful, can I see those curves. Hi Silky. What do you like?* Or *Hello, I love beautiful Nubian princesses.*

Hi, sugar. How are you today? I cooed to each of them. I knew how to work the IMs. I had software that managed up to twenty IMs at a time. Some men were seeking cybering relationships. Some were seeking friends. Still, others were hoping for a long term relationship. I didn't give a rat's tail. I had my own secret agenda, but I didn't want to get caught in any lies. Just as I had approached Mike under a different screen name, any of my online guys could have approached me under a different name and discovered my duplicity. The fastest and easiest way to keep my lies straight was to say the same thing to everyone: Copy and paste, copy and paste. I didn't have to be original until AddnMchn44. He broke the mold.

AddnMchn44:	SWM doesn't give a damn about looks but wants a sexy body.

Please. How can you not give a damn about looks? I was not a superficial woman. I did not want a pretty boy. Pretty boys made excellent magazine covers, but they did not excite me. Nor did the downright homely peak my interest. I preferred walkable men, men who did not cause shame to course through my body. I preferred men with wit and charm, men who always got a second look based on animal magnetism, men with presence like Lou Gossett, Jr., Robert DeNiro, or Matt.

SilkyDreamGirl:	I got the body and as an added bonus, I got the brains . . .
AddnMchn44:	So you are a smart, ugly chick with a sexy body.

SilkyDreamGirl:	Hmm, hope you have enuf brown bags.
AddnMchn44:	Brown bags?
SilkyDreamGirl:	To cover my head, sugar.
AddnMchn44:	ROFLMA Do you have a pic of your body?
SilkyDreamGirl:	Oh, yesssss. I can send you that.

I quickly cropped the head off my legs' photo and saved the revised picture under a new file name. I emailed a copy to him. While he downloaded the picture, I checked his profile. He was an accountant who enjoyed white water rafting and skiing. He was also separated.

AddnMchn44:	You have a body to die for . . .
SilkyDreamGirl:	I know but my face would kill you.
AddnMchn44:	I'm in Naperville. Wanna meet?
SilkyDreamGirl:	No, thank you.

He told me his name was Keith. I added him to my list of men. We chatted about his twin daughters and how he missed them dearly. His wife, he said, was unforgiving, heartless, and selfish. After his little affair (his words) with a woman in his office, his wife had taken the girls and moved to Kentucky. I thought about his wife, poor unfortunate soul, crying her blue eyes out and longing to see him suffer. I finally sent him the picture of my face.

AddnMchn44:	You're not ugly. You are gorgeous, a bit sad but gorgeous.
SilkyDreamGirl:	Uh huh. Did I send you the right picture?
AddnMchn44:	I think I love you.
SilkyDreamGirl:	Keith, I do believe I could look like a sideshow freak and you would still lust for me.
AddnMchn44:	I'm not lusting. I'm falling.

SilkyDreamGirl:	Oh? Are you through mourning over your wife?
AddMchn44:	I can only think of you.
SilkyDreamGirl:	Liar.

Enchanted as I was with my online flirtations, those flirtations did not churn electrons into silver coins to pay the landlord. Those flirtations did not produce a wondrous table laden with hot food for my sustenance. During the day, I used three job web sites to search for employment. I also answered every promising ad in the Sunday *Chicago Tribune* and *The Reader*. The classifieds in those two papers are the unemployed handbooks. My resume, plumped with real and imagined achievements, went out on good gray linen paper. The phone was silent for three weeks until I finally got a call for a position as a call center lead person. The salary was a big cut in pay from my days as a supervisor, but my belly was crying "feed me." So, I dressed with care, in a suit that was ten years old but it was the only thing that fit decently.

As the El rumbled downtown, I rehearsed possible questions and answers. I checked off reasons while I had to take a job in the loop although I despised the horrendous pace of downtown Chicago. Once I stepped off the El, I had to accelerate my steps and merge into the flow of pedestrians. In the loop people scurry like mad ants. The women stretch their meager checks to dress professionally, with spiffy shined shoes, coordinated suits and shirts, Gucci, Coach, and Dooney-Bourke bags. I really didn't want to step into that fashion rat race.

At Belmont I almost transferred over the trestle to the train heading back North to my apartment. Instead while the Red Line descended into the subway, I changed to the

Brown Line and rode past DePaul University, around the Merchandise Mart and got off a block from the Insurance Exchange. The Exchange ended the LaSalle Street canyon. Old banks and law firms are housed on LaSalle Street in stone buildings that are often shown in period movies like *The Untouchables*. Here the insolent haute-couture of people etching out a living was second only to those on working on Michigan Avenue. Here the Chicago power makers reigned and the wind, caught in this canyon blew harder and colder than any other part of the city. Here I made my way into the Insurance Exchange building.

The instant the Human Resources Director limply shook my hand, I knew that the job was not mine. Momentarily, he lost control of his hand. It flopped like a fish out of water. Once when he leaned forward, his perfect toupee slipped across his balding head. He self-consciously tried to adjust it without letting on that I knew he knew I knew it was a toupee. There was no way he would hire me. I could "tell" someone about his "perfect" toupee.

I stopped at the Corner Bakery on Adams and Dearborn for a recuperative lunch. I was biting into my chicken salad when my eyes connected with a pair of eyes two tables away. The man lifted his eyebrows, cocked his head, and studied my face. I dropped my eyes. Self-consciously, I dabbed my chin with my napkin. Did I have a big hunk of salad on my chin? He stood and lifted his tray. I quickly did a police assessment of him, carrot red hair, a telltale beer belly, six feet tall with knocked knees, and pockmarked skin. His eyes stayed riveted to my face as he made his way to my table. I held my breath, hoping he would bypass me.

"Excuse, me," he said when he reached my table. "I think we know each other. My name is Keith. You call me AddMan," he said. "You are Silky."

"Oh my goodness!" I exhaled. "How did you know me?"

"You have the most exquisite round eyes," he said. "I would know those eyes anywhere. May I join you?"

I nodded my head. I do not believe in ghosts, psychics, horoscopes, nor coincidences. Everything, I think, happens for a reason. There was a reason why AddMan and I were together in a downtown lunch joint.

"What are you doing here?" I asked. "I thought you lived in Naperville."

"I do but I work across the alley," he said and pointed to the white and silver Xerox Building.

"This is too wild," I said. My voice was liquid honey. I smiled into his jovial face. His face was red, round, and filled with barley-size pores. Thick red brows and lashes fringed his cerulean blue eyes. His nose sloped like an inverted strawberry above a thick handlebar moustache that curled at the tips like a villainous cartoon character.

"I've never met anyone from the web before and here you are," he laughed. His soft and raspy voice verged on hoarseness and contradicted the strength of his stout body.

"So, what are you doing downtown?" he asked. "I thought you were unemployed."

"I'm looking for a job," I said. "I had an interview by Union Station but I know I won't get the position."

"Oh?" he asked and took a sip from his coffee. I recanted what had happened and he laughed, just cracked up.

"No, hun," he said after his laughter subsided, "that job isn't yours."

"It was such a good opportunity," I sighed. "Maybe, my interview this afternoon will go much better."

"You are on a serious job hunt!" he exclaimed.

"A woman can't live by her charms alone," I teased. "I intend to have a job by the first of July."

By the time he finished his couscous, we were chatting like old friends. He told me about his job and his company.

He told me about his trip to Spain and the running of the bulls. He bragged about his daughters' dancing accomplishments. He told me about his dear wife, faithful as a lap dog, quiet as a spider, and long gone. He also told me that a woman from his office plied him with alcohol, seduced him, and wrecked his marriage. I lifted one eyebrow.

"Hmm," I said.

"What?" he asked.

"I want to see the Herculean woman who clubbed you, dragged you off to her lair, screwed the sap out of you, then sent you home dried as a raisin."

"You don't believe me?" he asked. His red skin turned three shades of vermillion then settled into a pale ruddy color.

"Hey." I shrugged my shoulders. "If that's your story, stick to it."

I lifted my Pepsi glass and toasted him. He sat back in his chair with a deep scowl on his face. He expected me to offer a sympathetic ear, a soft shoulder, or a foolish heart. I sat there with a quirky smile and one eyebrow raised in disbelief. He conquered his disappointment and smiled.

"So," he asked casually, "do you want to date?"

I tell you the Pepsi squirted out my nose and into the glass. I grabbed my napkin and wiped my face. So much for cool sophistication.

"Date?"

"Yeah," he said.

"Keith, you are crazy," I laughed. "I'm not dating anyone off line."

"Why not?" he asked. "We've had a pleasant lunch. I'm a good guy."

He leaned to one side and pulled a canvas wallet from his back pocket. He opened it and passed it to me. Credit cards and pictures stretched the seams of that wallet.

"See. Here's my ID with my current address."

I laughed and pushed the wallet back to him. His hand covered mine and I smiled to keep from flinching. He had big sweaty hands with coarse hair, the color of rust, across the knuckles. His hands felt like a banana slug, that thick slimy parasite indigenous to the California Redwood Forest. I knew how slugs felt because Regina had placed one in my pocket during a vacation. I had screamed and shook when I pulled out that slimy thing instead of my plum lipstick. Anyway, I gently pulled my hand out of Keith's. "If you noticed," he said, "there are gold and platinum credit cards in my wallet which means I'm financially responsible."

"Plastic means debts, sugah," I laughed. "You have debts."

He laughed and asked again, "So, how about dinner Saturday night?"

My destiny, I thought, was to make him pay for his wife's sufferings and for my sufferings. That day, that moment in time, I could have organized my sistahs, passed out pamphlets, and created large posters that read—US AGAINST THEM which stood for United Sisters against Thieving wHorish Evil Men. All organizations must start smart. It was up to me to set the standard.

"I would love to," I said, thinking of his pitiable wife. *Okay, girlfriend*, I thought. *This bastard will pay. He will desire me. He will fill my hands with treasures, and I will break his lying, cheating heart.*

***

Okay, okay, I was not the skank I tried to be, or rather I was a skank with standards and, that man was sleaze. We agreed to meet at Gaylord's, a great place for East Indian cuisine, plus it was well-lit and safe. As we waited for our dinner, the man's thick pink tongue slithered out his mouth and licked his lips not once but three times as his banana slug fingers crept up my naked arm.

"What soft skin you have," he said with saliva bubbling in the corner of his mouth.

I picked up my napkin and wiped my mouth. His fingers dropped away. Wet fingerprints remained on my arm. Although the night was a balmy eighty degrees, and the restaurant was comfortable, I shivered. I wondered if maybe my brain was off track. The man across from me was a repulsive, cheating, red-faced, slug-fingered sleaze. There were three billion, nine hundred and ninety-nine million other men that I could torture. That pitiable wife in Kentucky had to handle her own mess. Before the stuffed grape leaves arrived, I excused myself from the table, walked out the restaurant, and hopped into a cab.

The next online guy I dated flew in from Detroit. He was as funny as Martin Lawrence and looked like him, a short man with an infectious laugh. We spent Friday evening at the House of Blues. We spent Saturday evening at the Cotton Club. I was happy to see him go Sunday. The man had more nervous energy than a child with attention deficiency. Still, my experience with him paved the way for me to date another guy off line. And another. And another. Starbucks, the Corner Bakery, and Leona's Restaurant became my meeting places. Those shops provided a safe environment for me to meet and size up the men. I could always walk away. None of the guys had my home address or home phone number. All calls came through my cell phone.

The men wanted to touch me, kiss me, shower me with gifts, lavish attention on me, and take me to hotel rooms. I received offers of trips to the Virgin Islands, to Europe, and to Las Vegas. There were good dates and bad dates. There were wandering hands and lusty bulges. There were scary guys that I never saw beyond coffee at Starbucks.

For all my big talk, my last sexual encounter was a long distance memory, back in the summer of '98 before dear

Clarence departed. Now my body craved satisfaction. Yet, none of the men excited me to the point where I parted my legs, until I met a delectable morsel named Ben.

Ben was as chocolate as a Mounds candy bar with a heavy, trimmed, gray mustache. He had wide eyes and a strong voice. His law offices were minutes from my new job as office manager for a rival law firm. That's how we met. I was in tears at the elevator when he walked up. He asked me what was wrong. I told him that I had just interviewed for the job of a lifetime but didn't think I had a chance of getting it.

"Miss Lady," he said, removing a handkerchief from his inside breast pocket. "Think positively."

Without my permission, he tipped my head up and gently dabbed the tears on my face. He smiled and I saw edible lips under that thick moustache. Dormant longings stirred in my body. I trembled. I stood still as he smoothed my hair back. It was brushed back in a tight chignon. I thought that style would make me appear more confident.

"You have intelligent eyes," he said. "I'm a good judge of people and I say don't worry."

"Thank you," I said weakly.

It was a good thing that the elevator was packed with people, otherwise I would have ripped Ben's suit from his luscious body and had my way. In the lobby, Ben grabbed my hand before I walked away. His hands were dry but warm.

"You must give me your number," he smiled. "So I can call and congratulate you on your new job."

We exchanged telephone numbers. Ben and the job called a week later. He wined and dined me from the Mirador to the 95th floor and many other fine restaurants. We attended *Fosse*, argued about Chicago politics, and danced at a South Michigan Avenue night club. I liked the way Ben's muscular body pressed against mine, very much so. The first time Ben kissed me, he lifted my head very gently, placed a dry, chaste kiss on my lips, stroked my cheek, and walked away. Oh, yeah. Doris Day never had it so good. His next kiss, along those same lines, was followed by nibbles on my lips. When Ben invited me to his home for dinner, I was ready. I wore a short dress with a pair of lacy thongs underneath. I had walked through a shower of Bulgari perfume before I left the house. During the long drive from my apartment to his home in Beverly, I hummed. In my head I heard the words *gonna get me some, gonna get laid* repeatedly. After a year of celibacy, I planned to knock the boots, screw, get laid, make love, whatever you want to call it.

When I drove into Ben's driveway, my mouth dropped. Beverly was a neighborhood on the South Side of Chicago that consisted of middle-class and upper-middle-class residents. Ben lived in the latter. His home was a two-story red brick colonial house with a sweeping lawn and a curving driveway. *Oh, yeah*, I thought, *this is a place for seduction*. I hoped he wasn't into bondage or SM or some other fetish.

I checked my face in the mirror. Hungry brown eyes stared at me. I had smudged the liner until my eyes were sultry, seductive orbs. I wore fuchsia lipstick and a slight blush. Everything in that face shouted available, easy, hot, get it now. I was a fake Cleopatra, bordering on slut.

Heat crawled up my thighs as I walked toward Ben's home. I craved for chocolate, chocolate lips on my hands, chocolate melting over me, and chocolate oozing under me. Ah, dark men with muscular bodies make a sista holla— Ooooaw. I walked up those steps pulsating, throbbing across the widest veranda I've ever laid eyes on. I imagined myself the lady of the manor, sweeping down a curving staircase, sans Loretta Young, in an elegant but sexy gown by Versace greeting the Mayor and Mrs. Daley with a warm peck on each check. I would turn to Clarence, my ex-husband who would then be the butler, with a disdainful air and ask for another bottle of Pessac-Léognan Blanc, softly touching Ben on the arm, a sign of affection and possession. *Of course,* I would say to the First Lady of the United States, *I'm excited that Ben is considering the offer to be Secretary of State for the President's next term.* Oh, yes, we would entertain political leaders of the city, the nation, and the world. After all, with my nudging, Ben would run for the city council, for state senator, and yes, he would sit in the White House, one way or the other.

That fantasy flamed the desire in my stomach. My nipples hardened. If Ben answered that door, if he had given the maid, the cook, and the butler the night off, I would leap into his arm and beg him to take me now.

I pressed the door bell and a few bars of *Say It Loud, I'm black and I'm proud* flowed through the house. I shook my head. How tacky! A woman could not be elegant with James Brown emitting from a doorbell. That would be the first thing I change. I anxiously waited for the door to swing open on my new life. Ben opened the front door and my fantasies vanished. He had a bottle of Bud in one hand and a baby in the other. A BABY! I quickly scanned through my memory bank for any mention of a baby. Nope. None. Nada. Zip.

"Ben?" I asked tentatively.

"Come on in, Katie," he said. "I have to give little Ben to his mom."

His mom? I thought. Okay. Okay. Let's take a breather here. Tell me I'm crazy but how could he forget a baby and a wife? How could he expect me to sit down to a meal with both? Or would he relegate them to some dark tower room like Edward Rochester did to his wife in *Jane Eyre.* I looked from the baby to Ben. I knew puzzlement twitched on my once glamorous face. My eyelids jumped like Mexican jumping beans. My nostrils flared like a snorting boar. Oh, I knew brother-man could not be so bold.

"My daughter, Angela," he said, reading my thoughts. "Remember I told you about her?"

I nodded, vaguely recalling the name. I tried to remember what he had told me about his daughter. I followed him through a marble foyer filled with the aroma of fried chicken. On one side of the foyer was a huge dining room in a combination of moss green, deep purple, and a smidgen of taupe. A wonderful painting called *Generations* stood over the buffet. The painting depicted four generations of African-American women. I wasn't sure from that distance if it were a print or the original. It didn't matter because both were beyond my limited income.

I heard the stampede of elephants on the floor above us. Rambunctious voices barged down the stairs. I barely made out, *Stop it! Imma tell!* I threw a wary glance up the steps and wondered what creatures lurked there. The color scheme in the dining room continued into the living room. Two sofas face each other. On one sofa, a young woman, who I assumed was Angela, sat half on the lap of a young man. Angela had used a black liner on her lips followed by a dark berry lipstick. Her small eyes had a hard edge to them. Acne plagued her face. The dark side of the moon didn't have as many craters and bumps as Angela. She frowned as we approached. The man had on a leather jacket. A thick gold bicycle-like chain choked his neck. A mass of hickeys circled above the chain.

Between the two sofas was a large glass cocktail table. A cluster of Christmas lights flash from the bottom shelf. Around the top of the table ran a miniature trolley line. Inside the track sat all these wonder porcelain miniatures depicting black life. The arrangement was a beautiful, heart wrenching scene—out of place, yet so right. Now here's the glitch. Angela's boyfriend was using one of the figurines as an ashtray. I freaked when I saw that. I glared at the young man. I gave him that haughty disapproving look that only mothers know how to administer. He immediately pushed Angela off his lap, sat up straight on the sofa, and stubbed the cigarette out. Ben said nothing but handed the baby to Angela.

"Angela, will you take Lil Ben, please," Ben begged.

Angela rolled her eyes at him and whined, "Dad!"

"Come on Angela, I got to turn my chicken."

She grudgingly took the baby and sneered at me like I was Alley-Mae-the-Beggar. Her nose and lips lifted and twisted at one corner. I ignored her and followed Ben out the room. He had not introduced us.

When we reentered the foyer, the herd of elephants crashed down the stairs. The herd consisted of three children, a girl about six years old and boys about the same ages as CJ and Darius. They circled us. Ben, who obviously had much experience being corralled by wild children, threw up his hands in surrender. I guess the two chocolate boys belonged to Ben. Their ears stuck out like hands waving goodbye on each side of their faces. Their tiny teeth were spacey but brilliant white. As if any doubt remained, each tilted his head and examined me like Ben had that first day we met. The little girl, however, resembled no one in the house, not Angela, Ben, the boys, or the boyfriend. She had a walnut beige complexion and thick wavy brown hair. That moment, standing in the foyer with those rambunctious children circling me, the last thought of seduction, of being half of Senator and Mrs. Ben Moss disappeared. I could get sex anywhere, anytime, I reasoned.

"Are you my daddy's new girlfriend?" One of the boys asked.

"No silly," the other boy said. "She's his computer date."

"Really, grandpa?" the girl asked.

Ben laughed and ruffed the girl's hair. She was a beautiful child with downy baby skin that only the young possessed.

"Who are these children?" I asked.

"Oh, this is Zach and Terrence, my sons. This is my granddaughter, Nyta. My eldest son and his wife are in the Bahamas for two weeks. I have another teenage son and daughter who won't be home for dinner today. You know teenagers."

"You have six children?" I asked.

"Yeah," he beamed as if he were handing me the most exciting news of my life. You got to understand, after four weeks of intense dating, the man finally revealed his flaw—a large family. Indeed, he had mentioned briefly some problems with his daughter Angela. I thought Angela was an only child. I looked at him with a scowl on my face.

"I got to turn my chicken," he said hastily. "I'll be right back."

The man left me standing in his foyer with three children who seized that opportunity to size me up like I was a burnt cookie. The girl popped her thumb in her mouth and twirled a braid around her finger. One boy crossed his arm and rocked back and forth. The other simply stared at me. When I first entered the foyer, it had appeared spacious and empty. Now it shrank to the size of my bathroom.

"Dad says we're gonna have a new mom, soon," the boy with the crossed arms said.

"Well," I said. "I'm sure some lucky woman will fit right in."

I wanted to run out the front door and disappear from that half million-dollar home. What did I need with riches? I had peace, serenity, and a home that contained only me and silence. I made it through dinner, which was an affair at a pig trough. The little girl and Angela's boyfriend were the only members of that household who knew the proper way to hold a knife and fork. Angela ate most of her food with her fingers and a slice of bread, explaining that was how it was done in remote villages of Africa. The boys hunched over their plates like CJ and shoved fork full after fork full of food down their throats. They were noisy and displayed the table manners of trolls. They grabbed food, scraped their forks loudly across their plates, smacked, chewed with their mouths open, and I swear, one of them belched. Angela and her boyfriend ignored the children and the baby who crawled around the table. How could Ben, who had insisted that a waiter at remove all the crystal on our table at because of a spotted goblet, tolerate such mad gluttony? After dinner, I made some excuse about having an early morning. Once home, I signed online and wrote Ben a cordial thank-you note and a polite apology for breaking off the relationship.

Before I could sign off, I received an IM from Matt, MastrThief. My fingers froze on the keyboard. I had not chatted with Matt since that day in June when he had taken my heart and condemned it to misery. I typed a hello.

MastrThief:	What's wrong?
SilkyDreamGirl:	What makes you think something is wrong?
MastrThief:	You took forever to answer my IM.
SilkyDreamGirl:	Imma coy kinda girl.
MastrThief:	Don't play coy with me.
SilkyDreamGirl:	Don't take that attitude with me.
MastrThief:	Get off line. I'm gonna call you.
SilkyDreamGirl:	Where are you?
MastrThief:	Home.

| SilkyDreamGirl: | Where's the Girlfriend. |
| MastrThief: | May I call you? |

His words were breathtaking, as breathtaking as an arctic wind through a tunnel. Just like that, after I'd spent weeks gathering and pasting the pieces of me back together like a patchwork quilt, he click-clicked an IM, expecting what? A weak butt woman.

| SilkyDreamGirl: | Give me five minutes. |

I signed offline and quickly undressed. I viewed my body from the back, the side, and the front. Yes, I had love handles but most of the skin glowed from care. I slipped into shorty pajamas and climbed into bed with a ringing phone.

"What you do to me," he exclaimed when I answered the phone. "I'm going crazy with desire."

"Oh, so that's all I am?" I laughingly asked. "A quick rump in the old cyber bed?"

He laughed. "You are anything but a quick rump."

"What about the lovely Julia?" I pulled the comforter over my head, shutting out the slant of light through the mini blinds.

"Sweetie, it's possible to love two women at once."

"Matt, you're full of it," I laughed. My voice was light as a bee's wing and full of sexual undertones, hums, and sighs.

"I love you."

"Right and Mrs. Brady is stripper," I purred. I breathed in the soothing scent of the lavender and chamomile sachet permeating my bedding.

He laughed. "I've missed you, Katie."

"I won't let you break my heart again," I sighed.

"Did I break your heart?" he asked.

"Of course, but I'm cured and dating a lot."

"Really?"

"Really," I said and told him about Keith, Ben, and a couple of others.

"Interesting," he said when I finished.

"What?"

"All those men, and you still haven't found one to captivate you."

"Honey," I cooed. "This is my game. I'm just toying with the boys."

"You're bad," Matt said.

"Hmmm, I had great teachers," I said. I caressed a spot on the side of my neck and sighed. Slowly I rocked back and forth. Soon, I would hum, and my eyelids would shut off the sliver of lights coming through the mini blinds.

"Maybe I should fly to Chicago for a date with the infamous SilkyDreamGirl."

"Darling," I sighed. Sleep thickened my voice. "You can't handle the big girl." My hand crept underneath my top. I softly caressed my belly. My entire body relaxed. *Sleep, sleep,* my brain whispered.

"You think?"

"You've already proven it," I said and yawned.

"How?"

"You ran the first time," I said. "You fell in love and ran. Live with it."

Heat from my body spread and warmed the covers. Sleep now moved over me as I gently stroked my stomach. I shut off the sounds of the city, the traffic, sirens, and listened only to the rain falling against my window. First, nobody wants you. Then everybody wants you. I had sloshed off sixty-five pounds of self-pity and anger. I had build an impenetrable wall of self-confidence, and the wolves were blowing, huffing and puffing trying to tear my house down.

"Katie?"

"I hear you, Matt."

"So?" he asked.

"You want to be one of my boys?" I asked.

"You're being a shit!" he said.

"Nite-nite, Matt," I yawned. "I'm going to sleep now. I hung up the phone.

CHAPTER 16

The doctor restricted Georgie to complete bed rest for the last two months of her pregnancy. LaDell rented a hospital bed and set it up in the family room. He found these old-fashioned bed jackets for Georgie. Some were quilted. Some were lacy. Georgie wore them with elegance and her natural sparkly flair. Her peanut butter skin glowed under the soft light of the family room. LaDell had transformed the room into a multimedia wonder. A wide-screen television covered one wall. A stereo system that could compete with any sound stage lined a second wall. Georgie's handiwork was evident in the abstract art on the walls, the soft beige carpet on the floor, and the polished brass picture frames on the tables scattered around the room. The overstuffed, teal, leather furniture squatted against the walls. Palm plants and other foliage endowed the room with a tropical air.

Georgie lay in her hospital bed like Cleopatra on an

imperial barge, floating down the Nile. Like a queen she received her guests as if they were foreign dignitaries. Women
cooked and cleaned her house, combed Shanna's hair, and
pressed Terrence's blue jeans. They also kept Georgie
abreast of gossip from the church, the hospital, and the
world in general. Georgie, uncomfortable accepting the care
others gave her, was a lousy patient. She wanted everyone to
stop fussing over her.

On Sundays, while LaDell and the children were at
church, I entertained Georgie with my online and offline
escapades. The Sunday Mama stumbled into the family
room, clutching her chest like Fred Sanford, I had Georgie
in tears about Ben.

"Heaven help you, Katie!" Georgie laughed. "Didn't you
ask the man if he had children?"

"Girl, naw," I said and leaned back in the chair next to
the bed. "All I saw was Mr. Attorney. I imagined us dining
with the Daleys as Ben prepared to enter public office.
'Sides, Georgie, how many men with six children drive a
Porsche?"

"Goodness!" Georgie exclaimed. "Katie, you were too
busy looking at his wallet to ask about his life."

"No, I wasn't."

"Uh, huh," she laughed. "Well at least you're careful."

"Yeah, I don't want another Mr. Irresponsible, Mr. Jail
Himself, Mr. Dirty Old Man, and of course, my favorite, Jim
the Ho."

"You should have married . . . what was his name?" she
asked.

"Who?"

"The cop."

"Jackson?"

Yeah. Now that man was sharp.

"He wanted babies too."

"Oh."

"Nobody decides to marry a thousand times," I said. "Liz Taylor is probably just like me, seeking love from bad characters."

"Don't be so hard on yourself," Georgie said. She folded her hand over mine. "I can honestly say that you tried with Clarence. You took care of his children, when he didn't. You supported all his business deals. I'm no fool, Katie. I know the money put a big dent in your pocketbook. Now it's time for you to lose the rest of that excess weight, and I'm talking about Clarence and Mr. Pete's house. Get rid of them both. Start over. Hey . . ."

She stopped talking in mid stream. Her chestnut hair fell in her eyes. I saw the cogwheels turning behind her eyes. After a minute of thinking, she lifted one eye and asked, "Would you like to meet a nice man with two young daughters?"

"Whoa!" I shouted.

"Now, you know I don't go in for fixing up people," Georgie said, "but this Internet dating thing scares me."

"What happened to this man's wife?"

"She left him and the daughters for a beef cake and a line of coke."

"Are you serious? You want to fix me up with this loser?"

"His wife had the problems, not him," she said. "And to put it bluntly, Katie, you haven't exactly married any princes."

I didn't answer her. The back door opened and closed. Mama called out her presence and Georgie answered. I looked at my watch. It was 2:00 P.M. and time for me to leave before Georgie's church crowd arrived. I rose to go but Georgie put a hand on my arm.

"When are you gonna make peace with Mama Jeffries?" she asked.

"We're at peace, Georgie," I patted her hand. "We're not fighting."

"That's because you barely speak to each other."

"Oh," I smiled at her. "You miss the good old days?"

Georgie shook her head. We stared at each other. A glass crashed to the floor in the kitchen. We heard a stool scrape across the floor. I stretched. Georgie straightened the blanket on her bed.

"Katie," Mama hissed from the doorway. Mama's dark face was ashen. She kneaded her breastbone with her hand. Her eyes were glazed. Her breath came in quick gasps.

"She's having a heart attack!" Georgie shouted.

"Mama!" I screamed.

Georgie's hand automatically went to the cordless phone on her bed. Mama stumbled across the room. I rushed to her and caught her before she fell to the floor.

"Lay her down, Katie," Georgie shouted.

I moved Mama into a straight line and snatched a cushion off the nearest chair. I tapped Mama gently on the face. There was no response.

"Mama, Mama, are you okay?" I asked, trying not to scream or shout.

I heard Georgie in the background talking to the emergency operator. Mama looked so frail on the cold hardwood floor. I placed two fingers in the groove of her neck, next to her windpipe. I did not feel a heartbeat. I tilted her head back and lifted her jaw forward to move her tongue away from her wind pipe. Still, there was no breath. Mama Jeffries and I were not in a love fest, but we were about to kiss.

I pinched her nostrils with my thumb and index finger and covered her mouth with mine. I gave one slow breath into her mouth and paused. I repeated that step. My own heart beat fast, adrenaline pumped through me as fear swept over me. Mama could not, must not die. She had yet to apologize!

"Mama," I said.

Her chest did not respond, did not rise and fall with life. I placed my fingers in the groove of her neck again. Still, there was no pulse.

"Old woman, don't you slip away like this," I hissed.

I positioned the heel of my left hand in the center of her chest, where the lower part of the rib cage meets. I placed my right hand over it, interlocked my fingers, and pumped. I tried to remember to keep my elbows straight as I leaned my shoulders over my hands. I tried to remember everything I had learned in CPR. My mama was on the floor, slipping away from me.

"Mama, please," I whispered.

"The ambulance is on its way," Georgie said.

Fifteen times. Fifteen times, I heard the voice of my instructor repeating over and over. *Katie, a smooth, rhythmic manner, not jerky. Katie, don't rock back and forth. Katie, take your time. Katie, save your mama's life, so she can apologize to you.*

Again, I pinched Mama's nostrils and gave her two slow breaths. Again, I followed this with fifteen chest compressions. Again and again. I rechecked her pulse and there it was. The old girl was back. I rolled her whole body on her side. I sat there with my hand stroking her head.

"You did good, Katie," Georgie said.

I heard the catch in her throat. When I looked up, Georgie was sitting on the side of the bed and holding her stomach.

"Now, I think you better call an ambulance for me."

"Damn!" I said. "Do you think I'm Wonder Woman?"
We both laughed.

***

Late that afternoon, eight of Mama's church buddies crowded the critical care waiting room, including Mrs. Anderson and Mrs. Jordan. Some of the ladies walked and prayed, lifted hands, and hummed worship songs. Some of the women sat on the vinyl brown couches and whispered. I was lost in the midst of those praying women, so I stood by the large windows that stretched from one wall to another. We waited anxiously for word of Mama's condition. Mrs. Jordan trampled back and forth, from the critical care waiting room to the maternity ward, where, as I understood, Georgie's new daughter clung to the womb, as stubbornly as any Jeffries. I felt Georgie's pain each time Mrs. Jordan gave another report. Finally, a weary, soft-eyed doctor entered the waiting room.

"Are you the young lady that administered CPR to Mrs. Jeffries?" The doctor singled me out.

"She's her daughter," Mrs. Anderson said in an accusing tone. The other women stood apart from us, listening but respecting my time with the doctor, except for Pat Anderson. She marched over to us like she had some great stake in this matter. I looked the doctor in the eyes and nodded. My chest tightened. I wondered what steps had I missed. Had I murdered my own mother? A clump of fear wedged in my throat and I trembled. I had no words. Mrs. Jordan walked up to me and grasped my hands.

"Yes, doctor," Mrs. Jordan said. "Katie did CPR on Helen."

"Well," the doctor said. "You saved your mother's life. She was blessed to have you there."

"Thank you, doctor," I said. Mrs. Parrot Nose Anderson's face dropped. I had done something right. All the women listened as the doctor filled me in on Mama's condition. By the time he finished, I was leaning against Mrs. Jordan and crying. Mama's church buddies were in a round of praise the Lord and hallelujahs.

"She's resting now but you and one other person can see her. She may have two visitors for five minutes every hour. Understand?"

"I understand," I said to the doctor. "Mrs. Jordan and I will be the visitors."

"You go ahead, Katie," Mrs. Jordan said. "I need a word with Pat."

I walked into the hospital room and saw a fragile woman lying in Mama's hospital bed. Tubes ran under the sheet. Oxygen tubes invaded her nostrils. An IV needle invaded her right hand. All the trappings of the sick surrounded my mother. I sat by the bed and lay my head against the cold rail. I had never spoken a tender word to my mother in all my days. Now I had no choice. Mama could slip away.

"Mama," my voice cracked. "There's something I have to tell about the day you left me alone with Daddy. Mama, all he talked about was you. He said 'Helen was a mule down there in Mississippi. Working, working, working and taking abuse from her own kin including your Grandma Ann.' He told me that your big brothers were lollygagging. Your sisters were cooling in the shade. Daddy said when he saw you in that yard, hoeing your mother's garden while everybody else was cooling in the shade, he got fighting mad. He saw all the years of sorrow and neglect on your back. He said he fell in love with you then. He just wanted to take care of such a strong woman.

"Mama, you were always first with Daddy, not me. He said when he looked in my eyes, he saw you, he saw strength. He was happy that you had married him and blessed him with strong children. He was happy that he could take care of you, even if he wasn't there. I was so mad,

Mama, cause you went to work like he never did any of that. You went to work for a few dollars and daddy had provided for you. That's all he ever wanted to do was take care of you. And there you were scrubbing floors and cooking like he didn't provide for us, for you. I couldn't understand how you could throw all that love away."

The tears fell where my words had fallen—on my lap. I wanted that old woman well. I wanted to hear her fuss. I felt an arm around my shoulder. I looked up at Mrs. Jordan. She had followed me to the room. Tears ran down her face.

"I wanted to let her know how much my daddy loved her. How much I love her."

"Sh, girl. I think she heard you." She nodded toward Mama.

I looked at Mama. Her eyes were open. Her hand moved, and I gently squeezed it. The steady beat of the monitor, the whirring of the oxygen machine, and the hushed tones of the hospital, calmed my spirit.

"K-Katie," Mama said and closed her eyes again.

"She's gonna be all right, Katie," Mrs. Jordan said, tenderly. "You'll see."

When we returned to the waiting room, Donna and Mrs. Anderson stood by the windows. Of course, Donna was impeccable in a beige pantsuit. Mrs. Anderson turned up her nose and walked over to the group of women sitting on the couches. Donna gave me a weak smile. We had not spoken since she kicked me out of her car. She walked toward us.

"Don't let Pat and Donna ride you," Mrs. Jordan whispered. "Some folks got a core of bitterness in their soul."

I kissed Mrs. Jordan on the cheek. She nodded when Donna came over then joined the other ladies. I didn't say a word as Donna fidgeted with her gold chain. Mrs. Jordan was right. There was a core of bitterness in Donna. It was evident in the down turn of her lips.

"I'm so glad Mama Jeffries pulled through," she said.

"Thank you," I answered.

"Did Georgie tell you about Mike and I splitting up?"

I nodded and she plunged into details about the breakup. Mike had finally confessed his secret computer life. He had fallen in LOVE with someone from online. I tell you I had a brief moment of fear.

"So," Donna whispered. "He left me. He packed a suitcase and told me he was flying off to Tampa, Florida to meet the love of his life."

"Donna, I'm sorry," I whispered, relieved.

"Don't be," she said. "He came crawling home three days later. Miss Wonderful was anything but his ideal woman."

"So, you guys made up?" I asked.

"Hell, no!" she hissed. "I kicked him out. Why would I stay with a man that would leave me for an Internet woman."

"You wouldn't," I said. I didn't know what else to say to her. There was no glad-to-see-you-feeling in my heart. Her eyes crawled over me, over my hair wrapped in two braids, over my sweats, and over my beat up gym shoes. I saw the disdain. I realized how much peace I had without her in my life. I could not walk away from Mama because the old girl needed me to keep her on her toes. Donna was just a friend forced on me since birth.

"Well, I'm sorry to hear about your troubles, Donna."

"I'm sorry to see you're down to the bone," she said. "Folks are talking about how you're just wasting away crying over Clarence."

"Wasn't it your suggestion that I lose some weight?" I asked.

"Yeah, but you're dropping away to nothing."

"Donna, take care of yourself. And next time, get the gossip right."

I walked away from her and the rest of the women in the waiting room. I heard her gasp but didn't look behind me. I found the elevator and made it to the maternity ward just in time to welcome my niece, Regina Kay, in the world. LaDell and Georgie fell into each other's arms weeping, when I told them that Mama was okay. I missed my call time to the boys by two hours. I called collect and Darius accepted the charges.

"We thought you forgot about us," he said.

"How can I forget about my hearts?" I asked. "I'm at the hospital with Mama Jeffries. She had a heart attack."

"She's at the hospital," he said to whoever was in the room with him. "Mama Jeffries had an attack."

"Let me speak to your mother," I heard Clarence in the background.

"He and Raquel had another fight," Darius whispered before Clarence took the phone.

"Katie, what happened to Mama Jeffries?" Clarence asked.

I explained what had happened with Mama and Georgie.

"Do you want me to fly in with the boys?" he asked.

"There's no need, Clarence. It's probably too late to get a ticket, anyway."

"I can try."

"Clarence, it will cost a small fortune to get a last minute flight from there to here."

"I'm sure I can get half from Bertie, if you would lend me the other half."

"I'm sorry, Clarence. I don't have any extra money to spare. Could you put the boys on the line?"

"You don't want to talk to me?"

"I have to get back to mama. Let me speak to the boys."

***

I hope to live a long, long time, but if old age means a dark bedroom with heavy furniture and pictures of my children and grandchildren covering every inch of free wall space, somebody, somewhere, rescue me. My mother's bedroom was a museum holding the antiquities and treasures of one family. Pictures of the family stared down at us. Crayon drawings from her grandchildren, dried flowers, those ugly clay bowls, ashtrays, and sculptures every Chicago student must make before leaving second grade. A huge, dark mahogany four poster bed occupied the majority of the room. More family mementos crowded the top of the oversized dresser. The armoire held a photo of Daddy leaning against our front stoop.

Daddy was right. Mama was strong. Five days after her heart attack, Mama was home and propped up on a massive amount of pillows. Mrs. Jordan took care of her during the day. I stayed with her at night. I was conciliatory, respectful, and careful not to provoke Mama into a relapse. She suspiciously eyed me. She sipped and sniffed the water like she was looking for telltale signs of arsenic. We moved around each other like hens pecking for the same grain.

"I want you out of here, Katie," she finally said one night.

"I'm just trying to help?" I snapped and then bit my lip.

Mama shook her head and closed her eyes, "You're biting your lip to keep from saying what's on your mind. I'd rather you go home."

"Katie," she said as I stormed toward her bedroom door. I turned and looked at her.

"The money your daddy left is still in the bank, except the little LaDell used to start his business. I was too afraid to touch it, Katie. Too afraid that I would have to return to the

Delta and to my mama's house. I didn't think I could make it without Alex, without our nest egg."

"Mama. . . ." I started.

"Don't," she said. "If you need anything, if you want to start that catering business, I'll help you."

I walked over to her and hugged her. She flinched. I vowed to hug her more.

CHAPTER 17

At the end of my work day, I stood in my office window and watched a windy and velvet night descend on Chicago. The lights from the office buildings and the street lights cast a hazy glow on North Wacker Drive. Rushing commuters clung to briefcases, purses, and shopping bags as the wind whipped around them. Cars, SUVs, taxis, and buses trudged like a chain of creepy crawlers, their red and white lights strung out like gems. Somewhere out there Georgie's "really nice guy" waited for me.

I removed the vest over my black rayon dress, and draped a lime green, white and black print scarf over my shoulders and down my back, sans Audrey Hepburn. I waltzed through a spray of Bulgari perfume. I snatched the ponytail holder out of my head. I ran a brush through my hair. It fell in waves over one eye. Finally, I slipped on a pair of black stilettos with lime green patent leather tips. Those suckers cramped but would cause the man to drool.

Like a lot of women, I wanted a dashing, charming man who had street smarts, sophistication, and enough sex appeal to cool my wanton body. A few bucks in his pockets would be a bonus. No where in that description were the words, "nice man." Georgie's emphasis on the words "nice man," created an image of a portly, stoic, dull man with bland features. He was probably a pompous buffoon of a man. I would be polite, friendly, and flirtatious. The man, however, would never lay a finger on my velvet skin.

I agreed to meet Noah Watts at a dimly lit restaurant that boasted of great seafood. My plan was to dive into my dill salmon while Mr. Pompous went on and on about himself. Later, I would call Georgie and say, "You know, Noah is a very nice man but he's not for me."

I arrived at the restaurant a little late to ensure that he was waiting for me. The White Swan dripped with ambiance: Chandeliers, Waterford crystal, linen, china, and a wait staff in black ties and cutaway. I knew Noah chose that restaurant to impress me. I agreed because it had the best seafood North of the Chicago River. I checked my coat and smoothed the dress over my curves. I strutted up to the maitre'd. A couple was ahead of me, so I took the opportunity to scan the restaurant. Only one black man sat at the tables clustered in the center of the room. And, yes, he was every bit as homely as I imagined. I walked past the couple.

"Madam," the maitre d' called.

"Mr. Watts is expecting me," I said to the maitre d'. "I see him."

I groaned as I neared the man's table. The man had a huge round face. His nappy gray hair was brushed back like porcupine quills. His tongue snaked out and licked his puffy lips. One of his triple D's feet stuck out in the aisle. *Oh, my goodness*, I thought. *A man with stinky feet.*

"A gentleman usually stands when a woman approaches the table," I said.

"I beg your pardon," he said in this pompous voice, looking me up and down tips of my stilettoes to my perfect hair.

"I'm Katie," I said and held out my hand.

A glint shown in his eyes as he rose from the table. I was forced to lean back and let my eyes scale that mountain of a man. My head barely reached his chest. My mouth remained closed but my eyes bucked as I stared up past his chest and into gray eyes. Why would Georgie toss me in a pot with a pompous giant?

"Wilbert! Wilbert! Who is this hoochie?" a squeaky voice hissed behind me.

I turned and faced a Minnie Mouse of a woman with wounded eyes. Her thin legs with knobby knees wallowed in her low heels. Her dress was a tab too ancient with big square pockets and an empress waist.

"Lovebug," the man said. "I don't know this . . . this woman."

"Excuse me?" I asked.

"How could you?" she cried, twisting the ring on her finger. "You're still fooling around!"

She did a girly toss and sent the ring flying over my head and into his chest. He fumbled to catch it. Lovebug hitched the straps of her purse on her shoulder, wheeled around and stomped off. Mortification crawled up my back. I was frozen to the spot. I didn't want to add to the scene. The man dug his wallet out and tossed a few bills on the table. Patrons at the surrounding tables gawked. Deep laughter resounded from one of the booths.

"Here's my card," the pompous man said. "Give me a call." He stuffed the card in my hand as he brushed passed me, a little too closely.

I shook my hand as if the vilest slime clung to it. The card fluttered to the floor. Deep laughter roared from a booth. I turned toward that laughter determined to hold my head high. A strikingly dark man sat in a booth diagonally from the table.

"Katie Coomers!" The man called and waved to me.

My mouth dropped. I marched over to him and leaned into his booth. "Are you Noah Watts?" I asked.

He nodded his head and laughed so hard he held his stomach. Embarrassed, I slipped into the booth opposite him and moved to the far corner. I covered my profile with one hand and glared at him. Tears streamed from his dark eyes and sparkled on his thick curly eyelashes.

"You heard me introduce myself and you said nothing," I hissed.

"I was studying the wine list," he lied. "You have to admit the situation was funny?" And with seriousness, he raised his voice several octaves and imitated the Minnie Mouse woman, "Wilbert, Wilbert, who is this hoochie woman?"

I lost it. I burst into laughter. Tears ran through my heavy mascara. But I could not stop. "And that pompous fool had the nerve to shove his card into my hand," I laughed.

"Ooow!" Noah said. "So, big man is a playa."

"Yewl!"

"Now, please, Miss Katie, smooth out your feathers, and let me order you something soothing to drink. You ever had Chai tea?"

"No," I said, fumbling in my purse for a tissue. I dabbed at my eyes as he ordered the tea from a young waiter that sneaked glances at me.

"Now you look like a raccoon," Noah tittered when the waiter walked away.

"I know you don't expect me to leave this booth to fix my face?"

"Well, Georgie did tell me to expect anything." He shrugged broad shoulders draped in a well-tailored gray jacket with a black turtleneck underneath.

"Uh-huh. And she said you were nice."

"And nice translates to pretentious?" he asked.

"Don't start with me." I shrugged my shoulders and held up my hands.

"Relax," he said. "Let's enjoy the meal. Tomorrow we can call Georgie and say it didn't work out."

He looked at me knowingly. I could feel the blood racing up my face. I studied his face, which was well-chiseled with laughing eyes and sensuous full lips. The man was a neat package ripe for the right woman. Or was he?

"So," I said, stuffing my purse between me and the wall, "why did Georgie feel the need to match you up?"

"You know the old story," he sighed. "Single man with two growing daughters, a home, a business, and no apparent woman hanging around. All the sisters in the neighborhood either hit on you or fix you up with their poor desperate relative."

"Thanks a lot!" I snorted.

"Present company excluded," he said. "Cause Miss Katie, in that dress, in those heels, the word desperate does not come to mind."

"Oh, I think Georgie must have the wrong impression of you," I said. "You are smoother than a shot of Cuevo Gold."

"A tequila drinker?"

"Only in the safety of my own home."

"I don't see you playing it safe."

We chatted like that throughout dinner. We pulled out pictures and talked about our children. We did not bring up our estranged spouses. His interest in books leaned toward Ishmael Reeds, Henry Louis Gates, Jr., and other intellects I prefer not to read. His taste in music, fusion jazz, so of course, my love for Etta James didn't wash with him. We volleyed words and tastes and laughter until the place was emptying out.

"Thank you," he said after his last bite of tiramisu. "It's been a great evening without expectations."

"Hmmm, and here I had great expectations of at least a marriage proposal," I laughed.

"You are whacked!"

"My family will agree with you."

"Tell me," he insisted. "Why did Georgie set you up with a blind date?"

"Oh, she's bent out of shape because I've dated a few men that I met on the Internet."

"What?" he asked.

I waved aside his skepticism as I finished my crème brulee with raspberry sauce. He leaned back against the booth and studied me.

"You do keep a person on their toes."

"Some folks don't understand the different between sleeping around and dating."

"There's a difference?"

"Forget it," I said. "I'm not getting into a morality debate. All I got to say is out of the twenty or thirty men I've dated from the web only two have come close to getting into my Victoria's Secrets. I sashayed over to this brother's house and discovered six rugrats running around. Lying sap sucker."

"Ouch!"

"He was searching for a mom, and I was not it."

"And the other guy?"

"He's from Atlanta. He plans these weekend excursions to meet and sleep."

"So let the man come up and get your groove on."

"Man, first, he has a woman. Second, he's white."

"So?" he asked.

"I've learned the hard way that he thinks of me only as a booty call."

"Damn, that's a long distance booty call."

I laughed, "Yeah, it is."

"Well, I can help you out," he said and looked at me with affected lust, shifting his eyebrows up and down, hanging his tongue out one side of his mouth, and panting.

I laughed. "You are absolutely crazy."

"Let's call it a night," he said.

And we did.

***

Once upon a time there lived a tall man with amazingly strong legs. This man could leap great distance through the air, twirl a large orange ball on his fingers, and send it dead center through a net, high above the ground. He maneuvered around trolls and ogres of other towns. So striking were his skills, so magical was his feats that whenever he appeared the townspeople shouted his name, *Air Jordan, Air Jordan.* As with all great men, Air could not accomplish these feats alone, he was part of an incredible team called Da Bulls. Now, there lived a poor, meek woman named Katie, whose one dream was to witness the miraculous feats of this team. Yet, no matter how she tried to plow through the crowd and claim a view, she was stunted at every turn. And so it came to pass that . . .

. . . Watts invited me to a Bulls' game. I do remember telling him my desire to be a court side mom and a player's groupie. Unfortunately, that dream lived during the reign of Da Bulls.

"What do you mean tickets to the Bulls game?" I asked over the phone that I held in place with my chin. I was rubbing thick, creamy foot balm into my ankles. Night cream covered my face, and my flannel pjs shielded my body from the night chill. A call from Noah was not on my beauty agenda.

"Courtside," Noah said.

"And you think I wanna go?"

"You love the Bulls."

"I loved Da BULLS, you know that team from the last millennium," I said. I slipped heavy cotton socks over my feet.

"Oh, you are a true Chicago Fan," he smirked.

"Sho, you're right," I said and walked on my heels to the bathroom. I turned on the hot water and sudsed my hands. "I'm a flaky Chicago fan. The Bears lose; I root for the Packers. The Sox lose; I'm one huge Red Sox fan. Since the Bulls left town, I'm for the Pacers."

"Come on, Coomers, if you don't go with me, I have to take my brother Edwin and he'll blow the whole game worrying about his wife having an attitude."

"Yeah, yeah," I said.

"Coomers, do a brother a favor."

"Man," I said as I washed the balm off my hand. "I thought you were strong. How did Georgie sucker you into asking me out a second time?"

"Woman, please," he said. "I got tickets to the game, and you like the Bulls. It's a buddy thing."

"Uh-huh," I said and held my mouth under the faucet.

"Katie, don't flatter yourself," he said. "I'm not interested in you as a woman."

"Geez, thanks," I said after I swished the water around my mouth and spit.

"What are you doing?" he asked. "Do I hear water running?"

"Yeah, I'm going through my beauty routine," I said.

He laughed, "So you putting on a lot of goo."

"Lots," I agreed.

"Coomers, I thought you were different."

"I'm just an average woman, Watts, trying to stay young."

"The game will keep you young," he said. "Be a sport. You know the game, you're not interested in me, and I'm not interested in you."

I laughed, "But, Watts, I'm used to filet mignon, why would I settle for round steak."

"Because," he said with seriousness, "there's nothing else in the house."

I laughed, "Okay, round steak it is."

***

I was unimpressed by the salesperson sitting on the other side of my desk. Mondays were awful days for sales presentations, there were too many crises to extinguish. Sales people schmoozed me with trinkets and tickets to benefits, dinner on them, theater tickets, all day spa passes, floral arrangements, snow globes, desk accessories, and cookie-bouquets, only because I had the final say on new equipment, temp agencies, training classes for the clerical staff, and locations for conferences and banquets. Some, like the salesman who sat on the other side of the desk, pitched their products like I was dim-witted and in need of their wisdom to decide what was best for the firm. He was immaculate, with perfect blond hair that waved back from a low brow. His jaws, nose and mouth extended from his head like the face of an angora goat. The man spoke rapidly, like an auctioneer.

"Here we have the zee kay four seven eight nine model, able to print out twenty pages in a minute, capable of switching from black ink to color ink. I can arrange for you to visit our show room for a full demonstration."

I jumped in before he could speak another word. I closed

the file folder and pushed it across to him. He was the last sales person of the day, and I was tired of the game.

"Listen, there's no sense in wasting your time or mine," I said and stood. "We want a machine that can produce, with minimum down time, at least thirty pages a minute. This is the top of your line and it does not begin to meet our needs."

I walked around the desk. His small goat eyes narrowed. He made a strange sound in his throat as he stood. I extended my hand. He reluctantly shook it and dropped it. Grabbing his folders and stuffing them into his briefcase, he followed me out of the office.

"You're making a tremendous error," the man said. "Our products are top of the line."

"We need speed," I said as I waved to one of the clerks. "Wendy, will show you out."

I stepped back into my office and closed the door. Yes, I was rude, but I was also tired; tired of toting a heavy briefcase crammed with paperwork back and forth; tired of shifting cubicles, offices, and computers from floor to floor; tired of temperamental administrative staff, lawyers, devious sales forces, lost documents, missed calls, working from seven to seven while munching on alfalfa and apples; and tired of a job that sapped the life from me. How I envied the clerical staff's nine to five work day, voluntary overtime, and the camaraderie between them. My position, one step from the company financial controller, separated me from the support staff. Once in the ladies room, while sitting on the toilet, I was privy to a conversation about me.

"She's a control freak," one of the women said. "Can you believe all office supply orders have to go through her?"

"She reviews the phone records," the other woman said.

"She's taking away internet access from the word processors."

Heat ran up my face. In short, I was embarrassed. I couldn't move off the toilet seat. I breathed softly, afraid of discovery.

"Next it will be the secretaries, then the admins," the first woman continued.

"The firm was a top rated organization before she came."

Was I ludicrous? Why was I hiding in a stall? I had done nothing wrong. I was the office manager, the guardian of the till, overseer of the workers bees, manager of equipment, controller of space, and yes, the empress of my domain. Was it not my duty, my obligation, my right as office manager to put fear in the support staff? Quietly, I finished my business, stood, and eased my clothes into place. They never heard the sounds but continued their dissertations on my ineptness. One woman summed it up right before I flushed the toilet.

"Bitch!"

The water in the toilet swerved. I opened the stall and joined them with a smile.

"Ladies."

Their eyes widened and their lips quivered as "the bitch" walked to the sink. They looked at each other then dropped their heads. They were too stunned to move. I smirked. I washed my hands, dried them slooooowly, touched my hair, and then strolled to the door.

"Ladies," I said. "If your mentality is representative of a top-rated firm, then bless the day "the bitch" came on board. At least she has taught you to check the stall before plunging into a gossip session."

With my office door firmly closed on the last salesperson of the day, I sat at my desk and stared out the window. Gray clouds hovered above the buildings. The wind was so strong that the window rattled. I was tired but was facing a mound of work. My position with the firm was going downhill. The more hours I invested in the firm, the more desirable catering looked. I could work my own hours. I could dip my hands in silky flour. But, could I sell without Donna's help? Did I need a business degree? Did I need marketing experience? Fear pumped those questions and more through me. The familiar beep of an instant message broke into my thoughts. I had downloaded AOL into my computer at the law firm. Sometimes the only time I could chat was at work.

AmaskIwear:	Come help us. QUICK. Here's the link.

I clicked the link and was whisked into the private room with AmaskIwear a.k.a. Dee, TTSGURL a.k.a. Josey, Vanity-Fair28 a.k.a. Nancy, Porky2love a.k.a. Lori. Carol, Mush-Mouth, seldom came online since she moved to Seattle.

SilkyDreamGirl:	What's going on here?
TTsGurl:	Talk to Lori. She's the one with the big plans.
VanityFair28:	It's Lori. She's meeting some guy at a coffee shop tonight and driving to the coast with him.
SilkyDreamGirl:	Have you met him before?
Porky2love:	No, Katie.
VanityFair28:	They are meeting at 11 pm.
SilkyDreamGirl:	What!?!
AmaskIwear:	Send Katie the pic of him.

Lori sent the picture and I opened it immediately. The women's concerns were justified. The man stood in the middle of a murky creek surrounded by dense, dark trees. The sleeves of his shirt were rolled up. His biceps were as big as my head, and that was big. He wore army fatigues and a cap pulled low over his eyes. His entire face was hidden in the shadows. His features were unclear. Although it was evident there was no sun, he had on dark shades. He had a hunting knife hooked on his left side and a gun strapped to his right thigh. He could have been any nationality.

VanityFair28:	His name is John
AmaskIwear:	Or Juan and she doesn't know his last name!
SilkyDreamGirl:	Do you have any information on him besides his screen name?
Porky4Love:	His parents are dead.
AmaskIwear:	You will be too if you go off with him.
Porky4Love:	You are trying to scare me.
VanityFair28:	You should be scared, Lori.
Porky4Love:	Katie dates and nobody makes a fuss about it.
SilkyDreamGirl:	Don't be silly. By the time I go out with a guy I know everything except his mother's maiden name.
AmaskIwear:	What about that woman from the east coast? She met some guy from online and next thing you know she's dead!
VanityFair28:	Or that other woman in Texas who got sliced up in her own home.
Porky4Love:	What about Katie?

We chatted too long, trying to convince Lori not to meet John, Sean, whatever his name. She finally typed: *It's my life.* She signed off without saying goodbye. If all the world was a stage, why was my life vaudeville? Why did I accumulate the bizarre? Once my online chats provided intermissions, breaks from my continuous flux of trouble. I didn't want to worry about a stranger's craziness. I didn't need the drama. Nevertheless, all that week, I monitored the comings and going of the girls. Lori never signed on.

I moved around my tiny office from the crammed steel file cabinets to my overloaded desk, working on automatic pilot while my imagination grew wilder with each passing moment. I imagined the caw of vultures and the howling of carnivorous animals. I imagined Lori's pale mangled body floating like an oversize buoy in a dark, murky river. Her blues eyes, glossy in death, were fixed on a blinding white sun. Somewhere in my daze, in my daydream of death, came a low hum, a mourning song. I heard Mama Jeffries' church choir singing and I heard somebody wailing *Poor Lori*. At one point I imagined James Weldon Johnson leaning toward me and preaching:

Go down death, down to Texas and bore Sister Lori home.

Every time someone entered my office, I jumped. At one point, I closed my office door to eliminate surprise entrances. Yet, with every rap-rap on the steel door, I leaped-startled out of my musings. Every time the telephone rang, I was startled out of morbid visions of a dead Lori. So, it was when Watts called. I snatched the phone off the hook.

"Katie Coomers," I answered.

"I don't like your name," Noah said without any preliminaries.

"What?" I snapped.

"Katie Coomers sounds like a bad case of parasite infestation."

"Oh, I am enchanted," I said and shut down AOL. I started the add/remove program on the computer and deleted AOL.

"Next time you choose a mate, try one with a simple name like Jones or Johnson."

"Noah, you called to discuss my name?"

"No, I called to invite you to join me for a movie," he said. "I want to see *The Best Man*, but I hear it's not the type of movie to see with a spouse-seeking woman."

"And so you're asking me?"

"Damn skippy!" he exclaimed. "We understand each other."

"Uh-huh."

"And it's Dutch," he continued. "You pay your own way. Buy your own popcorn, pop, and JuJu Drops."

"Oh, I see."

"And to make sure there's no misunderstanding," he continued, "I won't take you home. I'll slam your butt into a taxi and say adios."

"Oh, you are so charming me into a yes, Noah."

"Okay, Saturday night at the Burnham Plaza."

"Yeah, yeah," I laughed. "I'm due for a movie. I haven't been to one since The Prince of Egypt."

"Wow, maybe a R rating movie is too strong for you."

"Good-bye, Noah," I said.

The rest of the week I exchanged email with the girls regarding Lori's disappearance. However, I didn't sign on to chat. I didn't want to worry. I didn't want to feel helpless. Yet, visions of Lori's face, twisted in grimaces of pain, danced through my mind. I imagined that her broken body was squashed in a small dank space. What a relief it was to finally receive email from her.

Subj: **Porky2Love**
From: Lori0923880
To: Amasklwear, MushMouth, SilkyDreamGirl, TTsGurl, VanityFair28
Please don't worry about me. I'm okay. I did not meet John. Instead I went over to my brother's place. He is awesome. He says he didn't know I was lonely. We are spending a lot of time together. He's helping me prioritize my life. He's encouraging me to become more

involved with our community. I did tell you he was a local council man, right? Thanks for being there when I needed friends, but I'm going to try reality for a while.

Reality, Lori had written. My reality was a dime novel, a melodrama with Mama and all my ex-husbands as the villains and me as the damsel in distress. The plot was my quest for a hero. Lori had the right idea. I deleted AOL from my office computer. It was time I dealt with reality.

***

Saturday, I took the rumbling el to Jackson and State and made a short stop at Garrett's Popcorn shop. As usual, the shop was packed with customer craving their world famous caramel and cheese mix. I bought a mini-mix, grabbed a wad of napkins, and stuffed everything under my makeup kit in my shoulder bag. Walking through the South Loop Area is not too dangerous on Michigan Avenue or Street, or in the summer time. In the late fall and winter, when the temperature drops and dark comes early, the area is a little spooky. Many of the buildings were vintage industrial buildings. Some were empty or going through renovations. I decided to hop a cab to Burnham Plaza which lay just at the edge of South Loop and the beginning of the Near South Side. Noah was not in sight. We had agreed to meet at the concession stand, so I bought a ticket and rode the escalator up to the second floor. Noah stood at the concession stand with a tub of popcorn the size of a small wash bucket, a large Twix bar, a hot dog, a half gallon jug of pop, and, I swear, a Hostess Ding Dong was sticking out of his jacket pocket.

"Katie Coomers, You're late," he greeted me.

"You're greedy," I said. "Why didn't you eat dinner?"

"I did," he said.

I shook my head and walked passed him. I caught a whiff

of his cologne and stopped myself from hungrily sniffing his body. Again, I was conscious of his well-defined body, and his blemish free dark skin. Honey, it's seldom that you see a man as creamy as chocolate frosting.

"Are you buying popcorn?" he asked.

"Man, I came to see a movie, not to have an indoor picnic."

"Don't stick your hand in my bucket," he warned.

After the lights were dimmed and the preview had started, I dug the mini-mix out of my purse. The popcorn was still hot. The sweet aroma of caramel rose from the bag. I stuffed a handful into my mouth and munched loudly. He sniffed.

"Is that a cheese and caramel mix?" he whispered.

I nodded.

"Are you gonna share?" he asked.

"No way," I said and shook my head.

"Aight," he said. "You're gonna get thirsty."

He took a big slurp of his pop. I ignored him and stuffed another handful of the mini-mix into my mouth. The combination of salt and sugar played with my tongue, satisfying and teasing it. It was ecstasy to indulge my craving after weeks of counting calories, but, the more I ate, the more I wanted. I was in Paradise with fine brothers on the screen, mini-mix in my mouth, and a man who wanted nothing more from me than company. Noah slurped, belched, and talked through half the movie.

"Why do women swoon over him?" he asked about Taye Diggs.

"The body, the face, the voice . . ." I whispered.

"You too, Coomers?"

"There are only two young brothers I hanker for," I whispered.

"Who's the second one?"

"Shemar Moore."

"I would figure you for a Denzel girl."

"Please, the man is settled," I whispered. "There's no thrill in his game."

"So, he's not exciting because he's settled?"

"I don't hanker over married men," I hissed.

"You're sick," he said.

Somebody shushed us before I could reply. By the time the movie was over, I was as thirsty as parched ground. I shoved my way through the crowd, ran to the concession stand, and actually managed to butt my way in line. I bought a large Seven-Up and sucked half of it down before I rejoined Noah at the top of the escalator. He laughed as we rode down.

"You should have shared," he said.

"No!" I barked and sucked the rest of the pop down.

Outside it was raining. People squealed and ran toward the parking garage or stood in the shelter of the theater. Noah pulled me through the crowd.

"Come on," he said. "I'll give you a ride home."

"No," I said and shoved my empty cup into his hand. I ran to the curb as a yellow cab cruised toward the theater.

"Woman!" Noah called.

"Taxi," I yelled and held up my hand.

"Adios, Watts," I said and climbed in.

Noah and I bummed around like pals. A couple of Bulls games, a scary movie, and once, bowling. He yakked about his plumbing business, his employees, his daughters, and his only brother who was married to a pretentious and controlling woman. Trust me, that's a story in itself. Although I freely discussed my Internet life, the rest of my story was tucked safely in a vault.

"Girl, you're dangerous," he said once after I gave a nonchalant answer about Clarence.

We were sitting in Gold Coasts Dog. I had a craving for cheddar fries. I had decided that a once a week treat would not hurt my weight. So I agreed to meet Noah there for lunch. Gold Coasts Dog was one of those downtown stands that offered a gourmet hot dog with the works for triple the price at a neighborhood joint. The place was packed with yuppies in designer suits and staid dresses. I had on a great Armani suit that I bought at the Crowded Closet, a resale shop in Evanston. Noah had on gray work clothes but the brother looked spiffier than all those executives in their Brooke's Brothers suits and ties.

"Why do you think I'm dangerous?" I asked. I licked cheese from my lips.

"Women talk, but not you" he said and bit into a thick double cheeseburger.

"Watts, we've had some very interesting conversations," I said.

"What happened between you and your husband?" he asked.

"He left."

"Why?"

"Ask him."

He shook his head, "Katie, I pity any man who falls for you."

"Yeah, yeah." I said. "At least I'm not as silly as those skanks you date."

"How's that?" He reached for one of my fries and I slapped his hand.

"Didn't you tell me you never bring them around your daughters?"

"That's just a matter of respect for my girls."

"Right but you can lay up in those women's beds with their children in the next room."

"I always offer to pay for a motel."

"You are a sleaze!"

"Beside it's not as many women as you think."

"Hey, I'm just your buddy," I said. "You owe me no explanations."

He laughed and grabbed a fry.

CHAPTER 18

"It's not going to happen," Darius said over the phone.

"Yes, it is," CJ said on the extension. "All the computers in the world are gonna crash. Right, mom?"

Outside my apartment, hard sheets of rain fell. Inside, steam hissed from the radiator, Curtis Mayfield crooned from the stereo, and the boys argued over the phone. I nibbled on alfalfa sprouts, provolone cheese, and red onions between slices of zucchini bread. A cluster of grapes and a bottle of spring water rounded out my meal. Longingly, I fingered *La Belle Cuisine*, a cookbook that read like a story. My job had me dreaming of baking cakes and cooking special meals. I shoved the book into the paperwork that covered the table. The novelty of my job had worn down to an irritating pebble. Thanksgiving was a few weeks away. I was anxious to hold the boys in my arms, to smother them with affection, and to be a mom again.

"Listen," I said to the boys. "Don't worry about Y2K."

"What if it's the end of the world?" CJ asked.

"Well, that will be that," Darius said.

I laughed. I was happy that Alexander Graham Bell had the vision to send sound through a tiny wire. "It's gonna be wonderful having you here for Thanksgiving," I gushed.

The boys said nothing. Their breathing wasted an entire five-cents-a-minute. Silent disappointment shrieked across the wire. A sob caught in Darius's throat.

"What wrong?" I asked.

"Dad said we can't come home for Thanksgiving," CJ whispered.

"What?" I asked.

"He said he can't afford to send us," Darius whispered.

"Put your dad on the phone," I said.

"Mom," CJ whispered, "he doesn't have any money for the tickets. Some men came in a truck and took all the furniture away. He and Raquel fight all the time."

"I'll pay for the tickets," I said.

"We told him that," Darius whimpered. "He said we were not going and that was that."

From the stereo in the living room, Curtis Mayfield encouraged me to *Keep on Pushing*, and, right then, I wanted to push my hands through the receiver, across three thousand miles of fiber optics and snatch Clarence's lying tongue out of his mouth.

"Put him on the phone," I said with controlled calm.

I toyed with a crust of bread while I waited for the fart-butt jerk to come to the phone. My temple throbbed. My mouth puckered. The words *Kill, Kill, Kill* flashed before my eyes like a neon light. "What's up, Kay Jay?" Clarence finally answered the phone.

"I want the boys here for Thanksgiving," I stated calmly. "I'll buy their airline tickets."

"This is not a good time to talk about that," he said.

"Why not?" I hissed. "You said I could have the boys for Thanksgiving."

"Things change," he said.

"What kinda things, Clarence?" I asked.

"Raquel is trying to get close to the boys."

"And?" I asked.

I stood and walked to the back door. The lights from the other building cast a ghostly glow through the thick rain. I cracked the door. The cold wind whipped through my kitchen. I shivered. Clarence was silent, breathing deeply in my ear like a telephone pervert.

"Clarence," I said. "I will see the boys at Thanksgiving."

"It's not a good time," he said.

"Clarence, you are a certifiable asshole!" I shouted. "Why are you forcing that baby girl on my boys?"

"She's not a baby girl," he said in a cocky voice. "She's just a little insecure now."

"Uh huh," I sneered. "She can stay insecure. They don't like her and they won't accept her, ever."

"Not if you drag them to Chicago for Thanksgiving. You are not being fair."

"They are coming home for Thanksgiving, Clarence!" I screamed into the receiver.

"They are home, Katie," he said and hung up.

His words hit a core. Suddenly, I felt like an impotent man must feel. Frustrated, bewildered, angry, and helpless. I wanted satisfaction but had no way of getting it. I pushed my low-calorie meal away. I felt tears itching to break forth. I've spent months, years struggling with bills, struggling to provide for Darius and CJ. How could a man watch you hold a child, love a child, protect a child, then steal that child from you? How could he do it twice? I trembled with rage. My head twitched. My legs were weak. Now, it was all clear. I had been nothing, nothing to Clarence. Would I never see the boys again? Heat spread across my face. I understood rage at that moment. I understood crimes of passion because as surely as my name was Katie Jeffries Cannon Smith Robinson Coomers, I wanted my hands on his throat. I wanted to be like those dangerous 1940's women who carried ice picks and straight edge razors. No man dared messed over them. Nice girl. Sweet person. Pollyanna. Who gives a rat's tail about those good girl titles? My life, when I examined it, was a hodgepodge of bad judgment, impulsive decisions, and trying to please everyone but Katie Jeffries. I'd done what I thought I had to do, every step of the way. Yet there I was Impotent! Impotent! I was miserable and powerless. I crawled to bed.

The next day was my first Saturday off in two weeks. Powerlessness and rage forced me into the kitchen. I whipped up a lemon meringue cake, using silky cake flour, extra large eggs, butter, sugar, lemon juice, lemon peel, and a couple of ingredients to make the cake light and fluffy. The cake was high, loaded with filling, and covered with a meringue frosting. All I wanted was to sink my teeth into something sweet and tart, and to plot. The cake cooled on the counter. The filling chilled in the refrigerator, and the frosting waited in the stainless steel bowl. In my head, cobwebs dropped from the rusty parts of my brain. Slowly, painfully, the cogwheels turned. Why should I be nice? Why should I let Clarence get away with so much crap? If I didn't pop something in my mouth soon, I would scream. I sliced a big hunk and poured a mug of milk. Eat, drink and be merry, lest I die of heartbreak, lest I crack up in tears, lest I . . . the ringing phone saved me.

"Katie Coomers," I snapped.

"Hey, woman. Lighten up. You're not at work. It's Saturday," Noah said.

"What can I do for you?" I barked.

"Are you all right?" he asked.

I was silent. I looked at the beautiful cake on the table. I was not one to wear my emotions like a wide-brim hat.

"Katie, privacy is one thing," Noah said. "But it's dangerous to hold things inside, to let your past dictate your life."

"What do you want me to say?" I asked.

"If you have to ask that question, then we're not on the same wavelength," he said. "What's your address?"

"Why?"

"I'm coming over," he said.

"No. I'm not one of your skanks!"

"No, I consider you a friend," he said tenderly. "You are wacky, Katie. We both know that. But woman, there's more going on inside your head than you show. You've got barriers up. You've got anger waiting to explode. Bitterness is ruling your life. I feel it through the phone."

I tsked like Mrs. Anderson and Donna.

"You know, brothers like me always have to clean up other men's garbage. Good women like you, Katie Coomers, always overlook men like me. You don't wanna talk to me. Cool. I know that your fancy law firm has mental health benefits. If you don't talk to me, if there's nobody else in your life you can talk to, use your benefits and get some help, girl. You're too fine a woman to lose it."

"Yeah, yeah," I said. "I really want you to stop trying to get in my head."

"Katie, promise you'll talk to someone," Noah whispered.

I was sobbing, quietly sobbing. What I didn't need was another man trying to tell me what to think, how to think.

What I didn't need was a man with little respect for women telling me I was sick. I didn't need that lemon meringue cake, excess baggage, Clarence Coomers.

"Good-bye, Katie," he quietly said and hung up the phone. My one offline buddy was gone.

After two weeks, I ache for my buddy. In three weeks, I resigned myself to another lost friendship. Still I had questions for Watts. *Tell me, Watts,* I whispered to my journal, *will therapy make me debt free? Will therapy give me sweet revenge? Most important, will therapy bring my boys home?* Thanksgiving was a breath a way, and I had not heard from Watts. During that time, I analyzed everything in my life and found that the footpath to my future had weeds and thistles. To move forward, I had to clear the path. To clear the path, I had to make decisions. The decisions I made were painful. The first decision was a call to Clarence.

"You're right, Clarence," were the first words out of my mouth. "I haven't been fair. I'm sorry I yelled at you."

I sighed, audibly sighed. Clarence spun the merry-go-round and I was off like a wooden horse. I opened the back-door and the rain whipped around me. I could cry like the sky or I could blow like the wind. I was playing the same old game with Clarence, and he was controlling the board.

"You don't know what I'm facing here," Clarence said.

"You probably have a lot on your plate with the boys demanding so much time. Then, there's Raquel's insecurity and did your, ah, business venture work out."

"No," he sighed. "Bertie isn't charging me rent, but she wants me to work in one of her yogurt shops."

"Oh?"

"Can you see me dishing up frozen yogurt?" he asked.

I laughed good-naturally, "No, Clarence. I can't."

"You understand me, so well, Kay-Jay," he said.

"Yes, I do," I whispered almost sexually. "You know,

honey, maybe coming at Christmas would be best for the
boys. That will give you and Raquel two weeks of privacy."

"Are you serious?" he asked.

"Uh-huh."

"Katie, you are a good woman."

"Thank you," I said sarcastically.

"I didn't realize what I had until it was gone," he said.

I heard the regret in Clarence's voice. I quickly asked to
speak to the boys so I could explain the new arrangement.
The boys willingly exchanged the Thanksgiving weekend
trip for a Christmas visit. I hung up without speaking to
Clarence again. Women are from Venus. Men are from a
loony bin. I laid the phone in the window and walked out
the backdoor. The Crisp autumn wind whipped the cold
rain around me, drenched me, cleansed me. The ghostly
glow from the porch light illuminated the bricks and concrete that surrounded me. The next apartment building
pressed against mine. A tall dark tenement sat beyond that.
I thought about the spaciousness of Clarence's house. I
thought about LaDell's big backyard with the blue patio
furniture. I thought about my boys so far away. I dreamed
dreams.

My brain ticked with ideas as I cleared the table, showered, then prepared for the next day. Liquidation became
the key word. Mama Verna's jewelry and the house in
Englewood had to go. I went online and researched the
Chicago real estate market. From the North Side to the
West Side to the South Side, communities boasted a healthy
real estate market as renovation swept through one dying
area after another. Chicagoans were falling in love with their
city again. Money poured into Rogers Park on the North
Side, Homan Square on the West Side, and Burnham Park
and Logan Square on the near northwest side. Even Wood-
lawn on the South Side, once home to the Blackstone

Rangers, shucked off its decay and neglect. Englewood, alone, seemed immune to the love fest. Property in Englewood was not selling. That heart wrenching data changed liquidation into salvage. I had to salvage what I could from Mr. Pete's property. I had to savage my sanity. I refused to be impotent. I refused.

***

I seldom visited Mr. Pete's property. The Gordons were great tenants. He was a security guard and she worked at a candy shop. Over the years we had reached a mutual understanding: They mailed the rent less the cost of any minor repairs to the house. When I pulled up in front of the house, the Gordons' love for the property greeted me. Small evergreen hedges barricaded the well-manicured lawn from the cracked sidewalk. New blue shutters framed the windows of the house. A swirly white wrought iron security door protected the house. I ticked off the monthly deductions: the lamp post in the yard, the awning over the door, the brass mail box, and the new drainage pipe. The old drab house had morphed into a cute Georgian bungalow.

"Katie?" Tina Gordon answered the door. She was a short woman, about five feet, if that. I towered over her at five feet four inches. "What are you doing here?"

"Is Curtis home?" I asked. "I need to talk to both of you."

"Come in," she said. "Rest your coat."

I stepped inside and she closed the door behind me. I slipped out of my coat and handed it to her. She hung it on a coat rack by the door and then led the way into the living room. Curtis, a tall lumbering man, stood when we entered the room. I leaned back and looked into his crossed eyes. He smiled and showed his crooked teeth.

"Have a seat," Tina said and pointed to a cream brocade love seat. Light brocade furniture exposed the couple's childless status.

During my reign as Mrs. Smith the walls had been a dingy gray, a color as old as Mr. Pete. The Gordons had poured love into that dingy place and transformed it into marital paradise. There was a sharp twist in my heart when I saw their handiwork: window treatments, hand stencil borders around the ceiling, and flower arrangements. The walls were painted a soft cream.

I sat on the love seat. Curtis reclaimed his large arm chair. His feet sprawled before him. Tina sat on the arm of the chair and leaned against him. He grabbed her hand and comfortingly squeezed it.

"I have really enjoyed having you as tenants over the years. The care and upkeep you've put into this property have not only preserved the value of it but also increased it. The problem is I need a place for myself."

"You want to move here?" Tina asked. Her voice quivered. She clutched her husband's hand. A lump formed in my throat as I witnessed the sweet tenderness they expressed toward each other after twelve years of marriage. I wished desperately for another solution to my problems. There was none.

"No, no," I said and threw up my hand. "My plans are to sell this house and buy out in the suburbs. I wanted to let you know before I contact a real estate agent. I didn't want you to come home and see a for-sale sign hammered in the yard."

"We understand," Curtis said. "In fact, we've been looking for a place ourselves. We've been preapproved by Southland Bank. Unfortunately, everything on the market is beyond our limit."

"I know that problem," I said. "When I look in the papers, I shudder."

"How much are you asking for this house?" Tina asked.

I told them my asking price. They looked at each other

then turned to me with beaming faces. "We'll take it," they said simultaneously.

***

I arranged to help Mama and Georgie bake pies for Thanksgiving. I also told them that I had an important announcement to make. First, I bundled Mama Verna's jewelry up and carted it to a quaint antique shop in Evanston. The antique shop sat on Dempster Avenue, a quaint shopping area where the hassle of crowds and unconcerned sales clerks were missing. On Dempster, many one of a kind shops, like that antique store, boasted of the old-fashioned personalized service. That's a good description of for Evanston, old-fashioned with a modern flair.

Inside the store, a rosy hue radiated from the 1908 Steiff red mohair bear, a rose patterned couch, ruby-red stem ware, and other trinkets. Although the dim lighting cast a dusky shadow over everything, the items sparkled with cleanliness. The shopkeeper, a small wiry man with round silver spectacles, stood beside a glass counter. Everything about the shopkeeper was gray, his hush-puppies, slacks, sweater, moustache, and his curly hair. Even the irises of his eyes had a soft gray film. He had a kind smile that revealed the straight line of dentures. When he spoke, his teeth clicked.

"May I help you?" he asked.

"I have jewelry to sell," I said. I set my bundle on the counter and unwrapped it. I unrolled the bundle and Mama Verna's gems sparkled under the dim light of a Tiffany lamp. Colorful baubles encrusted heavy white gold. He squinted his eye around a jeweler's lupe and lifted the emerald ring. Four curves of forty diamonds swirled around a stunning bright green center stone. His tongue touched the corner of his lip so quickly that at first I thought I had imagined it, but a tiny wet spot revealed his hunger for the ring. He picked up a flower motif band set with diamonds. That time I heard a tiny coo in his throat. He set the second ring by the first and picked up an antique sapphire bracelet. My brain whirred and clicked like an adding machine. Just maybe, the money I receive from selling the jewelry might redeem me. He picked up a ruby brooch, examined it, and put it aside. Like a Las Vegas dealer he shuffled through the remaining pieces until there were two piles.

"These are no good," he shrugged, "cut glass."

"What?" I asked. He stunned me. Mama Verna's jewels had been the very foundation of my feud with Mama.

"You take them to another dealer and he will tell you same thing."

"But the pieces are old," I said.

He shook his head and shoved the pieces aside.

"What about these," I asked and pointed to the pieces that he had set aside.

"These are very good pieces. This is a Colombia emerald ring, about four carats. This is too rich for my shop. You need to take it to Eduardo's Chest in Kenilworth. They will pay what it is worth. I can give you a good price for these."

He lifted the diamond ring and turned it over. The ring sparkled under the Tiffany lamp. "This is also good. I can give you about seventeen hundred for this and for the bracelet, three thousand."

I thanked him and returned all the pieces in the bundle. The clerk at Eduardo's was not as friendly or helpful. He appraised the bracelet and motif diamond ring for much less. After examining the ruby brooch, he looked down his long elephant trunk of a nose and shook his head. He dropped the brooch, wiggled his fingers like he was shaking off bugs and sneered.

"These are absolutely worthless," he said. He picked up the emerald ring and bared his wolf teeth as he examined it through his lupe. "We need your proof of ownership to purchase the other items."

I snatched the emerald out of his hand, bundled the pieces up, and returned to Evanston. I sold the bracelet and diamond motif ring to the gray man. The emerald ring, I slipped on my finger. The fake jewelry stayed in its bundle.

The drive from Evanston to Country Club Hills canvassed Chicago from the rich and famous Streetersville to the poor and infamous projects along State Street and finally, the distant southern suburbs on I-57. I practiced my speech during the hour and a half drive to LaDell and Georgie's. I planned to break all my news in one breath.

"I know you guys don't approve of me, but I have to do what's right for me," I would say. "I'm selling Mr. Pete's house. I'm divorcing Clarence and starting a catering business."

By the time I parked my car all my well-rehearsed words jumbled in my mind. Terrence and Shanna rushed out the door and past me with a *Hi, Aunt Katie.* The soothing aroma of cinnamon, cloves, and nutmeg permeated the air. Mama stood at the kitchen island with her back to the door and sink. She moved a paring knife around the apple in hand. A perfect curl fell from the knife. On the counter to her left was a beautiful Blue Willow bowl filled with granny smith apples. To the right of her, was a stainless steel bowl of pared and sliced apples. Georgie stood at the stove, slowing stirring the contents of a large pot. Winter sunlight slipped through the sliding glass doors, across the kitchen table where LaDell sat with sandwiches, chips, and a Pepsi. With one hand he held a sandwich and with the other hand he rocked the white bassinet at his knee.

"Late," Mama greeted me.

"We've been waiting for you to make the pie crust," Georgie said.

"I had to take care of some business," I said and walked over to table.

In the bassinet, Regina Kay wiggled and reached for the mobile above her. I set my purse on the table, slipped out of my coat, and threw it over the back of the chair.

"There's a coat rack," LaDell said. He stopped rocking the bassinet long enough to take a swig from his Pepsi.

"What kinda business you had to take care of on a Saturday?" Mama asked.

"How long has the mincemeat been cooking?" I asked Georgie and ignored Mama.

"About twenty minutes," Georgie said.

I walked to the stove and took the wooden spoon from her. Apples, dark raisins, and pecans were bubbling in rich brown liquid as deep and thick as molasses. I stirred a couple of times and turned off the fire.

"Well?" Mama asked.

"This is done," I said and moved the pot to a back burner.

"Sis, come on with the big announcement, so I can watch the game," LaDell urged.

"I've agreed to sell Mr. Pete's house to the Gordons and . . ."

"We've already heard that news," Mama interrupted. "You should have told us first."

"Mrs. Anderson told Mama a week ago, and Mama has been fuming ever since," LaDell said.

"Ain't fuming!" Mama snapped.

"Yeah, everybody in the old hood is buzzing about it," Georgie said as she moved to the sink. "Some old timers like Pat Anderson are talking about you like a dog."

"Mrs. Anderson will always hate my guts," I said.

"True," LaDell said.

"Mama," Georgie turned and placed her hand on Mama's back and rubbed softly, "Katie's here now. Let's listen."

They looked at me expectantly. I walked to the bassinet and picked up Regina Kay. I sniffed the sweet scent under her neck.

"Katie . . ." LaDell began.

"I'm moving . . ." I interrupted.

"To California?" Mama eyes widened and she clutched her heart.

"No ma'am," I said and sat on my jacket. "I want to find a house in the suburbs."

Georgie stopped rubbing Mama's back, walked around the island and sat on a stool.

"You in the suburbs," LaDell laughed and brushed crumbs from his mouth. His wide eyes lifted and he rolled them back and forth.

"It's not for me. It's for the boys," I said. "You know they're coming for Christmas vacation."

"Yeah," he said and leaned back.

I had everyone's undivided attention. Mama's hand covered the knife on the counter. Georgie folded her arms. Regina Kay wiggled against me and clawed my face.

"I don't intend to let them go back."

"Katie!" Mama said.

"Why should I?"

"So you are taking Clarence back?" LaDell questioned me like I was certifiably insane.

"I want my boys," I said and propped Regina Kay in the crook of my arm. "I let Mama have Alex. I have regretted that. You did a wonderful job, Mama, but I should have raised my own son. Do you know how many times I've thought how different my life would have been if only . . ."

"No ifs, Katie," Georgie interrupted. "You made decisions

based on what you knew at the time. Good or bad, don't live with regrets."

I pressed Regina Kay against me. "I want this now," I said and looked directly at Georgie. "I want my family, Alex, the boys, Mama, LaDell, you and your knuckle head kids."

"Why my children gotta be all that," Georgie laughed and threw up her hands.

"I want the warm fuzzy feeling of holidays," I said.

"So, what about Clarence?" LaDell asked.

"I'm divorcing him."

"You think the man will just hand over his sons?" LaDell asked. His full lips thinned into a disapproving sneer.

"It doesn't matter," I said. "One of the firm's lawyers has agreed to take my case. He says I have a seventy percent chance of winning custody. I'm going for it."

"And?" LaDell asked. He tipped his head to the side and slanted his eyes toward me.

"What?" I asked. His tone and his attitude puzzled me.

"You got that big old rock on your finger," he said. "Are you getting married again?"

"Goodness!" Mama exclaimed.

"Are you crazy? This was Mama Verna's ring," I said.

I told them about my morning with the antique shop and the jewelry store. During my narration, I placed Regina Kay in the bassinet and opened my purse. I plopped the bundled on the table and opened it. Mama burst out laughing. She walked over to the table and picked up the clump of fake jewelry. She was laughing so hard that tears ran down her face. LaDell and Georgie looked from her to me.

"You a silly girl," Mama said. "Of course it's worthless. There were only four real pieces in the pile. You think Verna would have you, Regina and Donna playing dress up in real jewelry?"

"After she died Mr. Pete said that she wanted me to have all her jewels. I thought it was real."

"All this time, you've been angry about fake stuff," LaDell said.

"Who? Me?" Mama asked. "Pat was the one kicking up the fuss. Verna told us that she was leaving it for a special girl. Pat thought she meant Donna."

"LaDell, if I get that crazy when I'm old, please lock me away," Georgie said and we all laughed.

"So, where are you moving?" Mama asked and wiped her eyes.

"I don't know," I said and wiped my eyes. "The Gordons and I are closing on the tenth. The boys will be here on the seventeenth. But I can't buy a house until I divorce Clarence. So I guess it will be about three months before I can look."

"Sis," LaDell said and pushed his empty saucer away. "Imma help you out. I'm working on a project for a guy who rents houses with the option to buy. I think this house is perfect for you. Would you like to see it?"

"Where is it?" I asked.

"About ten minutes away," he said and stood.

"Are you talking about the house on Ravisloe Terrace?" Georgie asked.

"Yeah."

"Katie, we can shop together. You can teach me how to bake cakes. You can keep Regina Kay on the weekends," George said.

Mama gave me a crooked smile and said, "It'll be good to have the boys back. You're doing the right thing."

***

As LaDell said, the drive to the house on Ravisloe was less than ten minutes away. A dismal yellow brick bungalow stared at us with empty windows. The drainpipe clapped against a corner of the house. Paint peeled away from loose shutters. The broken steps led to a rusty screen door. I didn't feel any love standing in the front yard. The sidewalk was cracked. Broken glass and trash littered the yard.

"Don't judge the cover," LaDell said.

He helped Mama up the broken steps and unlocked the door. We entered the house and he flipped on the lights. What horror chambers! Bits of tattered carpet covered the water-washed gray hardwood floor in both the red living room and blue dining room. A splintered window seat was underneath a large bay window. Some visionary had trimmed the ceilings with borders of pale green ivy In one corner were four five-gallon cans of paint, canvas drop cloths, brushes, pans, extension rods, and a step ladder. A carpenter's horse and various electric tools occupied the dining room.

"Remember, the owner only handles the basics," LaDell said. "You won't find anything fancy here. We've finished the upstairs. There are four bedrooms, a master bathroom, and a regular bathroom."

"That's good, right?" Mama asked. "If he doesn't put a lot of money into it, the asking price won't be ridiculously high, right?"

"Right, Mama," LaDell said. "Once you buy the house, Katie, I can make it your dream home."

I smiled and squeezed his arm. We walked past the equipment through the dining room and into a country kitchen. I was love struck. Light shone through a block-glass wall on one side and sliding doors facing a huge backyard with a birdbath in the center. In the northwest corner, a huge tree shaded the yard. In my dreams, I saw the boys running around. I stepped out onto the concrete patio and knew I was home. I turned and the expression on Mama's face confirmed it.

"Katie, this kitchen is huge," she said. "Look at the counter space."

"I could start my catering business here," I said without thinking. I had not shared that bit of news with my family yet.

LaDell and Mama looked at each other. Mama closed her eyes, placed three fingers against her temple and massaged the shock away. I walked past them and surveyed the kitchen. Cabinets lined the other two walls. A door in a corner revealed a pantry. The stove and the refrigerator were old. Eventually, I would have to replace them. Old-fashioned white linoleum with green diamonds covered the floor. The kitchen needed a butcher block island to diminish the size. "Are you serious about catering?" LaDell asked.

"Yeah," I said. "I'm never gonna write a book. Those half-finished canvases in Mama's basement are taking up space. I hate my job. The only thing I do well and enjoy is cooking."

"But you eat so much!" Mama exclaimed.

"Mama!" LaDell stopped her.

"I was miserable, Mama," I assured her. "I'm not miserable anymore."

"So, you're quitting your job?" Mama asked.

"Not yet, Mama. I have to get custody of the boys, get a divorce, buy a home, and have my ducks in a row."

"Katie, you are full of surprises," LaDell said.

"Are you and Donna going into this catering business together?" she asked.

"Donna and I are finished, Mama," I smiled and turned to LaDell. "I want to see the upstairs. If those rooms are as charming as the kitchen, we'll have to put this notion in motion, quickly."

"Sis, I know you gonna love it," LaDell said.

"Lord, to have my child settle," Mama prayed.

"Let's do it," I said.

***

It was the first of December. I needed more time, but I had no time. I bought round trip tickets for the boys. I signed the lease/option agreement with the owner of the house. I called Illinois Bell, ComEd, and People's Gas. LaDell and his crew put in long hours to finish the house. It was the fifth of the month, and the movers and I shook hands. Time, that dirty alley cat, plaintively meowed my days away. It was the sixteenth of month, and I was moving. My small bungalow with pale cream walls bulged with folks. After the movers dumped my belongings in the house, Tameka, Terrence, Shanna, Georgie, LaDell, Mama and I rushed about to put it all in order before the boys' arrival.

That night, my family and Tameka sat around my new butcher block table, under gleaning pots and pan. In spite of its spaciousness, the room was warm. Although, I had invested in state-of-the art restaurant style appliances, the kitchen retained its roominess. The red gingham valances were just the beginning of my theme. Once I purchased the house, LaDell would install an island and lay dull red ceramic tiles on it. That was in the future. That night, jokes, laughter, and rambunctious talk filled my kitchen as we devoured mounds of spicy fried chicken, dirty rice, red beans and rice, steaming ears of corn, and topped it all with Pepsi. Soon, the children and Mama were yawning. Everyone zoomed home and left me alone.

I found my faithful bottle of tequila and made my way to my office. Bills, checkbook, and postage stamps were stacked neatly by my adding machine. I wrote the final payments for debt after debt. Ninety-thousand-dollars worth of debt gobbled up my profits from the sale of Mr. Pete's house. Most of the proceeds paid off the mortgage. The rest went to my student loan, balance of my car note, two finance companies, a high-interest Visa, and a bunch of nonsense bills. Another stack of bills waited patiently for their turn. I ignored them. I had reduced my profits to a few thousand dollars. Enough to cover a difficult court battle with Clarence. Monday Clarence would receive divorce and custody papers. Even if Clarence might agree, Roberta would have a hissie-fit.

I stacked my neat little package of paid debts, set my checkbook on top of it, raised my shot of tequila, and kicked it back. The remaining debts were mine, all mine. I slept in my new home, sure for the first time that my decisions were the right decisions.

The next day, I shopped for groceries and filled the refrigerator with the boys' favorite food. Like a lazy cat time stretched and yawned as I waited for their flight to arrive. Finally, they were there and poured into my arms. We were about to step out into the brisk Chicago weather when I noticed their light jackets.

"Do you have heavier coats?" I asked.

"No, ma'am," CJ said. "This is all we have. Dad didn't buy us anything new."

If there was any doubt in my heart about getting full custody of the boys, it vanished with that statement. Clarence would be better off with no responsibilities. I would be better off with the boys. We stopped at Ford City. I dragged the boys through JCPenney's and loaded them with bags. Once we finished with the mall, we stopped on 79th Street for dinner and thick slices of French silk pie. The boys were exhausted and fell asleep in the back seat long before I hit I-57. I didn't wake them until I turned onto Ravisloe Terrace.

"CJ, Darius, wake up," I said.

They stirred slowly, stretching and looking around. I

waited for their reaction to the neighborhood. The block was lit with Christmas lights and decorations. Icicle lights dripped from rooftops, and Rudolph stood stranded in front lawns. Ravisloe Terrace blazed with lights.

"Wow!" Darius exclaimed. "Who lives over here?"

I turned into our driveway. I had allowed LaDell to string those icicle nightmares over my house. Yet, I stopped Georgie from dragging a tree into my living room. Instead small electric candles beamed from all the windows.

"We live here," I said. "Welcome home."

I clicked the remote and pulled into the garage. The boys were out of the car as soon as I cut the ignition switch. The garage door slipped back into place, and I led the way through the back door.

"Just bring in your bags," I said. "We can get the rest later."

The boys' mouths dropped when they entered the kitchen. Pots and pans hung from overhead racks. Wicker baskets and fake foliage peered from the top of the cabinets. CJ walked to the center of the room and turned around.

"Man, this is a big kitchen."

"CJ, come and look," Darius called. His face was pressed against the sliding door. "This back yard is mega-big."

"It's too dark to see out there," I said. "You can inspect the outside tomorrow."

The boys ran from the kitchen to the dining room and living room. In each room they said, "Wow." Finally, we climbed the stairs to the bedrooms.

"The two back rooms are mine," I said. "You can fight over the other two."

They each ran in opposite directions.

"Our own rooms!" Darius exclaimed in his doorway.

"We'll shop this week for new furniture," I said.

"That's okay, Mom." CJ threw up his hands and shook

his head. "We'll just keep the old stuff so nobody can truck it all away."

I dropped down on the top step. Like all adults caught up in a web of their own making, I had forgotten how hard this drama has been on the children. The boys watched the destruction of their family. They had suffered the humiliation of poverty and the insecurity of a broken home. Why was I concerned about Clarence? The boys were more important than his hurt ego.

"I'm going to pay cash for the few things we buy," I said. "So, if it's in the house, it belongs to us. Everything in here is all ours. Except the house. The house is rented, but you know I always pay rent."

CJ stepped down and sat below me. His eyes brimmed with tears. His bottom lip trembled. There was a moment of absolute quietness and stillness. Darius moved past me and CJ. He sat next to him.

"What's wrong?" I asked.

"It's only for two weeks," Darius said. "We can't stay here."

"Why not?" I asked.

"Dad won't let us," Darius said."A judge may tell your Dad that it's in your best interest to live with me," I said.

"Can a judge do that?" CJ asked.

"Yes, he can," I said.

"Well, call the judge!" Darius said. I laughed and rubbed his head.

EPILOGUE

The boys and I pulled into LaDell and Georgie's driveway. It was lit by tall, red plastic candles with yellow plastic flames. Small bulbs shone inside the flame. In the center of the yard Mr. Claus stood with a raised arm, beckoning us to *come join the festival*. Scattered on the lawn were large plastic toys like the props used in store displays. Elves peeped from leafless shrubs filled with gumdrops lights. Icicle lights dripped from the eaves while a miniature sled with eight reindeers trampled across the roof. All the windows were trimmed with running lights. In the center of each regular sized window were snowflakes, the kind made by spraying artificial snow over stencils. In the large picture window was a tall northern fir, burdened with ornaments, lights, strung popcorn and cranberries, gold angels, stars, homemade ornaments—just stuffed to overflowing. Mrs. Claus stood on the front porch with a platter of plastic cookies and a pitcher of milk. I clicked my tongue against the roof of my mouth. The house blazed with paganism. I shook my head and followed the boys up the steps.

"Now this is Christmas," CJ said.

"Santa Claus never left Baby Jesus a Tonka truck or a Buzz Lightyear," I said.

Darius shook his head and muttered under his breath, "Mrs. Scrooge knows Christmas."

I popped Darius up side his head. CJ laughed and pressed the door bell. *We wish you a Merry Christmas* emanated from the door bell.

"Help me get through all this merriment," I prayed.

Georgie opened the door and began screaming, "CJ! Darius!" She grabbed them in one of those auntie-hugs that you can never escape. Oh, was I ever glad to be fully grown. Shanna, Terrence and LaDell came out of the kitchen. An R. Kelly song competed with those voices. I walked past the group to the kitchen. A crystal bowl of red punch commanded the center of the kitchen island. I ladled a cup full and drank it down. It was syrupy sweet. I heard the voices from the family room. I refilled my glass, wishing Georgie had tequila or something stronger to get me through this holiday madness. I wanted family. I wanted the boys. I wanted the happy twinkle that George Bailey possessed at the end of *It's a Wonderful Life*. Yet, inside was the nagging fear of tomorrow and the call from Clarence after he was served with divorce and custody papers.

"Katie, wait!" Georgie called. "I forgot to tell you . . ."

Her voice dropped as I entered the family room. There was a room full of people. A few Jordans, a couple of Georgie's sisters and their family, other people, children and teenagers crowded in that space.

"We kinda stretched this into a bigger party," she whispered.

She put her arm around me to propel me into the room. I felt the tension knotting my nerves. Shanna and the boys flew past us and merged into the mob. I nodded stiff hellos to everyone and made my way to the wet bar.

"Any thing better than this," I said and held up my punch cup to one of Georgie's brothers-in-law who was tending the bar.

"There's nonalcoholic eggnog, nonalcoholic margarita, nonalcoholic wine, nonalcoholic Pepsi, but . . ." he leaned forward, "I got a little stash of something, that I can spike that punch with," he grinned and reached for my glass.

I held out my glass only to have it taken from my hands.

"The lady passes," Noah said. The man had on a blue jeans suit with a white turtleneck that accentuated the creamy richness of his dark skin. I focused on his eyes to stop my imagination from wandering.

"Watts, what are you doing here?" I asked.

"The children received an invitation."

"Yeah, yeah," I said. I cocked my head and looked at him skeptically.

"Woman, you got the biggest ego," he said.

"Katie, Mr. Watts," Tameka joined us before I could retort.

He acknowledged her presence. Excitement radiated from her. She chatted nonstop about Georgie's over decorated house. Silver tinsel was looped around the ceiling. Centerpieces, pictures on the wall, and even the snacks scattered around the wall had Christmas themes. From the wet bar we had a clear view of the entire room from the doorway to the stereo in one corner. I finally interrupted her and asked her why she was at such an old geezer's party.

"Grandma said I had to come," Tameka said.

"Damn, Coomers!" Noah laughed. "This is a mandatory party."

"Why don't you two just go dance the night away, and let me hold up the bar?" I said.

"Cause . . ." Tameka began and stop. "Alex?"

I followed her gaze to the doorway. Alex, in a full beard, surveyed the room. Mama stood next to him with her hand firmly on his arm. I hurried across the room and grabbed him. He hugged me so tightly that my bones popped against his arm. He pulled away and I looked into his eyes. The childlike twinkle was gone. Later he would tell me about beggars and women who were murdered with the sanction of their family. At that moment, he saw Tameka and moved away from me. They walked toward each other slowly, like love-stricken stars in a movie. They met in the middle of the room and Alex pulled her into his arms and kissed her. The room was in stunned silence until one of the children said, "Oooooh, they're kissing."

"Friends, indeed!" Mama guffawed.

Tameka blushed when the kiss was over but I noticed she stayed by his side, even when he moved around the room, accepting welcomes, hand shakes, and hugs.

Soon, the music was up and the dancing started. The young children worked hard at their steps. They concentrated on each movement, bouncing, gyrating like rusty toys, trying to imitate the teenagers and young people who moved fluidly. The adults mixed new steps with old steps. Finally there were the old folks with their stiff jerks and countrified steps. I even mixed the Errol Flynn with the bounce. For the first time in years, I enjoyed the season. I moved around talking to different people and sipping on eggnog.

"All we need is a shot of tequila." Noah walked up to me with a can of Pepsi.

"Oh, Watts," I laughed. "Are you trying to tempt me?"

"Katie," one of Georgie's sisters called. "Look up."

Sinister mistletoe dangled from a gold cord Georgie had draped the bough with a beautiful red satin ribbon. I shook my head. It would be a waste of time to tell Georgie, that mistletoe had pagan origins and that I thought she might as well dress up in a white robe like a druid. Slowly the other part of that pagan ritual dawned on me. I looked at Noah. He had a lecherous grin on his face.

"Don't you dare," I said.

"Sorry, Coomers," he said. "But tradition is tradition."

He pulled me toward him and leaned in. His lips were soft and moist. I closed my eyes automatically. In the background Donny Hathaway's voice crooned:

Fireside is blazing bright
We're caroling through the night
And this Christmas will be
A very special Christmas for me, yeah

And yeah, a surge of emotions, wants, naked wants flooded me. I leaned into that kiss and thought, *Oh, my goodness! Husband number five. Mama's gonna kill me.*

ACKNOWLEDGMENTS
AND THANKS

Special thanks to Brandy R. Johnson for the first read; to my writers group—Donna Chappell, Michele Friske, Lyn Purple, and Venice Johnson—for listening to all my literary woes. I'm forever grateful to John Schultz for the craft, and Betty Shiftlett for helping me fine tune the voice. I do appreciate my agent, Victoria Sanders, who encouraged me to give it a little more, and my editor, Toisan Craigg of Doubleday, who believes in this story and helped me polish it. Most important, how could I have done this without the support of my sons, Tyrone and Brian, who believed in me through the years? What wonders you are!